The Wolf King

Center Point
Large Print

Also by Marcia Lynn McClure and available from Center Point Large Print:

The Pirate Ruse
Sweet Cherry Ray
The Horseman
Divine Deception
Shackles of Honor
Midnight Masquerade
The Tide of the Mermaid Tears
The Romancing of Evangeline Ipswich
The Secret Bliss of Calliope Ipswich
The Bewitching of Amoretta Ipswich

The Wolf King

Marcia Lynn McClure

CENTER POINT LARGE PRINT
THORNDIKE, MAINE

This Center Point Large Print edition
is published in the year 2025 by arrangement with
Distractions Ink.

Copyright © 2016 by Marcia Lynn McClure.

All rights reserved.

All character names and personalities in this
work of fiction are entirely fictional, created
solely in the imagination of the author. Any
resemblance to any person living or dead
is coincidental.

The text of this Large Print edition is unabridged.
In other aspects, this book may vary
from the original edition.
Printed in the United States of America
on permanent paper sourced using
environmentally responsible foresting methods.
Set in 16-point Times New Roman type.

ISBN: 979-8-89164-452-6

The Library of Congress has cataloged this record
under Library of Congress Control Number: 2024948303

To My Sons, Mitch and Trent—
Two rare and heroic sheepdogs,
Protectors in a world of sheep and wolves.

To my hero and inspiration . . .
Kevin from Heaven!

• • •

"Territi sunt oves, et proximus sunt lupi rapaces.
Ego sum canis-intrepidus maneo."
(The sheep are frightened, and the wolves are close. I am the dog-intrepid.)
—Volk Royal Motto from *The Wolf King*,
by Marcia Lynn McClure

Before you begin reading *The Wolf King*, please note that the name Balian is pronounced *BAY-lee-un*.

Menace in the Meadow

"Please endeavor not to linger more than the hour, Minnette," Morgianna D'Angelville called to her daughter. "We must finish these lengths of lace before we lose the bright light of the day."

"Yes, Mother!" Minnette called over her shoulder, even as she hurried toward the meadow. "I'll not be long. I promise!"

Morgianna exhaled a heavy sigh, smiling as she shook her head. "She promises, does she?" Laughing a little, her amusement heightened as she watched three large, vibrant butterflies fluttering over Minnette's head as she disappeared into the forest tree line, Morgianna whispered, "At times, I do wonder if the girl has the slightest conception of time."

Yet Morgianna was not in the least vexed with her daughter, not in the slightest annoyed. For Minnette had been up far before the sun to feed the animals, milk the cow, and see to breakfast. She'd worked hard fashioning lace all morning as well—and whether or not there was still more lace to be made and herbs to be harvested and hung to dry, Morgianna knew her lovely daughter had well earned an amble to the meadow. Still, she laughed aloud, knowing that it would take Minnette near half the hour to reach the meadow—being that she would, no doubt, amble at a truly dawdling pace. Half the hour spent to the meadow and the second half the hour spent returning home allotted no time for tarrying in the meadow itself. Thus, knowing Minnette would indeed tarry in her beloved meadow, Morgianna surmised her beloved daughter would be absent far longer than the hour—and also that she must counsel with her daughter on the legitimate measurements of time.

Nevertheless, it was ever so heartwarming to see Minnette happy again—at last. When Minnette's father had died unexpectedly the year before, the crushing pain and mourning that had entirely enveloped Morgianna had found her in neglect of her daughter's own need for comfort and reassurance. It was a truth that haunted Morgianna still. Yet the past was past, and she could not change it. Hence, she prayed that Minnette had not suffered any unhealable emotional injury during those first few weeks of Morgianna's despondency.

"Oh, how I miss you, Stuart," Morgianna whispered. Her eyes were already tired from working lace half the long day, yet there was still half a long day of work remaining. Therefore, there was no time for tired eyes now—not since the burden of keeping the silk wares in plenty and the apothecary well stocked, so that she and Minnette could make their means, had fallen to Morgianna and Minnette alone.

Still, she was akin to her daughter in heart, soul, and longing, and the beauty of the day beckoned her just as it did to Minnette. Morgianna thereby deduced she would rest a while before returning to her task, as well—laze in the grass in the shade of the trees for a time. Rest would relieve her eyes—and perhaps free her mind of worry and fatigue in a measure.

Morgianna exhaled a long sigh of great weariness as she lay down beneath the large oak next to the cottage she now shared with only her daughter. Yet she smiled as she again thought of Minnette's promise to be away for mere the hour. "An hour indeed," she mumbled, grinning as she closed her eyes. "But I could not deny her the meadow. For she is my greatest treasure . . . and the only thing left to me in all this world."

It was so very refreshing to leave the confines of the cottage. Minnette knew she would not have a great deal of time to bathe in respite, to enjoy the sights and sounds the meadow afforded her. Yet the amble to the meadow and back would be invigorating and offer the much-needed rejuvenation her mind and body longed for. Working lace was a wearisome process, and even for the wonder and pride in accomplishment

Minnette always experienced upon finishing a length of the dainty adornment, it was work all the same—tedious work at that. Therefore, she was ever so grateful that her kind and understanding mother allowed her episodes of reprieve now and again throughout the day—for she felt it proved the saving of her very sanity at times. She considered that perhaps she would gather some herbs from the meadow and forest on her walk back—and thus feel as if not all of her time to and from the meadow had been simple leisure. After all, the apothecary stores were dwindling of several fundamentals. So in truth, Minnette mused, she was still toiling after a manner—only in different means than in fashioning lace.

As Minnette wove her way along the path through the forest—as the trees began to thin a little—she caught sight of the meadow ahead of her. Ah! The meadow! Its lush green grass, vibrant wildflowers, and small creatures making their homes there caused Minnette to fancy heaven itself could not be more lovely a place.

Several tiny rabbits scampered across the path preceding Minnette, and she giggled, thinking the soft, fluffy kits were assuredly the sweetest creatures she had ever seen.

"You see, there?" she spoke aloud as a lovely blue and yellow butterfly alit upon her shoulder. "Already the meadow is gifting us favor. For are not those little ones the most enchanting of creatures? I half expected to see fairies astride their backs, yes?"

She stepped out of the tree line and into the meadow then, inhaling a deep breath of all the fragrances the beautiful space offered any visitor. All things splendid in the green meadow's nature filled her senses with reprieve and recess. Minnette thought then that the color green was most assuredly God's own precious gift to the world of man—a color to soothe weary eyes and lighten heavy hearts. She thought that it was his intention to organize grass, tree leaves, flower stems, and so many other of nature's bounty in shades of green, for God did nothing by accident, and she wondered if perhaps green were God's favorite color, as well as her own.

"Thank you, God . . . for gifting me green, even in my eyes," she whispered reverently as she wandered farther from the forest and into the verdant meadow.

Minnette's smile broadened even still as she then looked up, gazing on the splendor and strength of Castle Vargar in the near distance. Surrounded by forest on the south and north with the meadow and forest beyond stretching out before it to the west, the castle and fortresses loomed in the east as a sentinel over all the land it surveyed—gifting a sense of protection and safety to the enchanting landscape all about. And as Minnette glanced back for a moment to the tree line of the forest between her and the village from whence she'd traveled, she looked back again to the mighty grandeur of Castle Vargar and was even still awed by its powerful presence. Castle Vargar's four white stone towers and turrets, its grand pinnacle, and its keep stood as stone giants within the impenetrable castle walls—powerful guards to both intimidate would-be enemies and reassure each citizen in the kingdom that Castle Vargar, and its king, Liam, would ever watch over and protect them.

Exhaling a breath of contentment, Minnette reached up, unpinning her long brown hair. As it cascaded here and there about her shoulders and back, she raked her hands through its length. Combing it with her fingers, she thought that even the very hairs of her head were tired of working lace—that even it felt free and rested as the soft meadow breeze gently tugged at a strand here and there in begging for a playmate.

Having always felt that meadow grasses were meant to be laid upon, slept in, or in the very least sat amidst, Minnette nestled herself in the soft, sweet-smelling verdure and again inhaled a breath, next exhaling a sigh of blissful serenity. The birds in the trees of the nearby frondescence joined with those hidden among the vivid meadow greenness to twill lulling descants, intermittently embellished by the aria of some particular songbird Minnette recognized as her father's favorite—the skylark. Even thoughts of missing her father, as desperately as she did miss him, did not diminish the loveliness of the meadow and its power to enchant her in those moments.

In truth, thoughts of her father proved to heighten her joy, for she was awash in memories of visiting the meadow with him—of one new spring in particular when the meadow had flooded and uncommonly cold weather had found it frozen. It was that spring, when Minnette had been near to seven years of age, that Minnette, her father, and her mother had visited the meadow, venturing out onto the frozen floodplain. All of them had been at once enchanted and next saddened when it was discovered that many of the smallest inhabitants of the meadow had been trapped in the sudden and unexpected ice. Tiny frogs, young meadow snakes, spiders, and diminutive shrews were frozen midst the stiff meadow grass, appearing exactly as if they might suddenly spring to life again once the sun had melted their icy tomb. Minnette's father had compassionately assured his daughter that undoubtedly many of the little creatures would indeed survive freezing and the consequent melting course. And though her father's words had comforted her at the time, she knew that his efforts were to soothe her—that most of the miniature wild things trapped in the meadow ice those years ago had indeed met their doom when the rains had flooded the place and the frigid weather had swooped down upon them, entombing them in ice. She knew now, and had known for many years, the reason her father and mother could not seem to find the time to take her to the meadow once the sun had warmed the earth long enough that logic would claim the ice had had time to dissipate. They had not wanted their tenderhearted daughter to race to the meadow only to find that death had indeed claimed so many tiny essences. No, they had waited days and days before taking her to the meadow again, time enough, she now understood, for the larger creatures of the meadow—the foxes, squirrels, and the like—to see to the refinement of their lovely habitat. Larger meadow dwellers that had easily survived the freezing had feasted on what the retreating ice had forsaken in its wake. And for all of it, Minnette loved her parents all the more: for letting the meadow remain as a dream world to their young daughter—a place where every beautiful thing flourished and harm came to nothing.

Of a sudden, Minnette's reminiscences were scattered when she heard a sound that was not native to the meadow. A whistled call of sorts—and definitely human.

Sitting up—for she had indeed relaxed to near sprawling in the grass while caught up in her reverie—Minnette frowned when the next sound to reach her was that of shouting—a man shouting.

Leaping to her feet, she looked to the tree line at the north border of the meadow in time to see a man come bursting from without the forest at a full run. He was tall—that much Minnette could distinguish from her distance—and he appeared in some sort of distress by the further look of him. His shirt, though white and bloused at the sleeves, hung open, and he wore no vest or coat about it. His breeches were black, but his legs were otherwise void of protection; he wore no boots or shoes of any kind.

Again the man shouted, as if tribulation were hot at his heels, and Minnette gasped as she then saw that it was indeed so. For as the man sprinted further into the open meadow, a pack of enormous white wolves, numbering at least five in brood, raced from the tree line in pursuit of the man! The wolves almost instantly overtook their prey, forcing the man to the ground as they pounced upon him, snarling and gnashing their teeth.

Minnette took hold of her kirtle skirt and, without pause, raced into the meadow toward the spectacle. The man would be dead before she reached him—she was certain of it! Yet she must try! She must endeavor to help him—to attempt to ward off the pack of hungry predators before they literally tore the man apart!

"Shoosh! Shoosh, wolves! Do you hear me?" Minnette shrieked as she ran toward what now appeared to be a mass of white fur rendering lost any remains of the man beneath their ravenous chaos. "Shoosh! Shoo! You brutes!" she cried as she slid to a stop. Reaching down and removing her shoes, she hurled them at the mound of white wolves. "Stop! Stop!" she cried. It was a paltry attempt at best, and Minnette knew it—tossing ladies' shoes at the predators. Still, she knew not what else to do.

And then, of a sudden, and much to her astonishment, the wolves did indeed cease in their apparent devouring of the man. Instantly, however, Minnette realized the consequences of her rash act of rushing in to meet danger—for all five sets of amber-colored wolves' eyes were now fixed upon her.

"Oh my," Minnette breathed. With the man they had been preying on now assuredly incapacitated at the very least, Minnette knew the pack of hungry wolves would turn their murderous intent to her—that she would become the subject of their feasting in the stranger's stay.

One wolf, the largest, lowered his head and moved toward her.

"There, there now," Minnette whispered. "I . . . I meant no harm to you, sir wolf."

But before she could utter another breath, the

wolf leapt at her, knocking her to her back in the meadow grass and pinning her shoulders to the ground beneath powerful front paws.

Minnette closed her eyes, not wanting to watch the wolf's dagger-like teeth descend to plunge into the flesh of her throat. No doubt the pain would be excruciating enough to indicate that her life was at an end. Thus, she had no desire to see her blood dripping from his fangs.

"Thor!" a deep voice commanded. "Stand down, Thor! At once! The girl meant no harm."

When Minnette did not feel the pain of gnashing teeth grinding into her throat, she opened one eye tentatively. The large white wolf—which had only a moment before been looming over her as a ravenous beast—now stood over her happily panting as if he were a simple village dog romping with a child playmate.

Minnette's attention was then drawn to the man who appeared to loom over her and the wolf—the stranger who had been the wolves' first victim. Yet without so much as a scratch about him, the man smiled down at her, reaching out to scratch the big wolf behind the ears.

"Y-you're not devoured," Minnette managed in a whisper of astonishment.

The man smiled. "No. I am not," he affirmed, chuckling as he shook his head. "But you are a brave lass indeed to run mad at a pack of enormous wolves to defend me." The man patted the wolf on the head and said something in a language Minnette did not recognize. The wolf released Minnette and rather bounded off to join the others of his pack.

"I am Balian," the man greeted, offering a strong-looking hand to Minnette to assist her.

"I am Minnette," Minnette managed, accepting his hand.

As brisk as a winter's wind, she was standing on her feet once more, staring up, up, up into the ethereally handsome face of the most comely man she had ever seen!

"Well, I thank you, Minnette . . . for my life," the man called Balian said. He swept a low bow before her, offering to her her shoes, which he had been holding in one hand behind his back. Minnette blushed, yet accepting her shoes and pulling them onto her feet as quickly as her trembling would allow.

"You must think me a fool indeed, sir," she said, glancing away from him a moment, "running at a pack of wolves as if I were some impervious huntress or some such nonsense."

"Not at all, milady," he assured her. "I find it quite heroic. But come now and meet the lads, won't you?"

"The lads?" Minnette muttered—though she full well knew the lads the man referenced.

"Thor! Delling! Komme pa en gang!" the man called to the wolves. Again he had spoken something to the wolves in a language Minnette had never before heard, and the pack instantly obeyed whatever command he had given them. Racing to her with all the intimidation of hungry wolves but with eyes that expressed no threat, the wolves gathered around the man Minnette now understood was their master.

"Do you mind?" the man asked.

"Mind what?" Minnette asked. He was quite astounding in his attractiveness—so astounding Minnette had near forgot that he was standing midst a number of enormous carnivores.

Without further explanation, Balian, as he was apparently called, reached out, brushing one hand over Minnette's forehead. He then offered his hand to the wolf pack, and she watched as each wolf sniffled at his hand in turn.

"This is Minnette, my brothers and sisters," he said. "Obviously she is friend, not foe, for she did endeavor to save me from the jaws of death." He paused, smiled at her, and added, "And quite literally, from her point of view.

"Husker henne," he said, and instantly the large wolves began to paw about the ground around Minnette as they smelled her clothing and hands. The largest of them, Thor, was so great that his head stood as high as Minnette's shoulder.

"They will not forget you now," Balian said. "They will never forget you."

Minnette forced a nervous smile. "And . . . and am I to assume that is good?"

Balian laughed, and when he did, his dark blue eyes danced with mirthful light. His smile was unguarded and pure—stunning as nothing Minnette had ever before seen. A square jaw was his, and a strong, straight nose. His brows were thick and dark, companions to thick and dark lashes to shade his cobalt eyes. His hair was also very, very dark—near black—stark contrast to the snow-white wolves surrounding him.

"Very good indeed," Balian assured her. "Perhaps the day may arrive when we can serve you in some way, milady." The handsome man's brows arched with wonderment as a large yellow and black butterfly alit on Minnette's arm and lingered.

Minnette blushed—flattered to near giddiness over his referring to her as a lady.

"Though today, we were merely frolicking," Balian added. He exhaled a heavy sigh akin to defeat. "One last breath of freedom before we . . . before we . . . well, before the day is through," he said—and she noticed his smile was not so bright as it had been a moment before.

Minnette startled as Balian turned toward the tree line from whence he and his wolves had appeared, put his fingers to his lips, and produced a loud, shrill whistle.

Instantly, an enormous black horse stepped

into the meadow. It was a magnificent mount, bedecked with such exquisitely decorated trappings and harness that Minnette felt her mouth fall agape in dazzled admiration.

"There you are, Ewan," Balian greeted the large beast. "We best make ready, eh?"

Minnette watched as Balian retrieved a gambeson padded jacket from the saddle at Ewan's back and pulled it on over his shirt. Next he removed two black boots that had been tied together with rope and hung across the saddle so that one boot dangled on either side of the horse. Removing a stocking from each boot and rather awkwardly shoving them onto his feet, Balian then pulled one boot onto each foot, securing his trouser legs in them just below his knee.

"Would that I had time to linger with you, milady," Balian said as he slid a jacket of mail from Ewan's back and pulled it on over his head. Minnette knew that either Balian was far stronger than most men in the kingdom or his mail jacket was lighter than others—for most men could not heft a mail jacket with the ease Balian did.

"But I've matters to attend to . . . people in wait of me," he added as he secured his mail at his breast. Last of all, he drew a tunic from his horse trappings—a royal blue tunic that had been rather chaotically tucked into part of the horse's harness. It bore a coat of arms that Minnette knew she should recognize at once. But the past minutes—the present moments—the realization that it was indeed a knight whom she had attempted to save from wild wolves—found her struck silent, unable to speak or to put memory to the coat of arms on the knight's tunic.

"You are a knight," Minnette breathed.

Again the man offered her a sweeping bow. "Balian of Vavassour, milady," he said.

"Sir Balian," she offered.

Balian of Vavassour shrugged broad, mailed shoulders. "It would seem, yes. And my thanks to you, Milady Minnette," Balian said. It was unexpected to Minnette when the knight dropped to one knee before her. She gasped as he took her hand in his, raising it to his lips and placing a warm kiss to the back of it. "I am in your service if ever you need me to be," he vowed in earnest. He stood, smiling at her and saying, "But for now, my friends and I must be on our way. Good day to you, my pretty lass."

Then, mounting the horse as if the mail weighed no more than a silken shawl, Balian took the reins, and he looked down to Minnette once more. "You may find wisdom in retreating closer to the tree line, milady, for at any moment the rest of my lads will arrive to escort me. Very well?"

"O-of course," Minnette stammered. "Of course."

"Again, good day to you, Minnette. I hope our paths cross again . . . and soon."

"As do I," Minnette said.

"Ewan!" Balian called then.

And there he rode—out across the meadow on his finely bedecked horse, with his five white wolves racing behind him.

"Goodbye, Sir Balian of Vavassour," Minnette whispered to herself as she watched him ride away. She reached with one hand to her opposing arm, pinching herself to ensure that she was indeed full awake and not merely dreaming of the handsome Balian and his white wolves.

Of a sudden then she heard chaos at the far tree line from whence Balian and his wolves had first appeared. Indeed, she did step farther back, though had she been able to gather her wits, she would have turned and run. For pure one hundred more white wolves emerged!

"It's a legion of white wolves!" Minnette breathed as she watched the massive pack of wolves race to join Sir Balian.

It was an awe-inspiring sight—Sir Balian astride his mount racing toward Castle Vargar with an army of white wolves at his back—if not also terrifying to her core! Again Minnette pinched her own arm, for the scene playing out before her in the meadow could not be real. Yet it was! Minnette knew it was real, for her vision was not her only sense to experience it but also her hearing, her sense of smell, every sense in her being.

"The king!" Minnette gasped as she suddenly realized that this knight and his wolves might mean harm to Vavassour's beloved King Liam and Queen Asta.

Yet she frowned next as realization slowly crept into her thoughts. "Balian? Sir Balian of Vavassour?" she muttered to herself.

Closing her eyes then, Minnette exhaled a long sigh of realizing her ignorance. The coat of arms on the knight Balian's tunic: it was the royal coat of arms—the coat of arms of the king—of the royal family! The silver shield on blue, the two stags on either side of the shield, the motto in banner above the shield, *Territi sunt oves, et proximus sunt lupi rapaces. Ego sum canis-intrepidus maneo.*

"The sheep are frightened, and the wolves are close. I am the dog-intrepid," Minnette whispered. "The motto of the Volk line of royalty. Balian of Vavassour is the long-absent crown prince of the kingdom . . . the Wolf Prince. There is no greater fool on earth than me."

How could she have been so ignorant—so completely dumbfounded by the appearance of a handsome man in the meadow, not to mention the white wolves that accompanied him, so affected by the man—that she did not recognize that the wolves were the very white wolves of near legend that all in the kingdom had shared stories of for near to six years past?

"The Wolf Prince," Minnette sighed as she turned toward the path through the forest. A new butterfly, this one in hues of pink and blue, landed on her arm. Raising her arm, she spoke to the delicate inhabitant of the meadow. "I have only just made the greatest fool of myself, pretty thing. I have endeavored to save the crown prince of Vavassour from his own pets." Stepping onto the path and heading into the forest and toward her mother and home, Minnette shook her head in self-disgust. "Yet I have not set my eyes upon him for this five years past. Thus how was I to know?"

Raising her arm in indicating to the gracious butterfly that it should flutter off and leave her to her own misery in humiliation, Minnette hurried along the path toward her home. She would gather herbs later in the day. For now there was lace to be worked—as well as a tale of her idiocy to confess to her mother.

"And he brought to me my shoes!" Minnette groaned, remembering the royal bow the Wolf Prince had offered her when handing her shoes to her—the shoes she had hurled at his pet wolves!

Minnette's shoulders slumped forward with defeat, even as the pretty blue and pink butterfly landed on one of them. "Minnette the imbecile—that is what they will dub me. That or the girl who threw her shoes at the crown prince's beloved pet wolves. Let us hope that the lace I work with

Mother today is the finest I've ever worked, else my moronic escapades in the meadow today find Mother and I without patrons for our wares. What means would provide for us then?"

Minnette found herself hurrying toward home, for gossip traveled faster than knights on horses with bejeweled harnesses—even faster yet than white wolves racing across a meadow after their royal master. And she would not have her mother told of her daughter's imbecilic antics by any other mouth but her own.

Thus, tears brimmed in Minnette's meadow-green eyes as she scurried along the forest path to the village to tell her mother that she had met and meddled with, the crown prince of Vavassour—Sir Balian the Knight—Balian the Wolf Prince.

The Tale of the Wolf Prince

"There came to Castle Vargar a pair of white wolves—a gift to King Liam from a great king of a northernmost kingdom," Morgianna began.

She reached across the small table at which she and Minnette sat inside their cottage. Taking her daughter's hands in her own, Morgianna smiled with reassurance. Minnette had been so distraught when she returned from the meadow—so distressed about her encounter with the crown prince of Vavassour—that Morgianna was endeavoring to soothe her with a telling of the story of the Wolf Prince. She was not certain that the story would calm her daughter's anxiety. Nevertheless she continued.

"Naturally, King Liam had the wolf pair added to his vast menagerie." Morgianna paused, quirking one brow as if she were revealing some mysterious secret to Minnette. "It is said the butterfly pavilion in the king's menagerie is also magnificent. And though it is not open to public viewing as the main menagerie is on occasion, I always imagine that the butterflies there would favor you, my sweet . . . just as all other butterflies do."

• • •

Minnette smiled, if only a little. "Do not attempt to flatter me into forgetting what an imbecilic fool I was before the prince, Mother." Her smile broadened, however, as she studied her beautiful mother—her brown hair and green eyes. Minnette hoped that she would age to be as lovely as her mother had, for her mother was truly a rare beauty indeed. "Nonetheless, pray go on with the tale, please, for it has been a very long time since I have heard it told."

Morgianna smiled, admitting, "It was your father who told the tale best. Yet I will attempt to make it quite as interesting as he always did."

"Thank you, Mother," Minnette whispered—though her heart experienced a vicious pinch for the loss of her father for a moment.

"As I said before, King Liam had the pair of northern white wolves sheltered and cared for in his menagerie," Morgianna continued. "And it was not long thereafter that it became obvious the she-wolf would soon bear a litter."

Minnette smiled and did indeed feel lighter of heart. She so loved anything that was in infancy—any child, any animal, any tiny living thing—and she could well imagine a litter of white wolf pups.

"Did you know that wolves mate for life, Minnette?" Morgianna asked.

Minnette nodded. "I remember Father telling me so."

"Well, it is true," Morgianna confirmed, "and no less true for the white wolves in King Liam's menagerie. Nevertheless, tragedy struck hard when the she-wolf birthed her litter. Four pups were born healthy as ever any new litter of wolf kittens were. Yet their mother, she did not fare well . . . and indeed died shortly after delivering her litter. Her mate, the mighty he-wolf, whom the young crown prince Balian had dubbed Thor, was angry, saddened, and no doubt frightened by the loss of his mate and mother of his pups."

"Thor?" Minnette exclaimed of a sudden.

"Yes," her mother affirmed. Morgianna giggled in slight. "Had you forgotten the tale of Thor, the prince's white wolf? Your father always and ever spoke of Thor when—"

Minnette shook her head, again humiliated by her own lack of wit when she'd met the prince in the meadow.

"I . . . I guess I had forgotten," she admitted, "or else I was so astonished by the wolves and the man . . . the prince in the meadow." She looked up to her mother, reaching across the table and taking one of her hands in her own. "For, Mother, the wolf that bounded to me, knocked me down in defending his master from my ignorant attempt to save him—why, the prince named him Thor! Do you think it is true? That I was pinned to the ground by the large, powerful paws of Thor, the he-wolf given King Liam?"

Goose pimples of affirmation raced over Minnette's arms and up the back of her neck as her mother nodded, answering, "If the prince referred to the wolf as Thor, then I am sure that Thor the he-wolf of the king's menagerie he was." Morgianna shook her head in wonder. "My, my, Minnette, my darling! You have had an adventure today the likes no one else in the kingdom ever has had!"

Minnette reflected on the enormous wolf who had pushed her to the ground. In her mind, she could yet envision the amber color of his eyes, remember the heat of his breath on her face as he'd stood over her.

"I think I nearly met Death himself today, Mother," Minnette sighed, "for was not Thor known to be a powerful, wild sort of wolf? After all, he was taken from the wilderness, was he not?"

"He was," Morgianna confirmed. "He was taken, with his mate, from their wilderness home in the north, penned up, and sent to King Liam. And when Thor's she-wolf had died—when his wolf pups were lingering in their place in the menagerie—well, it must have been that Thor knew his pups would surely die without their mother. For though it was not in his nature to be accepting of humans, the grieving male wolf,

Thor, allowed but one human being to enter his captive space to care for the pups."

"The young prince, Balian," Minnette offered—for it was well she knew the history of Prince Balian and his wolves. Even still, she was desirous that her mother continue reciting it, for she adored hearing stories from her mother.

"Indeed," Morgianna continued. "The he-wolf, Thor, accepted Balian for reasons no one could fathom. Thus, it was the prince, Balian of Vavassour, who fed and nurtured the litter of wolf kittens. And as he did care for them, Thor, their sire, began to hold Balian as beloved . . . as even a comrade. Naturally the wolf pups grew to hold Balian as beloved as well, and as their master. Years passed, and in the time before the prince left Castle Vargar, it was commonplace to see the prince running through the castle and grounds within the castle walls with his wolves at his heels—Thor included, though Thor ran beside the prince instead of behind him as the younger wolves did. It was quite ordinary, in fact, to hear the wolves howling at night, their far-off calls heard even here in the village. And even it was that Thor began to protect Balian as he did his own offspring. For once—and I know you know this part of the tale as well, Minnette—once a rogue wolf from the forest attacked Balian when he was riding alone on an evening. The rogue wolf leapt at Balian, leaving a brutal and bloody wound at his leg. And that was when everyone in the kingdom became aware of something."

"That Thor was ever watchful of the prince," Minnette interjected.

Morgianna laughed a little. "Yes! Yes! That was when everyone in the kingdom realized that Prince Balian never locked his wolves away, even for the fact that Thor had been bred and born a wild wolf. And because the prince allowed his wolves to roam here and there about the castle, Thor had begun following the prince . . . always following him. And it is why Thor was close enough to charge and kill the rogue wolf that had attacked his master. Thor had followed Balian even that very night and had, no doubt, sensed an enemy." Morgianna sighed and glanced away for a moment. "And of course, that is when the whispers and hearsays began. The gossips in the kingdom—and it seems that every kingdom, village, and town in all the world harbors gossips—but that event, Prince Balian being bitten by the rogue wolf, that was when—"

"People began to whisper of his being a werewolf," Minnette interjected. "That he turns from human to wolf during any and every full moon."

Morgianna nodded. "Yes. That is what some still say in Vavassour. And they whisper it is also the reason Prince Balian fled the kingdom five years past—though in truth no one is certain why he abandoned the kingdom. Still, it was when a little girl was found mauled—half eaten, in truth, and four fingers missing from her right hand—found exactly one month following the rogue wolf's attack on the prince. That was when the gossip began. The royal physician determined that a wolf had killed the child. At first, there were they who wanted to condemn Prince Balian's white wolves, in particular Thor, for the tragedy. Yet Prince Balian testified with utmost firm assurance that Thor and the other wolves had taken rest in his own bedchamber the night before the girl was found." Morgianna shrugged, exhaling a sigh of discouragement. "Nevertheless, King Liam's subjects would not be settled, and whispers caught current throughout the kingdom that Prince Balian himself had, although unwittingly and unwillingly, shifted his form from man to beast, from prince to wolf—and that it was he, not his white wolves or any other wild wolf, that had killed the child. In fact, it was not until the king and queen, in accordance with Prince Balian's request, offered to allow any and all who believed such absurdity to sit in witness the following month, that those who had accused were satisfied that the prince of Vavassour was not a werewolf."

"That was the October night when the prince was caged in the castle courtyard," Minnette said, "when all who wished to witness him there stood all through the long night of the full moon, waiting for the prince to change into a beast . . . or not change into a beast. I remember it—glimpsing the cage the prince was held in, seeing the prince himself dressed in naught but his trousers." Minnette smiled and lowered her voice to a whisper, adding, "I remember thinking the prince was far too handsome to ever be something so malevolent as a werewolf." Minnette's smile broadened as she supplemented, "He is far more handsome even now, Mother. Such broad shoulders has he . . . such a squared jaw. I suppose it was why I did not recognize him as the younger man who was kept in a cage all through a dark October night—for he has much changed."

"Five years is quite the length of time for the maturity of anyone, especially a youngish man the like of Prince Balian," Morgianna offered.

"I'm sorry to have interrupted, Mother," Minnette said, smiling. "Pray continue, please!"

Morgianna laughed with amusement for a moment and then indeed continued. "As you well remember, though you did fall very drowsy during the night we all stood watch around the caged prince, by sunrise it was plain proved that Prince Balian was not a werewolf. For there he stood, still a man, not a wolf, and having remained a man all the night long. Indeed, the night following the one of the October full moon, a huntsman killed a large wolf in the woods. And when they cut open the predator's belly, they found therein the vestiges of four small fingers . . . four child-like fingers. The child who had been killed—the child who had indeed been missing four fingers when found—it was the huntsman's prey that had killed her. Thus, all whispers of the prince's being a werewolf ceased. Almost all, that is. Even now, there still linger on the breezes here and there rumors whispering that it was why the prince rode away from his kingdom, castle, and family . . . that he truly is a werewolf and King Liam banished him in order to keep all who dwell in Vavassour safe from being devoured by the Wolf Prince."

"But it is not why the prince rode away, is it, Mother?" Minnette asked. She quirked one suspicious brow. "Why did the prince leave the kingdom? For I know that Father knew and that you yet know . . . though as you said, no one else seems to."

Morgianna sighed, and Minnette noted her cheeks pinked with discomfort. "Your father was sworn to secrecy, Minnette . . . by King Liam himself. He was granted only permission to tell me what had transpired and no one else . . . not even his own daughter."

"This I surmised long ago, Mother," Minnette admitted. "I remember the night, shortly after our family was invited to watch over the prince when he was caged. I know that the king trusted Father and his remedies, his powders and medicines, and that all in Vavassour respected my father. It is why the king wanted Father to witness Prince Balian in the cage, for no one would doubt Father's word. If Father said he had seen with his own eyes that the prince was not a werewolf, then all the king's subjects would believe it.

"Yet there was the night that a message arrived from the castle. I know you and Father believed I was asleep, but I was not, and I crept out to see one of the king's men speaking with Father. He said something of tragedy, of illness . . . of madness, I think. And Father left with him after gathering wares from the apothecary. It was not one week later that word spread of Prince Balian's having left Vavassour, his white wolves with him.

"Why did the prince leave, Mother? Only Father knew, didn't he? Outside of the royal family, only Father, who then told you—only you two know why the prince abandoned Castle Vargar. And it causes me to wonder—if only you now know why he has returned."

As the color fairly drained from her mother's face, Minnette felt guilt for pressing her so.

"Oh, Mother! Please do not concern yourself! I am so sorry that I was heartless, that I inquired of you as to why. Please put it from your mind, Mother, and forgive me for asking." Shaking her head with self-loathing, Minnette exhaled a sigh of discouragement. "It seems today is the day that my wits have abandoned me entirely. First I did not recognize the crown prince of the kingdom, and now I have caused you worry and discomfort, Mother. Please forgive me."

"There is nothing to forgive, my love," Morgianna said. As her smile began to appear once more, she soothed, "I wish I could tell you, Minnette. But I gave your father my word I would keep it secret all my days . . . even from you."

"I understand. Truly," Minnette assured her mother.

Still, it did not mean her curiosity was squelched in any regard. It had long been a mystery to everyone in the kingdom—the reasons for Prince Balian's abandonment of Vavassour, or else his father's banishing. But Minnette had always known there was something more to the mystery; she had always known her parents knew what the something more was. And being that the prince had now returned—the Wolf Prince of Vavassour, in his knightly garb, mounted on his knightly horse, and with his five white wolves and a hundred more in his wake—her curiosity was only fanned to fire.

"Tell me once more, Minnette . . . the words he spoke to you in the meadow," Morgianna asked with a delighted giggle. "Imagine, meeting the prince in the meadow as you did. I would barter you were the first in the kingdom to speak to him. Tell me once more what he said to you."

Minnette shrugged, blushing as she remembered her attempt to save the prince from his own pets. Smiling she said, "He told me I was pretty . . . and that he hoped one day he could serve me in some way."

"The prince was ever a gentleman, even as a young boy," Morgianna offered.

Minnette giggled as she reminisced aloud. "He referred to his male wolves as lads . . . as if they were simple playmates he'd met along the way." Minnette exhaled a long, breathy sigh of admiration, whispering, "Oh, Mother! I have never seen such a man! The prince is ever the most beautiful man on earth—I swear it to you!"

Morgianna laughed. "I have no doubt of it, my precious girl. No doubt in the least."

Minnette's smile faded to a frown, her brows puckering in disappointment. "I suppose I should be glad that I, no doubt, placed a mark on his memory. I'm certain no other silly maiden has tried to save him from his own comrades as I did today."

"You showed great kindness and caring for your fellowman, Minnette," Morgianna reminded. "And I am most certain that will be the reason Prince Balian remembers you when next you meet. For though there are many who serve the royal family—many who are kind to them, at least in appearance—there are not many whom the king and queen and no doubt the prince count as true friends. Monarchy can be a very lonely existence, Minnette—an existence where one is forever surrounded by people but never in league with true friendship. Therefore, hold no regret that you proved to the prince today you would defend even some stranger to you . . . and at such great risk of your own welfare."

"That would certainly be my wish, for I would not want him to remember me only as the silly girl who assaulted his pets and stood in the meadow with butterflies fluttering about as if I were spoiled fruit," Minnette sulked.

Morgianna burst into laughter. The expression on her daughter's face was that of miserable concern. Yet Morgianna had known Prince Balian near all his life—in the least since he was a child—and she knew that the Wolf Prince of Vavassour admired rarity above all else. And Minnette was indeed a rarity among young women.

"Oh, my pet," Morgianna sighed, still smiling. "You need not concern yourself. You are a beauty! A beauty in heart, in soul, in mind, and in body! Such a beauty that even the loveliest thing to take flight on earth is drawn to you as bees to honey—for butterflies have always followed you, my sweet, and they would not follow one who was not worthy to be followed. I am certain that you will meet the prince again one day . . . and that when you do he will smile at not only your loveliness but the memory of the girl who endeavored to save his life once. So let us forget our lace-making for now and perhaps stroll down to the baker and relish one of his sweet things, hmm?"

"But there is so much to be done, Mother," Minnette reminded. "And I have yet to gather herbs for our stores and—"

"A sweet indulgence with your mother is far more important, especially today," Morgianna interrupted. "After all, my daughter has caught the eye of the crown prince of the kingdom, and it is not every mother that can claim such distinction. Let us enjoy the baker's wares together first, and then we will both gather herbs for the stores. There is plenty of time on the morrow for working lace, hmm?"

Minnette smiled and nodded. What person would ever refuse the offer of a sweet cake or biscuit from the baker?

She remembered the prince's smile as he'd gazed at her then. Whether he was pleased by her appearance or simply amused by her ridiculous endeavors and her company of butterflies, he did smile at her—a handsome, alluring smile. And that was more than any other young woman in the kingdom had been able to lay claim to in more than five years.

"Very well," Minnette agreed therefore, "for it

is not every day a girl escapes the clutches of an enormous white wolf . . . and unscathed at that."

"This is true," Morgianna giggled as she stood from her chair.

Taking Minnette's hand as she also stood, mother and daughter left the cottage in search of a sweet baker's morsel.

As they ambled down the byway, several sizeable butterflies fluttered over Minnette's head. She took little notice of them, for butterflies had always accompanied her when their season was ripe to do so. Even as one particularly stunning butterfly of cobalt, black, and yellow alit on her shoulder, Minnette found nothing unusual about the fact. Yet other amblers the women greeted in passing smiled, delighted by the sight of the girl who was ever ringed in escort by the pretty fancies.

Even the singular white wolf watching from his cloaked space of thick brush near the forest tree line tipped his head to one side in seeming awe of the butterfly-garlanded girl whose scent his master had introduced to him. With a stealthy movement gifted to only those creatures Mother Nature favored, the large white wolf crept back into the forest from whence he'd come. As ever, not one human being had seen him stalk to the village. And not one human being would see him return to Castle Vargar—the home of his master, the Wolf Prince of Vavassour.

The Wolf Prince Returns

Those who lived within the walls of Castle Vargar were indeed curious. Rather they stood astonished—mouths hanging incredulously agape as Balian and his five white wolf companions rode through the outer gatehouse, across the outer bailey, and onward toward the great North Tower. For Balian's part, he grinned, amused. As he rode past the inner gatehouse, though not one person had spoken a word as he rode before them, he could in truth sense the breeze their excited whispers stirred in his wake.

"It would seem we are indeed a spectacle even yet, my friend," he spoke lowly to his oldest wolf companion. Thor glanced up to his prince in apparent understanding.

A quiet chuckle escaped Balian's throat as he mumbled, "Would that they should see a hundred others like you concealed in the forest in wait, eh? They would truly stand in awe then, yes?"

As he drew nearer to the great North Tower wherein he knew he would find his parents awaiting him, a substantial sensation of wistfulness began to enfold him. He was, undeniably, home. He had been born in the North Tower of Castle Vargar. The private chambers of each member of his family were cached in there—even his own—even the chambers of his brother, Phillip. Balian wondered then if Phillip still used Castle Vargar's clandestine passages to access his private chambers. He thought it was definite that he did, for he had no knowledge, had received no correspondence throughout his five years of absence from Vavassour, stating otherwise. It was therefore sure that all of Vavassour save the royal family and a very few others still believed Prince Phillip had died ten years previous—still supposed Balian's older brother lay at peace in the family crypt.

At the thought of his brother being forced to live the life of something akin to a ghost, a familiar vehemence rose within Balian's broad chest. A frown of near wrath puckered his brow. Still, he had promised to return to Vavassour and Castle Vargar. Balian had assured his father and mother, the king and queen of the kingdom of Vavassour, that he would return—that he was ready to reconcile the past heartaches, anger, and frustrations that had stirred between them, causing him to abandon Vavassour five years earlier—that he was, at last, ready and willing to take his place as the heir of the kingdom. Moreover, the deep, throbbing guilt he felt at abandoning his brother had ever weighed heavy on his heart and mind since the very moment of his leaving, and he meant to alleviate it—

even in the very least. Phillip needed Balian as an ally and champion. Even more imperative, Phillip needed his brother's companionship and affection. Hence, though Balian knew he would almost assuredly be fighting the same battle that had sent him riding from Vavassour in resentment five years previous, he felt he had grown, matured, acquired humility, experience, and patience—virtues that were now potent within him that had been somewhat lacking in the character of his younger self.

It was then he heard something nearly forgotten yet deeply familiar, something carried over the breeze as commanding as ever: the roar of the lion. The powerful roar echoed majestic and menacing from the menagerie near the West Tower.

When Thor paused a moment—his adult offspring Ullr, Freyja, Delling, and Nótt also pausing—Balian laughed. "Have you forgotten old Apedemak, friends?" Balian nodded toward the West Tower, adding, "It sounds as if our old lion friend is demanding his midday meal."

Of a sudden, and quite unexpected to both Balian and his wolves, the powerful roar of a second lion echoed over the castle grounds. Balian raised one eyebrow, speaking, "Ah! It would seem old Apedemak has had one son in the least of it in our absence. It would appear the Monk of the Menagerie has proved himself an able keeper of lions." Looking down to his wolves once more, Balian nodded once. "You well remember Apedemak, do you not? We are his allies. We, none of us, will fear him or his pride."

Having been soothed more by the calm of Balian's voice than his words, Thor and his counterparts moved on once more.

Reminiscently Balian mumbled, "I wonder if the Monk of the Menagerie is with old Apedemak now, perhaps spoiling him with beef today."

The older lion roared again, bringing further thoughts of the king's menagerie and the monk who tended it to Balian's mind. He grinned as he thought then of the butterfly pavilion, his mother's favorite fraction of the menagerie.

At once, visions of the lovely young woman, Minnette, whom he had encountered in the meadow lingered in his mind's eye, and he reflected on the fanciful butterflies that had gathered around her—alighting on her head, hand, or shoulder as if she were the most beautiful of flowers, spilling out the sweetest nectar of heaven for them to savor. The notion struck him that he would indeed enjoy watching the butterflies in Vargar's pavilion were pretty Minnette thrust into their house. He wondered for a moment if the lovely winged things might, in some form, attack her—desperate to taste the nectar promised by her soft beauty.

The trumpet sounding tore his thoughts from the beauty of the girl in the meadow and back to the moment at hand. Indeed, Balian looked up to see his father and mother standing at the solar balcony, looking down upon him and waving. Both wore smiles of love and relief on their faces, and his mother was weeping with joy.

"Come up and greet us, son!" his father, the king, called to him. "Do not delay a moment longer, please!"

Balian's mother, the queen, nodded with emphatic encouragement, even as she dabbed the tears from her cheeks with a lace handkerchief.

Balian's stomach knotted with more guilt then. What kind of fool had he been to abandon his family and kingdom so easily? He had been weak and selfish indeed. But the past was behind him, as it was for every living creature, and forward was the path he had determined to tread—reparation.

Thus, nodding to his parents, Balian Volk, the long-absent crown prince of Vavassour—the Wolf Prince, the Wolf Knight—dismounted his majestic horse, spoke, "Vent her," in the language in which he most often commanded his wolf comrades, and strode into the foot of the North Tower.

As Thor and the other wolves that had accompanied him remained outside the tower, Balian climbed the stairs that led to the solar, whereon his parents had stood in beckoning him. The past was full in his mind, even as he determined to leave it behind him.

Visions of the day ten years previous came to his mind—the day his elder and beloved brother, Phillip, was thrown from his mount, his head striking a large stone as he fell to the earth—images of the pool of blood threatening to drown his unconscious brother, Balian's first sight after having dismounted his own horse to rush to his brother's aid. This memory struck Balian's heart with renewed pain, as ever it did when it nested in his thoughts. This painful reverie was in an instant followed by visions of Phillip lying in his bed, pale and unconscious for near to a fortnight afterward. Just as wretched were the memories then of the day Phillip awakened from his unconscious state—the day it was revealed to Balian and his royal parents that great, harmful damage had been done the eldest prince of Vavassour. Tears brimmed in Balian's eyes as he climbed the tower stairs, remembering Phillip's inability to speak clearly—his slowness of mind and thought. Balian's brother had survived the fall from his horse and being struck in the head by the rock, but his eloquent speech and keen mind had not survived with him.

It was not that Balian did not understand the reasons the king and queen chose to tell the kingdom that their beloved Prince Phillip had died. That they had chosen to protect their son from ridicule, hardheartedness, and cruelty, he did understand. After all, Balian himself could well imagine the gossip that would have followed Phillip wherever he walked, the malice heaped upon his brother by monarchies of other kingdoms, and the criticism his parents would have received, even for the fact that the cruel tragedy that had befallen Phillip was the fault of no one. Yet in Balian's opinion, Phillip's life course following his injuries had been more difficult perhaps, for his brother had been secretly hidden from the kingdom for the past ten years. For ten years, Phillip Volk had not been free to wander the castle or its grounds. Phillip had no companionship, save his parents, Balian, the occasional visit from the village apothecary and his wife, and one young maidservant who had been sworn to secrecy on peril of her life.

It was in that moment of reflection that Balian was again thankful for his brother's unusual way with animals. Had it not been for Phillip's apparent kinship to the creatures of the earth, he would have had nothing to look to for delight and happiness, nothing to nurture and tend to, no friend outside his family.

Yes, Balian had befriended Thor—been accepted by Thor and his orphaned pups. Yet it was Phillip who owned the affections, respect, and loyalty of not only the lions in the king's menagerie but of every creature therein. From the great white bear of the north to the smallest red fox from the west, every creature in the menagerie doted on Phillip's bidding—protected and looked after their keeper as if they indeed understood their master's tribulation.

For the decade since Phillip's tragedy, it was the one freedom allowed Balian's brother by his parents—to care for the menagerie. Nonetheless, it was only allowed as long as Phillip remained ever hidden, as long as he never spoke to another human being while he was tending the menagerie, and as long as he was ever clothed in the dark robe and cowl of a monk. Thus, Balian's prince brother—he that was once, by birthright, the true heir to the throne of Vavassour, he that was once Balian's mentor, powerful exemplar of strength, intelligence, and all that was good in men to be admired and emulated—lived in veritable isolation, ever robed and cowled, with only a few who knew he even yet existed, and with animals to keep him in best company.

For the first five years following Phillip's injuries and consequent isolation, Balian had pled with his father to allow all who dwelt in the kingdom to prove that goodness dwelt in their hearts—to be given the opportunity to accept Phillip as he had become, instead of thinking of him only as the great prince who had tragically died. But King Liam would not hear of it. King Liam feared the ridicule that would surely fall upon Phillip—the sneers of disgust that would no doubt follow in his wake wherever he walked. King Liam had stood adamant that he would not see his eldest son—his son who had once been so powerful and wise, who would have been king—treated with any measure of disrespect, mockery, or scorn. Balian tried to assure his father, the king, that the people of Vavassour would have compassion for their once first prince, that they would accept Phillip as one who had known tragedy that, for no fault of his own, had taken his strength of mind from him and love him as they always had. But no matter how strongly Balian pled his brother's case, the king would not be swayed.

And then, when on another tragic day, as King Liam's ire had fallen upon Balian's wolf companion Thor—when his father had ordered Thor's execution before the truth was known—Balian had had enough of his father's fear and what Balian saw as weakness, and he had abandoned Vargar and Vavassour in search of justice and a measure of peace of mind elsewhere.

As Balian ascended the last of the stairs leading to the uppermost rooms of the North Tower, he thought of the day he had taken his five wolves—including Thor, who the king had ordered be put to death for killing a castle guard—the day he had left his mother sobbing, having collapsed to her knees with heartache—the day his father's face had been crimson with anger at his youngest son—the day his own brother, Phillip, had wept in begging him not to leave. In those moments, Balian felt more shame in his own anger and in the hurt he had caused those he loved than even he had before.

Thus, he paused before entering the room in the North Tower wherein he knew his parents awaited him. Would they truly accept him home? Gather him into their loving arms and be grateful only to have him back, having forgiven him his selfish abandonment of family and kingdom? He thought sure they would; else why would his father have written asking him, yet again, to return home?

Balian mused that his mother would love him and be jubilant to see him again, no matter the past. Yet he worried over his father's being earnest in welcoming the prodigal back—even if he had asked it many times over.

"Balian? M-m-my brother?"

At the sound of Phillip's beloved and familiar voice, Balian turned, and all doubt was washed away as he gazed into his brother's brilliantly blue eyes. Phillip appeared as strong and able as ever he had—perhaps a bit older, but only a measure. He stood straight and tall, with broad shoulders that mirrored the breadth of Balian's.

His jaw was square and firm, and to look at him—even as he stood in his black robe with a length of rope at his waist and a cowl hanging at his shoulders and back—Balian himself would not have conceived that his mind was not whole had he not known so already. Tears were fresh on Phillip's cheeks as he smiled at Balian in mingled disbelief and joy.

"Yes, Phillip," Balian spoke. "The prodigal son has returned."

At once Balian found himself gathered into Phillip's powerful embrace as the man wept onto his shoulder, moistening the fabric of his tunic.

"Phillip," Balian said, as tears traveled over his own face. "I am so sorry, my brother. I was weak and—"

"N-n-no!" Phillip interjected, however. "Y-you were ever my . . . my . . . my champion, Balian. Y-you are . . . are . . . ever . . . m-my b-b-brother."

In truth, Balian had forgotten how slow of speech his brother was. And yet it did not sadden him but caused his heart to swell with gladness that he was with him once more. Oh, how he had missed Phillip!

Of a sudden, it was as if Balian's senses had been imprisoned and had instantly known liberation! He was keen in awareness then of the scents of the castle and of Phillip—of the cool air wafting through the tower windows, of the scent of bread and pastry rising from the castle kitchens, of the mellow essence of animal fur, of lions. He could smell the courtyard grasses, and there was the lingering essence of candle wax and flame, of warm fires in hearths. Of a sudden he was aware of the laughter and excited talk of kingdom subjects that had gathered in the bailey beneath the North Tower, heard their cheering. Balian had returned to his home, his parents, his brother, and his responsibilities and, in doing so, knew he had been changed to a far better man than he had been five years before.

    Balian did not have to open the door before which he and Phillip stood, for it was opened from within by his father.

    His mother was on him in an instant, sobbing as she clung to him and to Phillip. "My boys! My two boys! Oh, how I've missed you, Balian! How Phillip and I have missed you!"

    After having kissed his mother several times, holding her for long moments as she wept, he looked up and to his father when the king said, "As have I, my son Balian. As have I."

    Balian sensed no lingering bitterness nor resentment as his father embraced him, kissing his cheek over and over again. There was only love and unspoken regret for time apart. His father was sincere in his gladness, and Balian felt as if some heavy thing had been lifted from his heart.

    "Come," Liam of Vavassour said, gesturing

that Balian should precede them all in entering the room.

Balian smiled as he stepped into the familiar surroundings, the room he'd loved more than any other as a boy. This was the room where he and Phillip had spent many evenings together in discussion, light conversation, or even playing at amusements of games and reading. Always it had been filled with love and comfort and privacy for the royal family. Even though guards oft had stood outside the door to the family solar room, it was the place where Balian and Phillip had felt most happy, as well as the least imprisoned by being royal. In the solar, there had always been laughter, delicious food for mere indulgence, instruction from their father, and nurturing from their mother. Balian and Phillip spent time together playing in the solar on their own whilst growing up as well. On the soft carpets they played with carved soldiers and horses, leading epic battles and winning pretended wars. And as he glanced about the familiar room, Balian's smile broadened once more. It had not changed, not in all his five years of absence. Even the chest filled with the wooden soldiers and horses he and his brother had cherished stood in its fixed place by the hearth as if waiting for new battles to commence.

"You look well, Balian," his father said.

"B-b-bigger," Phillip said, smiling.

"Oh, he is still a little boy in my eyes," his mother offered, still weeping.

"As do you, Father," Balian said with a nod. "And Phillip and Mother, as well. I am thankful to find you all in good health and otherwise well."

And it was true! Balian had worried in excess over the condition of his family in his absence. He was given information and of course received correspondence from his father and mother. But he had worried over them just the same. Yet to see them now, with color in their faces, strength in their postures—even for his father's temples being a bit more grayed and his mother's lips not quite as pink as they once had been—they, all of them, looked no worse for his having been away, and he was thankful.

"F-Father s-s-said . . . h-he t-told . . . that I . . . that I . . . I-I t-told h-him of . . . of . . ." Phillip struggled.

Balian frowned, his heart aching for his brother. Phillip endured even more difficulty in speech when he was desperate to say something. He watched his brother shake his head with frustration, inhale a calming breath, and continue.

"I-I t-told F-Father . . . the . . . the g-guard wh-wh . . . whipped me. N-nine l-l-lashes. I-It is wh-wh-why Th-Th-Thor t-took h-him b-by the . . . the . . . the throat, k-k-k-killing h-him."

Balian smiled, placing an appreciative and

supportive hand on Phillip's broad shoulder. "I know, dear brother. And I am so thankful that you did . . . grateful for your testimony on Thor's behalf."

Phillip frowned, however, adding, "B-but you st-stayed aw-away."

"I did, brother," Balian admitted as his heart began to ache once more. "And I am sorry. Will you be able to forgive me? One day perhaps?"

Phillip smiled then and nodded as he placed a strong hand on Balian's shoulder. "I-I h-have n-nothing t-t-t-to for-for-forgive, br-brother."

Balian exhaled a sigh of relief. Nodding, he said, "Thank you, Phillip. And know that Thor will be very glad indeed to see his old friend Phillip. He is waiting with Ullr, Freyja, Delling, and Nótt below in the courtyard. I will send them to you when we have had our full reunion, very well?"

"Y-you w-w-w-will send th-them t-to the m-m-menag-gerie," Phillip instructed.

"Of course," Balian agreed. "They will be happy to be with you again, my brother."

Phillip smiled. "Apedemak s-s-sensed th-the w-wolves app-approaching," he managed.

Balian chuckled, "Ahh! Is that what induced his roar? I thought perhaps he was summoning his meal."

Phillip shook his head. "N-no. It w-w-was

Th-Th-Thor's r-r-return," he confirmed with his own amused expression.

"Come, darling," Balian's mother, Queen Asta, began, taking his arm. "Come and sit with your mother a while. Tell us of your journey home to us."

"Yes, son," Balian's father, King Liam, agreed with a nod. "Are you weary? Your room has been prepared, freshened, ready whenever you need take your rest. And . . . and you will join us for supper . . . your mother and I, yes?"

Balian's smile faded somewhat, though he forced its remnants to stay upon his expression, for his parents' sake. Yet with his father's mention of supper—of the obvious exclusion of Phillip being named as an attendee—Balian felt the old anger begin to rise in his chest. He looked to his brother and received exactly what he knew he would—a nod of reassurance that he should say nothing in defense of him. It was as Phillip had done since his injury—ever encouraged Balian to accept Phillip's state of near ghostly existence. And although Balian knew nothing had changed where Phillip's secret continuation was concerned, he found his heart ached just as brutal as it had five years before for the sake of his brother's unquestionable loneliness.

"Perhaps," Asta began, "perhaps you would enjoy visiting with your father and I for a time . . . and then retire to Phillip's chambers for a visit of length with him alone, Balian. Before supper, hmmm?"

Balian saw the pleading in his mother's eyes—the tears brimming in their beautiful blue. This too was familiar, for his mother had ever endeavored to keep Balian from argument with his father where Phillip was concerned.

"Of course, Mother," Balian said, at once remembering every instance when he had ignored the pleading in her eyes and caused her pain while at variance with his father. "That is a wonderful idea."

He watched his mother sigh with relief, and she smiled and squeezed his hand with appreciation.

"Come then, Balian," Liam said then. "Tell us the tale of your travels to return to us. Of certain there is something of note to share."

Balian felt his own brows arch, as the first thought to leap to his mind was of the pretty village girl he had met in the meadow just beyond the castle. The truth was he had had many intriguing experiences on his way to Castle Vargar, some of which even involved those in other kingdoms he crossed. For when discovering he was Prince Balian of Vavassour, some had run in terror, being there were those scattered throughout all the lands and kingdoms that bordered Vavassour who still whispered of the Wolf Prince—the werewolf prince who, when the full moon rose, changed into a vicious beast that feasted on human flesh.

Yet it was the vision of the lovely butterfly sprite, Minnette, that gave him pause.

Grinning at his mother, Balian said, "I suppose it would not be comfortable for Mother if I were to begin with a tale of a pretty maid I met along the way, now would it?"

"Oh my!" Asta exclaimed as her cheeks pinked. "Are you in earnest, Balian?"

Balian laughed, as did his father and Phillip.

"Of course not, Mother," he fibbed. "It is only that I have missed your girlish blush and wished to see it once more."

Asta blushed a more scarlet hue, lightheartedly slapping her son on one shoulder. "I had quite forgotten what a terrible tease you are, Balian. How dare you discomfit your mother so."

Still, as his mother giggled with delight, Balian's father winked at him with approval, saying, "Go on now, boy. Tell us a tale."

"Very well," Balian began as he and the others took seats near one another. "I came near to being burned at the stake in Cevalon."

"What?" the queen exclaimed as all remnants of her previous blush drained from her cheeks.

"I said I came near to it, Mother. Only near to it," Balian assured his mother.

"Why?" his father asked.

Balian shrugged. "They knew me, and it would

seem that many in Mirermith still believe me to be a werewolf and not a normal man."

Balian did not miss the exchange of worried glances that passed between his mother and father. Yet he chose not to inquire as to their thoughts—not in that moment.

And so he continued his tale—himself taking note of the way Phillip's hands would clench into powerful fists as he spoke of battling the men endeavoring to bind him with intentions of burning him alive.

Yes, Phillip was as strong as ever he was in body. In his silent thoughts, Balian took note of the fact, for he knew it would serve him when the opportunity did arise for his brother to know freedom. Balian was determined that Phillip would one day be free from the darkness of Castle Vargar's hidden passages and the robe and cowl of a monk. One day, Phillip would wear armor and a royal tunic of blue marked with the family crest and motto.

Balian Volk of Vavassour had found wisdom and humility in his five years of isolation from his family and kingdom. Nevertheless, he was of the same mind regarding his beloved and most-deserving brother, where Phillip's liberation was concerned. That had not changed, and it never would. Balian would see Phillip freed from darkness and hiding. He would see him accepted by the people of Vavassour. He would see him dressed in the garments of a prince and wearing a prince's armor.

Even as he continued to tell his own tale of danger and escape in Mirermith, most prominent in Balian's mind was his resolve to see his brother's deliverance.

The Monk of the Menagerie

The royal family had spent near to three hours together in the solar, reminiscing, laughing, and sharing forgiveness, however unspoken—of disagreement and heartaches of the past. Yet all the while, Balian sensed that Phillip was desirous of private audience with him, and Balian himself grew impatient in wanting solitude with his elder brother.

Therefore, when at long last Phillip had inquired of his parents, asking that he might accompany Balian to the menagerie, that his brother could know what he had been about in his absence, it was Balian found himself exceedingly glad, and relieved as well. He had quite forgotten how incessantly his father could talk—how Balian's temper was so easily pricked for what he viewed as his father's neglect of his mother.

Yet added joy washed over him when his father gave permission for his two sons to view the menagerie together and Phillip asked whether Thor and the other four original wolves of Castle Vargar might join them. He relished the obvious joy the wolves experienced when, having been summoned, Thor, Ullr, Freyja, Delling, and Nótt arrived to greet Phillip with all the excitement of new puppies being reunited with their mother.

Balian smiled, overcome with amusement as he watched the large wolves romp about Phillip, jumping up to lick his face and hands and panting with elation. It was always the wolves had adored Phillip; even it seemed they understood that he had suffered great tragedy, and they loved him all the more for what he had endured.

For his part, Phillip was himself overjoyed to see the wolves and stroked their furry heads, scratched them behind their ears, and even fed them pieces of dried meat he carried in the pockets of his robe. As Balian continued to watch the merry reunion, he wondered—although he well remembered why—how he could ever have left his brother for any length of time, let alone five long years. He could only hope that what he had gained in humility, strength, and wisdom whilst away would serve Phillip and the kingdom well one day. It was his hope—it was his prayer—it was his only manner of hunting after forgiveness of himself.

As the two princes of Vavassour, along with their white wolf companions, made their way to the West Tower via hidden passages inside the castle walls, it further comforted Balian to know that, as it had been before, he found his mind heard Phillip's speech as unimpeded. Even for the truth that it was still impaired, somehow Balian heard Phillip's voice as ever he had—clear, defined, and without stammer.

"Apedemak's family has grown in your absence, little brother," Phillip said, smiling with pride.

Balian nodded. "We heard another lion roaring as we approached," he offered. "How many new males in the pride now?"

"Two," Phillip answered. "And twelve females. I do see Apedemak's sons beginning to challenge his rule. Apedemak is aged, and he is weakening, albeit slowly. I think it will be Armani, his eldest son, that will rule one day. Though Morocco is but one year the younger than Armani . . . and very strong as well."

"And the menagerie is still large enough to keep them when there are so many?" Balian asked.

"Yes—though I fear not in great comfort." Phillip seemed pensive for a moment and then added, "It is many the times I have contemplated taking the lions south . . . releasing them . . . perhaps living away from Vavassour myself for a time as you have done." He grinned with a rather sad sort of expression and said, "It would also put Father and Mother's need to keep me hidden to rest."

As Balian's angst was renewed at once, he grumbled, "It would devastate them, as well you know. *And* me. But I promise you this, brother: I will fight to see the day that you are free . . . that the entire kingdom knows you yet live and that you are strong and able. You *are* strong and blessed with many gifts and much to offer the world and our people."

Phillip drew his cowl up to cover his head and face. Then, placing a comforting hand on Balian's shoulder in an obvious effort to calm him, he said, "I *am* strong and able, Balian. For after the guard showed such disrespect of me, lashing me as he did—after Thor was so falsely accused of brutality when he was only protecting me and you fled in protecting him—I began my training once more . . . and I have never ceased. I daresay I could match broadswords with even the likes of Balian, the Wolf Prince of Vavassour, again. But do not set your sights on changing Father's mind. He is a man of stubbornness, determination, and considerable pride. Therefore, do not fret for my sake any longer, Balian. I am well." Phillip smiled, adding, "We are together again, and that is what matters. Now come, let me show you what the mysterious Monk of the Menagerie has accomplished whilst you were away, hmm?"

Balian's frown softened, though it did not entirely disappear. Placing a firm hand on Phillip's shoulder, he said, "You are a Prince of Vavassour as well. And one day, the kingdom—nay, the world—will know it again. It is my oath to you, my brother . . . my most deserving brother."

Phillip nodded, though Balian sensed his doubt that his vow would see fruition. Still, this was meant to be a glad visit with Phillip. Thus, Balian nodded and said, "Show me, Phillip. If the lions have thrived so well under your care, I am certain every other creature has as well."

Pushing at one wall in the passageway, Phillip stepped into a well-hidden space in the menagerie. Balian and the wolves followed, and at once, Balian was astonished at the change in the great menagerie of King Liam of Vavassour. Not only had the lay been exceedingly extended to a near massive venue of display, but also its ethereal beauty was astonishing.

Large boulders had obviously been brought in and situated throughout the various habitats and environments isolated from one another by iron posts and fencing, assuring the animals and any visitors were safe in separation from one another. It appeared as if no animal was chained, as many had been upon Balian's departure from Vavassour. Indeed, each intriguing captive of the menagerie roamed unreservedly within a habitat designed to allow them to do so. The large brown bears wore no shackles and chains, and the excitable monkeys were not tethered on ropes but rather sat in the branches of trees that were enclosed in immense iron cages.

Furthermore, flora and fauna thrived everywhere throughout the menagerie. Flowers, herbs, and vegetables could be seen both within and without each animal's territory. But most impressive of all was the enormous waterwheel drawing water from the moat, fed by the Vavassour River, and pouring cool refreshment into a series of raised waterways fashioned of wood and iron. The system of waterways, all of which were ingeniously masked by abundant green and flowering vines, presented fresh water in the form of small waterfalls into several of the various animal domains. From where he stood, Balian could see that the great white bear from the north was floating in a vast pool of cool water. The magnificent apes that had been a gift to his father many years before lay in plush, green grass, soaking their feet in the water cascading into their realm. The grounds and lair of the lions were the most immense in the menagerie, and Balian could see Apedemak himself sunning atop an immense rock as the rest of the pride stretched out in plush grass below him or lingered near a watering hole that was also being fed by a trickling waterfall.

Naturally, being that the menagerie was contained in what had once been the west bailey, the sun shone bright and warm upon it, allowing the animals to bask in warmth but also rest in the shade of the trees that had been added in Balian's absence. There was no strong stink in the area the like there was on occasion in the past. And Balian assumed that his brother had also found a way to manage the animals' waste and divert or vanquish the stench of it.

Looking to Phillip, Balian shook his head in admiration. "Brother," he began, "you are an architect from heaven itself. I have never seen such a place! Your brilliance is well evident . . . as well as your sincere care for the beasts herein." Balian laughed when he glanced down to Thor to see the wolf cock his head to one side rather inquisitively. "Even Thor now wonders why he followed me into oblivion when he could have remained here and savored such pampering."

Phillip chuckled, reached down, and patted Thor's head. "Oh, I am certain the adventures you and your five wolves have had far outweigh any pampering in captivity. Eh, Thor, old boy? And I do think that if animals that are not of a domestic nature naturally are to be kept imprisoned for the mere amusement of the king, then they should have as much comfort as can be allotted them. Yes?" Phillip then arched one curious eyebrow and as he scratched behind Delling's ears asked, "I am surprised you do not have twice or three times this many wolves, brother. It seems with two males and two females other than Thor, several litters may have come to you in five years' time."

Balian smiled. "Oh, several litters have indeed come to me, brother. And more litters than from just Thor and his brood."

"Indeed?" Phillip inquired.

"Oh, most certainly indeed," Balian laughed.

"Well, where are they? Are they free wolves then?" Phillip continued.

"Freer than they would have been had they been born in the menagerie, I would say," Balian answered. "And they are nearer than you might think . . . though unseen."

Phillip frowned. "How many? And if near . . . where are they near?"

Balian paused, uncertain as to how much he should reveal to Phillip—not so much as to the number of wolves he commanded but as to why he had decided to bring them back to Castle Vargar with him, as opposed to simply setting them on their free path altogether.

"Let us tour your great menagerie first, shall we? And then we will discuss the wolves. Agreed?" Balian suggested.

Phillip's eyes narrowed, and Balian knew his brother sensed his discomfort. Still, "Agreed," Phillip answered.

"Marvelous!" Balian said. "I want to see everything. But in particular, I am interested in the butterfly pavilion. I see it there, at the north end of the menagerie. Is it still fraught with butterflies and moths?"

"Oh, more so than ever before," Phillip announced proudly. He paused then, quirking an eyebrow once more. "But what finds you so interested in the butterfly pavilion, brother? As I remember, you did not favor it before you left."

"In truth, I would still rather play with lions than butterflies," Balian admitted. "But on my way here—through the meadow beyond the moat, in fact—just this day, I met the most . . . the most interesting young woman. And albeit somewhat unbelievable perhaps, she was flocked round about by butterflies. Even as we stood talking, they lit every which way upon her limbs and in her hair . . ."

"Ah, then it was Minnette you met in the meadow," Phillip said, smiling.

"What?" Balian exclaimed. "You know the girl? For indeed Minnette is the name she gave."

Balian frowned, confused. How could his brother know of the lovely Minnette when he was not privileged to consort with anyone other than his father, mother, and personal maid? Surely there were craftsmen and workers that had built the menagerie up per Phillip's instructions. But Balian had assumed Phillip appeared to these men only cloaked and cowled. How was it that his brother knew of Minnette?

Phillip laughed. "Ah, little brother!" he chortled. "You have given yourself away! You were smitten with the girl, were you not? And you are astonished that *I* should know of her . . . being that I am a veritable prisoner of the castle."

"In truth, yes . . . on both accounts," Balian admitted. "How *do* you know of the girl?"

Phillip's laughter subsided. "I am thinking she did not tell you her surname then? That you have no knowledge of her parentage?" he asked.

"No. None whatsoever," Balian admitted.

Phillip offered each of the five wolves in their company another luxury from his robe pocket. "Her name is D'Angelville . . . Minnette D'Angelville," he said as Thor and his counterparts enjoyed his dried meats.

The surname of the lovely butterfly girl from the meadow was far more than merely familiar to Balian: it was well known and respected, and for a decade.

"D'Angelville. She is the daughter of the apothecary then? Of Stuart D'Angelville and his wife?" Balian inquired in awe.

Phillip nodded, the front of his cowl sweeping low as he did so. "She is."

"And . . . and you're acquainted with her?" Balian asked.

"Not at all," Phillip said, "only through what her father and mother have told me of her over the years during their visits to administer to me—through what only her mother has told me this past year . . . for her father is dead."

Balian's mind quickly traveled back to the day Phillip had been injured. The royal physician had inadvertently poisoned himself and died one week before, leaving the royal family without assistance after Phillip's accident. Balian's father had often called upon the apothecary from the village, and he sent for Stuart D'Angelville that very day. It had been Stuart D'Angelville who had cared for Phillip, tended to his wounds, and watched over him night and day until he awoke. Save the royal family and his brother's personal maid, only Stuart D'Angelville and his wife, Morgianna, knew that the prince Phillip Volk had lived. Stuart and Morgianna had tended to Phillip whenever he was ill or in need otherwise of a physician's attention—since the very day King Liam had announced that Phillip of Vavassour was dead.

"And she does not know that you are yet living?" Balian asked.

Phillip's cowl moved side to side in indicating that the girl did not know he was alive. "Though I am told by her mother that the girl often visits the place where I fell when the horse threw me . . . that she leaves wildflowers there in my memory. It is apparent she is very tender of heart." Phillip paused and then added, "And her mother has mentioned to me that her daughter does seem to be made of nectar and honey . . . that butterflies find her no matter where she hides."

Balian was silent for a moment—pensive—somewhat envious that his brother should know more about the pretty young woman in the meadow than he.

"It is why you inquired of the butterfly pavilion

when there are lions to witness," Phillip offered. "You are wondering what would occur were Minnette D'Angelville to enter therein, hmm?"

At last, Balian smiled once more. Nodding in admittance, he said, "Yes. Indeed, it is a sight I should like to behold." He paused, frowned a bit, and then added, "Of course, I would not want the things to devour her or some such catastrophe."

"Oh, I do not think they would intentionally harm her," Phillip offered. "Though, from what I have heard from you and her mother, they may indeed flutter her to death, yes?"

Both brothers laughed, amused by the thought that butterflies could ever harm anything, let alone a grown woman.

"I have missed you, Phillip," Balian said as his laughter subsided. "Painfully, I have missed you."

"And I you, Balian," Phillip offered. "But the past is behind us. Therefore, let us relish today and look to the future with hopeful hearts, eh?"

"Yes," Balian agreed. "Now show me your lions, Phillip. Unless you think old Apedemak might not recognize me and choose to have me for his evening meal instead."

"He already recognizes you," Phillip said as both he and the wolves approached the lion enclosure. "See how he stands to greet you, his gaze resting on Thor now and again? Oh yes, Apedemak is aged but not so much he does not recognize true and trusted friends." With a low chuckle, Phillip added, "At least, let us hope."

Balian smiled, glad to be back in the company of his brother—sincere in his pleasure to be home.

"More than a hundred?" Phillip exclaimed in a whisper. "How came you by so many, Balian?" Phillip looked to Thor a moment, puckering his brow and muttering, "Surely Thor did not—"

Balian laughed, albeit quietly. "No, no. Thor is mighty, but he is no philanderer." Scratching Thor's chin where his head lay on his lap, Balian explained, "There were several litters from each of Thor's progeny—Ullr, Freyja, Delling, and Nótt—for each of them has a mate, it is true. However, the first winter I was away, I came upon several litters up north that had been abandoned or whose parentage had been killed or captured. Of course, we added them to our brood, raising them as our own. They then matured and begat more wolves, who matured and begat more. Also, each year in turn, I would return to the land of the north, and each year I found more and more abandoned wolf pups. I could not leave them to be killed, for every beast deserves a fighting chance. Do they not, Thor?"

Thor licked Balian's hand with affection, as if he understood exactly what his human friend was talking about. Balian knew that Thor did indeed understand him. He did not know how the great wolf knew his mind—just that he did.

"But so many," Phillip said. "Even a hundred? Why had so many pups been abandoned? Did you ever discover a cause?"

Balian nodded. "Indeed I did." He frowned with lingering anger as he continued, "It seems one family in that kingdom had lost a child to a white wolf. The child had been taunting a mother wolf that was protecting her litter, and the wolf attacked the child. The wounds inflicted were fatal. Therefore, the men in the family became vigilant in killing as many white wolves as could be found." Balian paused a moment, remembering the sight of blood-soaked snow near one wolf den wherein Thor had found an orphaned litter. "It was each winter I spent north that I would find bloody carnage seemingly everywhere—carnage and, in its wake, a litter of white wolves near to starvation. Until this past winter, that is."

Phillip cocked his head to one side, frowned, and inquired, "Why was this last winter different?"

Balian grinned. "I ended the slaughtering of white wolves in that kingdom to the north."

Phillip grinned as well. "You? How?"

Balian stretched his legs out on the ottoman before the fire, leaned back in his brother's large comfortable chair, and said, "I found that there is advantage to not only having a hundred wolves at one's beckoning but also in tales that abound of a Wolf Prince from the east who is, by all accounts of outlying kingdoms, a werewolf."

Phillip smiled. "You frightened the hunters into submission to your demands?" Phillip laughed with approval and triumph. "What? Did you appear with your hundred wolves and threaten to bring bloody carnage to them in your alternate wolf form if they did not comply?"

Balian smiled and laughed as well. "I did. Though I think it was Thor and his hundred soldiers that frightened them into submission more than the implication that a werewolf would linger in their midst did they not comply."

Phillip laughed again, sighing with satisfaction when his laughter subsided. "Oh, that I could have had such adventures with you, my brother."

Balian nodded. "Yes! What terror we could strike into the hearts of any harboring ill will toward our people, eh? The two princes of Vavassour—Phillip the Lion Prince and Balian the Wolf Prince! What fear and trembling would precede us and would we leave in our wake, yes?"

"Yes! That is it!" Phillip near shouted. "What a pair we would be indeed!"

"Excuse me, sire."

Balian startled at the young woman's voice sounding unexpectedly behind him.

"Would you be ready for your evening meal now?"

"Good evening, Arianna," Phillip greeted. "You do remember my brother, Balian, don't you?"

Balian fairly leapt from his comfortable seat as he stood to greet Phillip's maid, Arianna.

"Yes. Good evening to you as well, Prince Balian," Arianna greeted with a perfect curtsey.

Balian bowed, even as his brows rose in astonishment. "Good evening, Arianna. It pleases me to see you again."

The girl had matured—considerably. When last Balian had laid eyes on Arianna, she had been no more than a thin little thing of seventeen, with large green eyes that appeared far too big for her face. Yet now she stood before him a lovely woman indeed.

It was that Balian had always known guilt and heartache for Arianna's sake in similarity to what he felt for his brother. Upon deciding that the kingdom should be told that the prince Phillip had died from injuries sustained by his fall, it was also decided that whoever was chosen to serve him would never be able to speak to anyone concerning her responsibilities at the castle. Therefore, though Arianna's family had been quite satisfied to ask no questions about her duties at the castle when she was a mere twelve years of age and accepting of the task—no doubt because of the large sum of wages she and her family were both rewarded—by the time Arianna had turned fifteen, her family had taken it upon their own evil-thinking selves to decide she had become a scarlet woman. Her father had publicly denounced her as his daughter, claiming he had testimony from a castle guard that Arianna was kept as mistress to whomever was desirous of her company.

Having sworn never to speak of what her true duties were, Arianna was forced to abandon her family completely—to live in solitude much the way Phillip did—and it had always grieved both Phillip and Balian.

"If you have brought my supper, then of course I am ready for it, Arianna," Phillip said.

And it was as Arianna smiled, as her green eyes were lit with a flame of admiration—admiration in the very least of it—that Balian finally understood why Arianna had been so willing to stay and serve Phillip.

As she smiled at his brother, her cheeks pinking with delight—as she nodded and turned to retrieve the cart and tray she had left just outside the door to the room—Balian turned to his brother, arching his brows and silently mouthing, *Is there something I should know, Phillip?*

But Phillip shook his head, his face expressing that Balian was a fool as he said aloud, "Of course not."

As Arianna laid out a setting of plate and

utensils and then food on the small table in the largest of Phillip's rooms, Balian watched her every movement—watched her steal glances whenever possible at his brother.

"May I do anything else for you this evening, sire?" Arianna asked.

"I do not think so, Arianna," Phillip answered. "Your time is your own, to do as you like."

"I would ask a boon, if I may," Balian interjected, however.

Phillip looked to Balian, a puzzled frown puckering his brow.

"Of course, sire," Arianna said.

"I would beg that you stay with us, just for a while, that I might learn of what life has brought to my brother, as well as to you, these past five years of my absence, Arianna. If that is tolerable to you," Balian explained.

"Certainly, sire," Arianna agreed. "If . . . if that is what you both wish of me."

Phillip smiled. "Yes! That is a wonderful notion, Balian. Do join us, Arianna. Come . . . sit here next to me."

Balian grinned with understanding as the girl blushed. The flesh of her arms broke into goose bumps as she accepted the seat next to Phillip on the long chair next to the one in which Balian sat once more.

"What is it that you wish to know, my prince?" Arianna asked. Her hand trembled as she tucked a strand of loose hair the color of sunshine beneath her maid's cap.

"Well, tell me something of Phillip," Balian began, "some mischief he may have been about whilst I was away. For I know there is mischief in him . . . thicker even than runs through my own veins. Surely you have a tale to tell me of Phillip's mischief."

"I . . . I wouldn't want to disappoint my lord in any manner," the girl stammered.

"Oh, go on, Arianna," Phillip chuckled, however. "Tell a tale on your old Prince Phillip. It will amuse Balian, after all."

Blushing once more—eyes sparkling as if stars lingered in them as she gazed at his brother—Arianna said at last, "Well, there is one incident in particular that leaps to my mind."

"Very well. Let's have, please!" Balian encouraged gleefully.

Arianna giggled as she asked Phillip, "You know of what I speak, sire?"

"I do," Phillip said as he began to devour his meal. "Forge ahead, dear girl. For Balian will not rest until he hears of it now."

As Arianna began to tell of how Phillip had nearly been discovered by a child who had come to visit the menagerie and somehow become separated from royal parents, Balian heard little of what she said—not for the reason that he was not interested and not because he was impolite, but for the fact that he was far too intrigued with the interaction between Phillip and his pretty little maid. They shared laughter and smiles as they each told tales of humor or tragedy, and Balian began to think that perhaps his brother's misery in solitude was not so harsh as he had thought these past few years.

Furthermore, as Balian lay in his bed in his private chambers late in that night, he found he could think of nothing but the young woman in the meadow—the butterfly girl, Minnette D'Angelville. Why could he think of nothing but her? he wondered as he tossed in his bed. Thor was snoring, so deep was his sleep on the rug on the floor. Yet for all that the day had brought—for all his worries over the wolves lingering in the forest to watch for anything that might threaten Vavassour, for all his concerns for his mother and Phillip and even kind Arianna—it was the girl from the meadow kept lingering in his mind. Even he wondered if she truly did taste of nectar. Perhaps it was why the butterflies of the meadow admired her. Perhaps her berry-pink lips would taste of ambrosia were a man to steal a kiss from her.

Yet Balian had no plans to steal kisses from Minnette D'Angelville or any other young woman for that matter. Not while his brother was still a prisoner in Castle Vargar, not while the mutterings he had heard while in Mirermith still echoed in his ears—mutterings against King Liam and his weakness in loving his people far too much. Mutterings against the fact that it was said his son Balian was returning—that the Wolf Prince would dwell in Castle Vargar once more—that a werewolf was rooted there and must be cut out.

Still, even as Balian's mind fought to concentrate on possibilities of danger from neighboring kingdoms or of his determination to see Phillip liberated from a life like unto exile, visions of Minnette in the meadow swirled about in his mind. He smiled as he thought of her bravery—of her throwing her small shoes at wolves, mighty wolves the like of Thor, Ullr, and Delling. She was courageous, it was certain. And she was beautiful—soft and fragrant like a dream.

Turning over in his bed, resolving to force himself to sleep, Balian wondered for a moment if he had somehow weakened upon his return to Vavassour and Castle Vargar. After all, what man allowed a woman to distract him, even for a moment, when so much turmoil was in him—responsibility to his brother, his father, his kingdom? Why, only three days previous he had been battling Mirermithian soldiers who had followed him with intent to slay the Wolf Prince so that he could not return to Vavassour to one day reign in terror as a werewolf was bound to do.

Yet, as he closed his eyes, he felt his muscles relax—felt sleep begin to court him. Then, images of battle, of blood, of the necessity of might and muscle were vanquished as the sensation of sun warm in the meadow washed over him. Fleeting thoughts of the apothecary and his wife flittered through his mind—a vision of meadow-green eyes, berry lips, hair the color of roasted nuts in autumn, and a countenance and feminine beauty that beckoned nature's most delicate winged things to worship—and sent him to a quiet, content unconsciousness of slumber he had never known before.

Encounter in the Meadow

Minnette had begun to believe she had only dreamt her meeting with Prince Balian. And she had certainly begun to doubt that she had seen a hundred white wolves in his wake when he rode away from her. For although there was much talk within the strong walls of Castle Vargar among those who dwelt and sold their wares there—although everyone in the village was spending most of their day in gossip and speculation about why the prince had chosen to return when he did—not one soul mentioned having witnessed the prince with a hundred wolves in his company. Certainly everyone noted that Prince Balian's five white wolves had returned with him, as many had seen him riding through the castle courtyards and beyond the castle itself, and ever were the five white wolves in escort. No one had seen even one more white wolf, let alone a hundred.

Oh, there was much continual discussion of Prince Balian preparing to take the throne. King Liam was not so old as to be expected to give up the ghost any time in the near future. Yet men that were meant to be kings one day had much to learn—that is, if they intended to rule well and be beloved and respected of the people. Thus many in the village that thrived with Castle Vargar as a protective sentinel in Vavassour thought surely it was the reason Prince Balian had returned—to prepare to one day take the throne.

And yet talk as they did of the Wolf Prince, not a body spoke of having seen a regiment of wolves with him. Thus, Minnette did indeed begin to wonder if she had dreamt the hundred wolves. She mused that perhaps she had fainted as Prince Balian had ridden away from her that day in the meadow. In being so overwhelmed by his very presence and astonishing comeliness, perhaps she had lost consciousness for several minutes. Perhaps there were none but five wolves with the prince and she had simply dreamed up the wave of white that had appeared from the forest.

"No!" Minnette said aloud as she sat beneath a large tree laden with emerald leaves in proliferation at the edge of the meadow. "I saw them. I did! There were pure a hundred wolves with him!"

A beautiful blue and yellow butterfly alit on her hand, and she gazed at it, smiling. "Well, you are a pretty lady, are you not?" she spoke to the winged thing. "Surely you were here that day. You saw the hundred wolves, did you not? Please tell me you did, else I may begin to believe I am truly mad."

The butterfly did not speak, of course—simply opened and closed the expanse of its wings as if trying to convey an answer to Minnette, an answer she could not recognize.

Minnette smiled at the pretty flutter-by (as she had referred to them as a child). "Do you know I have come to the meadow every day since I came upon the prince here? I had hoped he would again ride this way . . . that I might be blessed with another visit with him. But he has not ridden this way when I have been here. No, sweet flutter-by, he has not. And my disappointment in that fact is . . . well, rather immense. Perhaps I will never meet him again. Perhaps I will never be so fortunate as to have another chance to study his handsome face, be sent to waves of gooseflesh rippling my arms in gazing at his magnificent smile. Perhaps I was only meant to meet him once . . . and therein daydream of him for eternity, hmmm?"

Of a sudden, the blue and yellow butterfly took flight once more. Minnette watched it go—watched it flutter and flit in the direction of Castle Vargar. And that is when she set eyes upon him again. Riding across the meadow—yet still quite a ways off—was a tall man, astride his magnificent horse. Even if the five white wolves had not been keeping pace beside him, Minnette would have recognized Prince Balian merely by the manner in which he sat his horse.

Her heart near leapt from her chest with instant excitement and delight! Yet she found anxiety welled in her, as well. For what would he think of her wasting time in the meadow when all worthy young ladies were at home sharing the labors of their other family members? If he found her lingering in the meadow once more, he might indeed think she was naught but a lazy lass.

She was certain he had not caught sight of her where she sat with the large tree between them, so she hurriedly climbed up into the branches of the enormous tree, concealing herself among the dense leaves it boasted. She did not know what had come over her! She had waited in the meadow for an hour each day—a full eight days consecutive—in hopes of seeing the prince again. But now she wanted only to go unnoticed—for Prince Balian and his wolves to pass her by—that she could avoid inevitable humiliation at the hands of her own insipid absurdity.

"Hush, please," Minnette whispered to a small orange butterfly as it alit upon her nose. "Do not make a sound . . . else we be found out."

As she clung, motionless, to the large tree limb on which she had perched herself, she closed her eyes, willing herself to breathe shallowly—even as she heard the leather of saddle and harness moving closer—even as the rhythmic drumming of hooves grew louder, ever nearer.

Balian could not keep a smile of utter amusement, and of course delight, from spreading across his face as he reined Ewan to a halt near the large maple. Oh, he had seen a figure glance at him from behind the tree's trunk only moments before—seen the leaves of the tree rustle as the same individual scampered up into its strong boughs to conceal herself. Yet even had he not seen the young woman peering at him—had he not seen the tree limbs shake, their thick veil of leaves shimmering with movement—he still would have found her out. For just beneath the one portion of the tree—the same portion wherein leaves and limbs had been rustling moments before—there gathered a veritable flock of butterflies!

At a quick count, he marked thirteen. And yet more were gathering every instant.

"Methinks you are perhaps of a sudden bashful toward me, miss," Balian called, unable to keep from chuckling as he did so.

When Minnette did not answer, he continued, "Might I tell you that I do not think you will ever be successful in hiding from any person for all your life. For your winged friends follow you no matter where you roam, it would seem . . . even up into the arms of a tree such as this great one."

Balian heard the young woman exhale a heavy sigh and drove Ewan to stand directly beneath the place where she was attempting to hide herself.

"I am not so terrible as to warrant this behavior, am I?" he asked, looking up at her—laughing as he saw she clung to a limb with both arms and both legs locked round about it. "Unless you are one who still believes I am cursed . . . that I am part wolf and alter my being at the rise of each full moon."

"Oh, of course I do not believe that, your highness," Minnette assured, speaking at last and thus owning to having been found. "It is only that I just . . . I just changed my mind where the possibility of another chance meeting between us was concerned, you see."

"Why so?" Balian inquired, his brow puckering with not only disappointment but also concern.

The beautiful young woman now fairly flocked in butterflies shrugged. "You are the crown prince of Vavassour, sire. Who am I to think you would wish a visitation with me? I am but one of your subjects . . . a commoner."

Balian grinned. "Oh, there is nothing common about you, fair butterfly girl," he said. "Pray come down and talk with me a while. I very much enjoyed our last encounter. After all, it is not often a man meets a woman willing to risk her own life in defense of his, now is it?"

She blushed, and Balian thought her all the more lovely.

"I am a silly goose most times," Minnette said as she began to descend from the tree.

"Pray, do you need assistance?" Balian inquired too late. For as the words left his mouth, Minnette daintily, yet very ably, leapt to the ground from the lowest branch to which she could descend.

"No. But your gallantry is duly noted, sire," she said, smiling up at him. "And most pleasing, as well as esteemed."

Balian was nothing less than entirely bewitched, enchanted, and enthralled with the girl.

Quickly he dismounted, letting Ewan's reins drop, and as the horse began to graze on the lush grass of the meadow, so Balian said, "Hvile, Thor. Rest, all of you. Hvile," and his wolves immediately sat on their haunches in the shade of the maple to wait.

Minnette could not help but take a step backward as Prince Balian strode near to her. He was far too intimidating to meet with confidence. She studied him for a moment—boot to brow. He was, in truth, the sort of prince of legends—tall and broad-shouldered, with dark hair and piercing blue eyes that seemed to gaze directly through Minnette's very flesh even to gaze upon her soul! His jaw was squared and strong-set, the bones of his cheeks high and perfectly sculpted. His nose was certainly unique, for it was neither too big nor too small, nor crooked in the least. It was a flawless nose—a rarity indeed—at least in Minnette's own experience.

Her attention was suddenly drawn from the

study of his long, muscular appendages to the faultless set of his mouth—the artistic form of his lips. Indeed, as she looked at him—as he moved to stand directly before her—Minnette again wondered if perhaps she had slipped into a dream state while sitting beneath the meadow tree, for could a man such as this, even the crown prince of Vavassour, truly be standing before her? Looking at her? She thought not. And thus she brazenly reached out and pushed at his arm with one finger.

The man laughed, saying, "Did you think you would find my arm soft and weak?"

Certain now that she was not dreaming—that she was indeed awake and that Prince Balian was there with her—Minnette shook her head. "No, sire. I did not think to find your arm wanting in musculature. And indeed it is not wanting . . . not in the least of it. I . . . I only thought that perhaps you were imagined. That I had fallen asleep and dreamt you up."

The prince smiled with being amused, she was certain, and Minnette blushed, silently scolding herself for her own preposterousness.

"And why would you think you dreamt me up?" he asked.

Minnette's eyes widened then, and she tenderly brushed a small butterfly from her forehead as she burst into explanation. "Because, sire, I am willing to swear that when last we met, when you left me here in the meadow . . . I swear I witnessed a hundred white wolves bounding in your wake as you rode toward the castle! Yet there has been no mention of them from anyone else in the village or within the castle walls. Hence, I can only surmise that I dreamt them up. Thus, I thought perhaps I had dreamt you up as well." Laughing a little, she added, "After all, sire, truly, who would believe the crown prince would pay heed to a simple village girl who does naught but work lace? The daughter of the village apothecary, hmm? Therefore, I thought sure I dreamt you up." She paused, leaned forward, and asked him, "Though if you are truly standing here now, and if I truly stood with you before in nearly this very spot, what of the hundred white wolves I saw?"

Minnette's eyes widened as the prince leaned toward her, bent in putting his mouth very near her ear, and whispered, "You did see a hundred white wolves in my wake, miss. You did not dream them up."

Minnette found she was breathless—her entire body riddled with gooseflesh at the sense of Prince Balian's warm breath to her ear, cheek, and neck.

"I . . . I did not?" she choked in a whisper as she felt her forehead break into perspiring over his nearness. His presence was somehow enveloping her in a warmth of exhilaration. She could hear her own heart beating, its mad drumming echoing in her ears.

"No, you did not," he assured her, rising to his full height and straight, commanding posture once more. "You did indeed witness a hundred white wolves accompanying me that day."

Minnette frowned. "Then why has no one else seen them? Why is there no talk of a wave of white wolves in great number roaming about the kingdom?"

The prince's handsome brows puckered with a frown. "The reason is simple. You witnessed the *ghosts* of white wolves—great north wolves that had been slaughtered by cruel men in a far-off kingdom. Their spirits find respite in lingering near me, for they know of my affection for their kind and kin."

For a brief moment, Minnette took his answer to heart. But the moment was indeed brief and fleeting. Not for the fact she did not believe in ghosts and spirits—she did, well knowing every living thing owned a soul. But to be told of a hundred ghost wolves—not to mention the light of mischief that flashed in the sapphire eyes of the Wolf Prince—he was in jest, entirely.

"Do you think that, just because a few butterflies accompany me hither and yon, my head is filled with nothing but moths as well?" she asked, smiling at him.

"Not at all, pretty lady," Balian chuckled.

"Then tell me, sire . . . if you wish to, of course," Minnette ventured. "Did I see a hundred wolves with you that day in the meadow . . . or did I dream them up?"

The prince's expression softened into something that appeared to be admiration—though Minnette was certain she misinterpreted his countenance.

"You did indeed see a hundred wolves with me, lass," he admitted. "And you are right. No one else in all our kingdom . . . has yet discovered they are here."

Minnette frowned. "How is that possible? There were so many! Where are they? If they are real, where then are they kept?"

The prince strode further beneath the canopy of leaves provided by the great tree. Sitting himself down in the grass beneath the maple, he leaned back against the strength of the solid trunk, exhaling a sigh of fatigue or contentment—Minnette was not sure which.

"They are here in the kingdom," he said. "They are not kept by me, but they are led by me . . . and by Thor," he explained, nodding to the largest and oldest of the white wolves that accompanied him. "They are the fruits of my labors during my long absence, for I did, in truth, travel north to find cruel men slaughtering matured white wolves for sheer hatred's sake. The hatred of these men, their thirst for revenge, orphaned more litters of wolf pups than I care to count. And with no adults to raise them . . . my friends and I took them in."

The prince reached out, patting Thor on the head with great affection and obvious appreciation.

A soft smile curved the corners of Minnette's mouth, even for the frown of sadness puckering her brow.

"An heroic undertaking indeed, your highness," she said.

"Oh, I did not do it for the sake of notice, pretty lass," the prince said. Thor, the great white wolf of fame, moved, placing his head on one solid thigh of his master. "I did it because the pups would have died without assistance and care, and the people in that north kingdom would have bid them good riddance. But not I . . . not us. Life is precious . . . all life. And although nature, tragedy, sickness, hardship, and war strike life down, there are opportunities given each of us to preserve it. Or so I believe." The prince looked up to Minnette, and his cobalt gaze caused renewed waves of gooseflesh to engulf her skin. "You there, with your trick of attracting the most beautiful of flying things—it is well you could capture them, pen them up, kill them even, and then adhere them to some means of display and peddle them as wares . . . could you not?"

Minnette frowned. "It's a malicious notion," she mumbled.

"Indeed," Balian said. "Yet there are those who do exactly that to those pretty things alighting on your shoulders, yes? And what harm do butterflies cause? Even wolves kill human beings at times. At least they kill only for food, protection of family, or fear. But butterflies? What harm do they cause, I ask you?"

Minnette's frown softened. "And the same can be said of baby wolves, hmm?"

Balian chuckled. "I will not deny I hold an affinity for the wolf . . . the white wolves. Perhaps because these wolves did not abandon me when accusation was thrust upon me. Or perhaps it is because I see strength and power in them. I admire their cunning and will to survive." He shook his head, adding, "Whatever the reason, I feel bound to protect them." The prince's smile broadened as he said, "It is the same for my brother, Phillip. Only his affinity is for lions, not wolves."

"You mean to say your brother held the great lions in the menagerie in high esteem as you do the white wolves?" Minnette asked.

Balian attempted to look unaffected, although he silently scolded himself for being over verbose—far too comfortable with the girl—and making the mistake of referring to Phillip.

Forcing an expression of reminiscent sadness, he countered, "Yes. Yes, that is exactly it. Phillip held a deep affinity for lions . . . just as I do for any white wolf."

"I am so sorry he was lost, sire."

Balian looked up to see Minnette's eyes brimming with tears. His own eyes widened with astonishment as he witnessed a sudden change in the butterflies surrounding her. Near instantly, the butterflies that had not already alit upon her person did so—in her hair, on her shoulders, arms, and hands. In truth, it appeared as if the fragile fluttering things were attempting to console the girl.

"Thank you," Balian said. "That is very kind. I sometimes believe the greater population of the kingdom has forgotten Phillip altogether."

"Oh, I promise to you, we have not," the butterfly sprite assured him. Sitting down in the grass next to him, her eyes filled with the moisture of emotion, as well as sparkling sincerity, she said, "I remember when Phillip was injured. My father was the apothecary in the village, as my mother is now, and he was summoned by the king to tend to your brother, Prince Phillip." She shook her head, mumbling, "Father always told us that the royal physician was an imbecile and had managed to somehow poison himself to literal death the week before. So the king called upon my father, as he did many times thereafter." She paused, adding,

"Until Father died, of course. Thus, now it is my mother who is summoned."

Minnette gazed into Balian's eyes until he was most certain she had bewitched him—for he could not look away from her, even if the desire had been in him to do so.

"My father promised me that Prince Phillip was at peace when he gave up the ghost," Minnette said. "I do not know, in truth, if he told me that simply to comfort me . . . or if it was true. He only knew that I was, like all in Vavassour, devastated at the loss of our great prince."

She looked away from him, and Balian studied her lovely profile at his leisure for a time.

"I still visit the place . . . gather flowers from the meadow on my way and lay them in the space where Prince Phillip fell," she almost whispered.

Balian watched, rapt as even more butterflies alit upon Minnette's person. She, however, seemed completely unaware of them, and Balian surmised that it must be such a common occurrence for her that she had grown unaware of it.

She looked back to him, smiling. "You really are a kind prince to sit here in the meadow sharing in conversation with a lace worker."

Prince Balian grinned, even as his eyes narrowed in studying her face. Minnette grew warm in her entirety under his appraisal.

"You really are a kind lace worker," he said,

"and brave as well . . . to sit in conversation with a werewolf."

Minnette laughed. "You are no werewolf, sire! I beheld you all through the night at my father's bidding, and not once did a large tooth suddenly spring from your lips. Not once did you grow fur before my eyes or howl at the moon."

"So you were witness to my test, eh?" he asked, his handsome smile broadening.

"I was," Minnette answered.

As he continued to study her, Minnette leaned closer to him, her own eyes narrowing as she whispered, "And you still have not told me where you have spirited these hundred white wolves away to, your highness. I must know! I swear to you I will run mad if you do not tell me how you have hidden them away!"

Prince Balian laughed, reached out, and tugged at a strand of Minnette's hair that had escaped its pin. "Well, I would not want you to run mad, pretty butterfly sprite," he said.

Minnette could not draw breath for a moment! His touching her hair, his nearness—she thought sure her heart would burst from her chest with its rapturous beating!

"They are here," he said in a lowered voice. "Everywhere in the kingdom. They will come to our aid if they are needed. And if they are not, I will send them to every part of our kingdom and those that surround us, that they may live wild and make of their lives what they will."

"But why are they not seen?" Minnette managed to ask. Though she wondered that she could speak a word—for the prince was charming her to near fainting!

Unexpectedly, Prince Balian whistled, one loud, sharp whistle. Thor raised his head, as did the other four wolves in his company. And as Minnette's mouth fell agape in wonder, ten white wolves emerged from the forest just behind the tree under which she and the prince were seated.

The prince whistled again, and the ten wolves lowered their heads, making their way with apparent prudence toward their master.

"You see? They are here. They are all here, or near enough to hear should they be called to protect . . . or to battle."

One of the ten wolves approached Minnette—then another and another, until each wolf in turn had sniffed at her in excess.

"Husker henne. Husker henne," the prince spoke to the wolves. "Remember her. Husker henne."

A moment later, Balian, the Wolf Prince, said, "Gå skjule. Go hide, take refuge. Tilflugt." And the wolves hastened away, disappearing into the trees from whence they had come.

Reaching out, Prince Balian placed a hand beneath her chin, gently pushing it upward, until

Minnette realized her mouth was still agape and closed it.

"And thus, pretty Minnette who works lace, is why no one but you has seen the hundred wolves I brought back to Vavassour upon my return," he said. "Because I do not want anyone else to know they are here." His smile faded, and he lowered his voice once more as a frown puckered his brow. "I would beg you to keep my secret, sweet butterfly sprite. For the safety of the wolves . . . and our people."

"Of course, sire," Minnette said. She near took a little offense at his feeling the necessity of having to ask for her confidence. Still, she knew that many in the world could not be trusted—and felt of a sudden not offended that he should ask her to keep his secret but privileged that he had entrusted it to her and no one else.

Without warning or obvious cause, Thor and the four other wolves accompanying the prince leapt to their feet, their ears stiff as they turned to face Castle Vargar.

Rising to his feet and offering a hand to assist Minnette in doing so, Prince Balian exhaled a heavy breath. "It appears I am being sought after at the castle," he rather grumbled.

The very moment Minnette accepted his hand, the warmth and power of his grasp caused a sudden thrilling shiver to travel throughout her entire self! And the words that he uttered next pure dumbfounded her to momentary silence.

Offering a smile of such allure it was near to playing at seduction, Balian, the Wolf Prince of Vavassour, asked, "What would your opinion be of a man who was himself so utterly fascinated at how butterflies flock to you that he desired to taste whatever nectar drew them to you for himself?"

"N-nectar, your highness?" Minnette stammered in a whisper.

Prince Balian's smile broadened. "There must be something about your person that lures these delicate creatures to you. It is obvious you own beauty. But many things own at least a measure of beauty—many flowers, many people. Thus, I must surmise that you taste as delicious as you are beautiful."

"Taste, sire?" Minnette breathed.

"Just days ago . . . seven perhaps," the prince said as he moved to take her face between his powerful hands, "I was thinking of you . . . wondering what would happen if I were to bring you into the pavilion of butterflies kept in my father's menagerie. I wondered for a moment if the butterflies therein might indeed devour you, being that there are so many that crave nectar. Being that at this moment it is what I desire, lovely lace worker that you are, Minnette—to devour you, as it were."

Minnette felt an intoxicating dizziness begin

to overtake her. She well understood his implication. Yet she was so overwhelmed with his provocative, enticing allure and attractiveness that she could little react other than to gaze up at him helpless as a butterfly in a net.

"Y-you wish to feast upon me, sire?" she stammered as her breath returned to her—quickened.

He smiled, a pleased chuckle emanating from deep within his chest as he said, "Only to taste you, Minnette. To know if you are woman . . . or some ethereal being contrived of ambrosia and nectar."

"You are my prince, sire," Minnette whispered. "I . . . I suppose you may taste what you wish."

"I may?" he asked, his head descending toward hers.

"You may," Minnette breathed an instant before his lips pressed hers in a careful and soft kiss.

Such a wave of titillation washed over Minnette she was certain consciousness would be lost to her! The sensation of Balian's lips to hers—warm, firm, yet somehow cautious—was as nothing she had ever before known! Balian, the Wolf Prince of Vavassour—the most powerful, fascinating, and handsome man in all the world—was kissing her!

And then in the next moment, Minnette gasped, conquered by theretofore unfathomable bliss as Balian pressed his mouth to hers—not just his lips but his parted lips. Made feverish by the fiery awareness of his mouth coaxing her lips to part in joining his, Minnette felt her knees threaten to give way beneath her—for her legs were numb, as were her arms.

Full consciousness was harsh in restoring itself to her when the prince stepped back from Minnette, ending their rapturous exchange.

"You are not entirely human as are the rest of us, Minnette D'Angelville," Prince Balian said. "Of that I am most certain."

A low growl emanating from Thor's throat drew Minnette's attention away from the prince.

"I shall have you to the castle soon, pretty lass," Balian said, sweeping a low bow before her. "For I must have you in my father's butterfly pavilion."

"I beg pardon, sire?" Minnette asked—even as her senses continued to swirl with the intoxication washing over her, resulting from his kisses.

The prince smiled, mounted his horse, and offered, "I mean to say, I must see what happens when the royal butterflies in my father's pavilion are introduced to you—she who is formed of ambrosial nectar and not mere flesh and bone." As his horse began to move about with impatience, the prince gazed at Minnette a moment longer and then said, "Thank you for the kiss, pretty butterfly sprite. I have never in my life partaken of anything so delicious and satisfying. I will send an invitation for you to visit the pavilion soon. Good day to you, my beauty."

Minnette felt her mouth fall once more as she watched the Wolf Prince ride toward Castle Vargar, his five white wolf companions in his wake. Had the prince truly kissed her?

"I did not dream that, did I?" Minnette asked a large yellow butterfly that sat still on her shoulder. "Yet I know I did not . . . for my skin is still tingling from his touch, my mouth still savoring the very flavor of his."

Glancing to the small blue and black butterfly that alit on her arm, she whispered, "Eight days consecutive I waited in hopes of seeing him again." And as a smile of pure delight and zeal captured her mouth, Minnette spun round and started back to the village, saying, "Yet now I know that I would wait eight *years* consecutive to have him kiss me again!"

Minnette paused for only a moment—paused to look back at the meadow and then to the forest beyond—paused to listen. For she thought she had heard something—a strange noise. Not a bark, yet not a human sound either. She frowned, feeling that what she had heard was not the sound of joy but rather the sound of pain. But when it did not occur again, she pushed the strange sensation of something dreadful having taken place to the back of her thoughts and hurried home in a bevy of butterflies. For she had lace to work, an astonishing tale to tell her mother, and most of all dreams to dream—dreams of the handsome Prince Balian who had endeavored to taste her, to kiss her, and had so very blissfully succeeded.

A Kiss and a Darkness

"Prince Balian kissed you?" Morgianna exclaimed in an astonished whisper.

Minnette felt a blush rise to her cheeks—but a blush of delight in memory, not of shame or regret.

"Yes, Mother," Minnette affirmed. She laughed as her mother's mouth dropped agape in wonderment. "And it was ever so much the most glorious sensation I have known in all my life!"

"But, Minnette, he is the crown prince," her mother needlessly reminded. "He will marry one day . . . and to royalty, which he no doubt must, and—"

Minnette shook her head, interrupting, "Oh, Mother, please do not think you bore and nurtured an ignoramus. It is well I know the prince will one day be king. And well I know all that will come with his being of royal lineage. But does it mean a common girl from the village cannot forever cherish the sweet memory of once being complimented and kissed by him?"

Her mother smiled and nodded, and Minnette was soothed.

"No, it does not," Morgianna agreed. "For he sees your beauty, both body and spirit, it would seem. As well as your inexplicable draw to butterflies that even I do not understand. So why not savor the truth that our handsome prince of Vavassour found you quite irresistible, eh?"

"It is my way of thinking," Minnette giggled. "And, oh, was it a moment to be forever relished in memory! Several moments, in fact. I swear to you, Mother, if he were not the prince, I would undeniably give my heart to him—whole and willing."

Morgianna smiled and returned her attention to the lace she had been working. "Oh, indeed, I am certain that you would." She glanced up quickly to Minnette a moment, asking, "But you have not, have you? You will remember that he is the crown prince of Vavassour, will you not? You will not allow him to break your heart . . . or tarnish your virtue, correct?"

"Mother!" Minnette scolded, scowling with offense. "How could you even think it of me? You know I would surrender my innocence to none, save he that is husband to me! And as far as my heart is concerned—you have raised a wise daughter, Mother . . . you and Father. And I will not lose myself to one whose heart I cannot own in return."

Morgianna smiled, though Minnette thought she did not appear truly convinced of her daughter's assurances.

"I know, my darling," Morgianna said. "A

mother simply worries always over her children . . . their well-being and happiness. It is our calling in life, you see."

Minnette sighed and returned her attention to the lace in her own lap to be worked. "I do know, Mother," she said. "But please may I enjoy the memory of Prince Balian's kiss for a time? He so intrigues me, after all . . . and he is so wonderful to gaze upon." She paused a moment and then offered, "He spoke of you today . . . of you and Father."

"Did he?" Morgianna mumbled as she worked her length of lace.

"Indeed, he did. He spoke of the day Prince Phillip was injured and of Father's being summoned to the castle to attend him. He spoke of you as well." Minnette concentrated on a difficult stitch before continuing, "And he spoke of his brother for a moment, as if he were not dead at all."

"Did he?" Morgianna asked. "How terrible sad."

"Indeed," Minnette agreed. "It is fair obvious he misses his brother to a terrible length. Is it true that Prince Phillip was to lions what Prince Balian is to wolves?"

"It is true," Morgianna answered with a nod of assurance. "The old lion in the king's menagerie, Apedemak, took to the prince Phillip at once. Before he was killed, it was not unusual to see Prince Phillip wrestling Apedemak when visitors were touring the menagerie. Of course, Apedemak was not more than a young cub when he was gifted to King Liam. I suppose he thought of Prince Phillip as his brother or some such similar relation."

"Thus, Prince Phillip's death was a great loss to the old lion too, I suppose," Minnette noted.

"I suppose so," Morgianna agreed. "But the old lion seems content enough now. After all, the Monk of the Menagerie has cared for him all these long years. The lion pride is quite large last I toured the menagerie."

Minnette worked lace for several minutes. Yet her mind was on the king's menagerie—her thoughts lingering on Prince Balian's claim he wished her to visit the butterfly pavilion therein. And again the Monk of the Menagerie entered her thoughts.

"Have you ever seen his face, Mother?" she inquired.

"Whose face, darling?"

"The monk's. The man who cares for the king's menagerie. And I am certain I know of no one who has heard him speak . . . not in all these long years he has kept it," Minnette said.

"No, I have never seen his face nor heard him speak. He is, after all, a monk, Minnette," Morgianna reminded. "And as I am to understand, monks take vows of silence, as well as isolation, so it is not unexpected that no one has seen his face or heard him speak."

"Do they cut out the tongues of monks, I wonder? Or are they simply so thorough in their self-discipline that they are not tempted to speak?" Minnette asked. "For I would assuredly have to have my tongue cut out if I were to take a vow of silence."

Morgianna laughed in agreeing, "I believe you would indeed. Yet I think how sad the world would be without your pretty voice upon the air."

"Thank you, Mother," Minnette said, smiling. "You are kind to your daughter, even though she is a silly goose who allows the prince to kiss her and . . . oh! I discovered something else, though I have promised to tell no one. Yet I have already told you . . . told you before I promised not to tell. So is it breaking a promise if I tell you what I know . . . even though I promised to tell no one . . . being that you already know?"

Morgianna smiled with amusement. "I suppose not. What is it that I already know that you are not supposed to tell anyone?"

Lowering her voice and leaning closer to her mother, Minnette whispered, "I did not dream the hundred wolves that were in the meadow with the prince when first I met him. There are, in truth, a hundred, at least."

Morgianna frowned. "But none but you has seen them. I thought, in certain, you had fallen into slumber in the meadow and dreamed such a vision as a hundred white wolves."

"As did I," Minnette said. "But there are a hundred white wolves with the prince. Only they are hidden throughout the kingdom." Minnette frowned, lowering her voice further. "And I think Prince Balian has brought them here as a measure of protection for the kingdom. He did not say it to me obvious, but I felt he is troubled over some unseen, unspoken threat. I saw it as well, in his countenance . . . heard it in his voice when he spoke of it. Yet he asked me to hold the secret safe, for he wants no one to know the wolves are here . . . including the king, I think."

Morgianna frowned. Not only was Prince Balian an able—nay, a supreme—soldier, but also his abilities in directing militia and preparing them for battle had been noted by the king and, in fact, the entire kingdom from his adolescence. He seemed to own a sixth sense that alerted him to any impending threat. Yet Vavassour had not had any incident requiring battle since Balian was a boy. Thus, why would the prince feel the kingdom needed unseen protection in a hundred wolves hidden away?

A strong sense of disconcert began to rise in Morgianna's bosom, and a sharp pang of fear in her husband's no longer being with her and Minnette as protector pricked her heart.

Yet she hid her concern and worry, saying only, "Then hold his secret you shall, Minnette. For if the Wolf Prince senses something is amiss, then I believe that something indeed is."

Her mother's tone of voice had changed. Minnette did not miss the sound of trepidation that accompanied her words. Still, averse to unsettling her mother any further, Minnette simply returned her attention to her length of lace. Further, she began to hum a tune that both she and her mother adored. It was often they had sung the song after Minnette's father had died, finding that it comforted both their broken hearts for some reason they could not name.

Minnette's worries over her mother's disconcerted countenance began to ease somewhat as her mother glanced at her, smiled, and began humming in unison.

After several minutes of humming together and working lace, Minnette smiled when she heard her mother giggle of a sudden with no apparent rationale.

Curious, Minnette looked to her mother and inquired, "And what is so very amusing, Mother? Did I miss a brownie scampering across our floor or a fairy sprite?"

Morgianna shook her head, continuing to smile. "No. It is just . . . well, I will confess it to you now. I am a proud mother in this moment, in knowing that the crown prince of the kingdom endeavored to seduce my beautiful daughter. What a prize indeed, my girl—a kiss from the handsome Prince Balian! It is every woman in the kingdom would delight in such thing as that. And yet it was you, my own lovely Minnette, who triumphed and won every woman's dream for herself."

Minnette smiled, blushing with enchantment at the mere memory of the prince's sublime kiss. Oh, it sent her skin to rippling with gooseflesh once more! Just the thought caused her mouth to water with wanting of another kiss from him.

Yes, she would continue to visit the meadow each day—hope that the handsome and powerful Wolf Prince would once more ride out alone from the castle to the meadow and find her. Yet she would not hide from him if he did. Nay! She would fairly stand in the meadow's center, wildly flailing her arms in beckoning him if she were to see him riding out again. For prince or not—one-day king or not—whether he married a princess from a neighboring kingdom or not—Prince Balian had stolen her heart already. She could not let her mother know of the fact of it, of course, for she knew it was folly and could only end badly for herself. But she would not deny herself even one more minute in the company of the Wolf Prince of Vavassour—no, not even if it were true he was a werewolf. Even then she would risk her life in going to the meadow in the hope of meeting with him again.

Minnette thought then of the prince stating he would send an invitation for her to visit his father's butterfly pavilion. She had not told her mother of this when reciting the details of her visit with the prince. For the first of it, she feared her mother would deny her permission—that she would, for some reason, kindly inform the prince that Minnette could not attend him. Oh, she knew her mother would be gracious and polite, concocting some imaginary excuse to give to the crown prince. Still, for some reason she could not name, Minnette feared her mother would deny her the pleasure.

For the second part, Minnette had not wanted to tell her mother the prince had spoken of an invitation if no invitation were ever to arrive. She knew that her mother was more pained by disappointment endured by her daughter than she was disappointment of her own. Therefore, as she had been ambling back to the cottage from the meadow, Minnette had decided to tell her mother all that had transpired between her and Prince Balian, all but one detail: his mention of an invitation to the king's butterfly pavilion.

And yet she would hope for it in her own mind—and in her heart. Even she would pray for it: that Prince Balian would indeed have an invitation dispatched to her and that she would find herself in his handsome, alluring company once more.

Minnette wondered for a moment how solitary was the pavilion. Was it solitary enough to afford the prince the opportunity to taste of her lips a second time? She blushed at even the very thought—yet hoped for the miracle of its being so, all the same.

"I feel it, Phillip," Balian said in a lowered voice.

"But have you any evidence, brother?" Phillip inquired. "For it is well you know the stubbornness and pride of our father. He will not hear you unless you have more than your keen senses to offer him."

"Oh, it is well I am aware of that fact," Balian grumbled. "And no, I do not have evidence to lay at his feet . . . not yet. And that is my very fear—that it will take evidence, pure tangible evidence, bloody carnage as evidence, before our father will hear reason. I am the one who has only just returned from touring our border kingdoms, and I tell you, in the very least Mirermith is a threat to us."

"For the mere fact that you are a werewolf?" Phillip said, smiling with amusement, in an attempt to lighten Balian's heavy heart.

Balian smiled and shook his head. "Sadly, no. If that were their only loathing of Vavassour, it would not be difficult to address. No." Balian exhaled a heavy sigh and said, "It is the core of our kingdom they are loathe to endure, Phillip. It is Father himself. They judge him a weak king, for he has not attempted to extend our lands in battle. They think him proud and pompous, pathetic and overconfident in his presumption our boundaries and borders are solid, impenetrable, and ably protected. And they see all this as opportunity, Phillip—opportunity that must be seized while it may be seized. Seized before . . . before . . ."

"Before *you* are made king and rule with wisdom, prudence, and strength that might thwart their intentions to expand their own borders," Phillip interjected.

Balian nodded—nodded with a feeling of defeat that had not been familiar to him for the past five years.

All at once, perhaps in an effort to rejuvenate his strength, his resolve, Balian frowned as he looked to Phillip. "Why have you not challenged him where your circumstance is concerned, brother? It is pure obvious you have the strength of an ox, that you communicate ably. Perhaps your speech is slowed and disjointed, but you do communicate and can be understood. And your mind is not so slow as Father has always attempted to lead Mother and I into believing. Thus, why do you stay hidden as this Monk of the Menagerie when you have yet so much more to offer . . . to contribute to our people and our kingdom?"

"You think me weak," Phillip mumbled.

In an instant, Balian was regretting his eruption. Shaking his head, he offered, "I do not think you weak, Phillip, and well you know that. Rather I think you stronger than you allow yourself to believe." He looked to where his brother sat in a large chair next to his own—studied Phillip a moment. "And that is my frustration, I suppose—in that I know your power still . . . but you do not believe it yourself. And certainly Father does not believe it, though he must witness it daily."

"No. He does not witness it," Phillip said. "I have kept it from him. And even were I to prove my physical strength, were he to witness that I am full as capable a soldier in battle as ever I was before . . . he would not confess it to be true. You look beyond what was lost to me that day we were riding and I was thrown. You still see Phillip, your brother . . . the same man you rode out with that morning. My difficulty in speech and in some processes of thought—you do not see them. But it is all that our father sees, and it shames him. I have long known that the reason I have been isolated was for the sake of Father's pride, not for his fear of how I would be treated by his subjects in Vavassour."

Balian rose to his feet, his old anger returning. "Then why not force his hand, brother? Force him to see the man you are, the power in your body. And though your mind may not be as quick as it was before, you are intelligent still. Father's menagerie as it stands now is evidence of that!"

But Phillip shook his head. "The menagerie has been improved under my furtherance. That I own, no matter if Father perceives it. And I am proud of what I have accomplished in accordance with it; even it was far more difficult a thing to do with the bonds of silence and facelessness upon me. But I am not so unhappy as you might think, little brother. For I have come to value isolation . . . and the lack of being driven to become something I do not want to be."

"You mean you are satisfied with being alleviated of the expectation to rule one day?" Balian asked.

Phillip nodded. "I am. Even when you were but fifteen years and I nineteen, even before I was thrown and my eloquence of speech taken, my quick wit exiled to oblivion—even then it was you who was best suited for the throne. Even then you were more suited than the very king who sits in ruling Vavassour now. And I never desired to be the great mind of stratagem and battle that others are. That claim belongs to you, Balian . . . and I do not envy it. Not in the least, I do not. For such keenness of mind heaps great expectation and responsibility on the bearer."

"Phillip—" Balian began to argue.

Phillip raised a strong hand in gesturing he did not wish to argue with his brother.

Still, Balian continued to champion his elder brother—even as he always had. "Very well, Phillip. I will not press you further just now. But I will tell you this. Vavassour is not so secure in her quiet peace as our father assumes. There is something threatening—something just beyond my vision and touch. And if the time comes—nay, when the time comes, as I know it will—when the time comes that our kingdom must be protected from whatever enemy we own, however unknowingly we own it, I *will* have you at my side, Phillip. I will ask you to defend our people and our kingdom, and Father can hang me for disobedience to his will . . . but only after Vavassour has been championed."

Phillip's eyes narrowed as he studied Balian a moment. Then, slowly, a smile began to curve his lips.

"Very well, my brother," he said. "If there does arrive a threat to our kingdom, I will defend her in battle to the death . . . with you as my captain."

Balian inhaled a breath of calming. He nodded and sat down in his chair once more.

"Now then, brother," he began, "let us discuss your Arianna, shall we?"

Phillip frowned and asked, "My Arianna?"

"Yes," Balian assured him. "We have talked too much of battle and Father's pride today. Let us turn our conversation to a more . . . shall we say, a more pleasing topic."

"And Arianna is this topic?" Phillip asked. "Why not Minnette D'Angelville? You did see her today, did you not?"

Balian's brows arched with astonishment. "Indeed, yes, I did see her . . . in the meadow, in the same place where last I saw her." Shaking his head with wondering, Balian asked, "Yet how did you know that I had seen her today?"

Phillip chuckled. "For one, there is about you the look of a man who struggles with distracting thoughts. And there is the large yellow butterfly wing crushed against your baldric there at your chest. And if I am to assume that each butterfly on earth is bewitched by Minnette D'Angelville as I have heard it is, the reason would answer . . . you were in the company of the butterfly princess today."

Balian smiled, and his smile broadened as his mouth remembered the sweet ambrosia of Minnette's kiss.

Brushing at his baldric with one hand, in an effort to wipe away the crushed remains of a butterfly there, he said, "Indeed. I did see her today. Moreover, I could not restrain myself . . . and I kissed the pretty thing."

"Ah!" Phillip chuckled. "And there it is, sitting so near to me . . . a man smitten by a lovely maid in the meadow."

"I will not have you sit in attempt at making me loose-tongued about the encounter," Balian said, smiling. "Not until you full admit to me that your maid, the lovely Arianna, is thoroughly smitten with you, her charge."

Phillip grinned, though Balian marked it a sad and wistful grin. "That is exactly what I am to Arianna . . . her charge. The pathetic, secreted prince, whom his father is loath to remember siring. So do not mistake sympathetic pity for fancies of romance, my younger brother."

But Balian was undaunted. "I make no mistake, my elder brother. The eyes of Arianna are only on you, and not because she brings you your supper and makes your bed." Leaning closer to Phillip, he whispered, "Will you lie to me and tell me you have never thought of her as anything more than friend? Will you lie and tell me that, even as we sit here, you do not desire to take her in your arms and—"

The loud beating on the solid door of his chambers startled both Balian and his brother.

"But wait, Phillip—" he said.

Nevertheless, his brother had already pulled his cowl down over his face and moved toward the hidden door near the hearth.

"Who disturbs me thus?" Balian called, even as Phillip nodded to him, pressing a stone in the wall to cause the hidden door to unlatch.

With one final nod of understanding, Balian

watched as his brother disappeared into the passageway, closing the hidden door in his wake.

"It is Lanval Mordoc, sire—captain of the royal guard . . . and your friend," came a deep and familiar voice in response.

Without further pause, Balian drew the bolt and opened the door to his private chambers. At once, Thor, Ullr, Freyja, Delling, and Nótt were on their feet, ears stiffened. A low growl rumbled in Thor's throat, and Balian knew at once what provoked it.

On the threshold to his private chambers stood Lanval Mordoc, captain of the king's guard and true friend to Balian. In his arms he carried a white wolf—dead—its once pure fur marred with evidence of deep wounds and blood.

"What is this brutality?" Balian shouted. "Who had done this? I demand to know who the murderer is, Lanval! Who has—"

But in a lowered voice, Lanval said, "Sire, there is something here you must see."

"Bring him in, at once," Balian commanded.

Lanval stepped into Balian's chambers; Balian closed the door behind him.

"What is it, my friend?" Balian asked.

With great respect, Lanval laid the white wolf down upon a nearby rug. Thor growled once more, and a quiet whimper escaped Freyja as Balian felt moisture rise in his own eyes. Near to tears was he—tears of instant loss and mourning, tears of vehement fury.

"A huntsman found the wolf in the forest . . . already dead, sire," Lanval explained. "He is wise and felt that a poacher would not have left the carcass . . . not when its pelt could bring a pretty price."

"No. No one would leave such a pelt behind," Balian agreed. Tenderly he stroked the wolf's coat, for he did recognize him. He had been his friend, one rescued from certain death in the north country four years previous. Again he stroked the softness of his fur and whispered a prayer for his life that had been lost.

"And then, sire, there is this," Lanval said. Taking the wolf's head in hand, he turned its face toward Balian. There, on the animal's forehead, some iniquitous being had carved an X.

"Her teeth—the long ones, the fangs I would think they were—they have been removed as well," Lanval stated.

Balian frowned. "A murderer's trade that would be," he said. "They take the teeth to prove their strength . . . to prove their kill. I have seen it before, Lanval—the mark, the manner of death, the extraction of the teeth."

Lanval exhaled a long breath. "It is as you thought, your highness, is it not? Malice is lurking in the morning mists."

Balian nodded as he continued to stroke the fur

of the dead wolf. "There is a darkness moving nearer, and though I will not have you speak of it—for it is not yet the king's will and may be construed as treason if you do speak of it—I will tell you. Prepare your men. Vavassour is not so safe as my father believes. Say nothing of my asking you to prepare our soldiers, but prepare them you must. You must ready them for defense of the kingdom . . . for battle."

"Yes, sire," Lanval agreed. "And . . . and what would you have me do with the . . . the victim, your highness?"

"Leave that to me, Lanval," Balian growled. "If this is not evidence enough to gain my father's ear, then I fear the worst for the people of his kingdom!"

Hefting the dead wolf onto one broad shoulder, Balian ordered Thor and the others, "Vent her. Stay here. I will deliver this evidence to the king, alone."

And with that, the Wolf Prince unleashed markedly restrained disapproval of the king—allowed his concern for the people and his anger toward his father's arrogance to carry him toward the solar, wherein he knew King Liam lounged, pompously devouring rich foods and lingering in prideful ignorance of the very existence of any malicious adversary.

A Looming Storm and the Sheep's Folly

"What in the name of all that is good is *this*, Balian?" King Liam bellowed as Balian strode into the solar, the carcass of a bloody wolf draped over one shoulder.

Ceremoniously dropping the dead wolf at his father's feet, Balian answered, "Evidence of that which I have been attempting to convey to you, Father." Taking hold of the wolf's fur at the top of its head, he directed it to face the king. "This, Father—this X carved into the forehead—it is a mark left by those who believe in and seek to destroy werewolves. A mark of warning . . . a promise that death will come." He released the dead animal. "There is a dark threat stirring ever closer to our kingdom, Father. And though this be only malicious mischief set to test our alertness, what will follow will no doubt be . . ."

Balian ceased in speaking as King Liam stood, frowning with stern disapproval at him. "It would seem to me, Balian, that this . . . this malicious mischief is not set to test me but *you*. You are the only accused werewolf in five kingdoms. Is that not so?"

Balian gritted his teeth and exhaled a heavy

breath in attempting to soothe his desire to attack his father with harsh words.

"Yes, Father," he near growled. "But this is not meant for me. This is not a threat to me alone. And although someone with less wits than a damnable toad would brand it, in the very least, a message to your royal highness that some other kingdom does not want you to allow Vavassour to fall to a werewolf's rule . . . I vow to you, Father, I have seen this before, and it is far more than that. It is not I this is meant for, and it is not even a warning in regard to me. It is the first rung in a ladder being assembled to depose you as king, Father."

"Enough!" King Liam roared.

Balian glanced to his mother, the queen, shrinking further into the chair in which she sat.

"You will not stride into *my* solar, deposit a dead animal at *my* feet, and suppose to accuse *me* of defect in sight when it comes to protecting *my* throne in *my* kingdom!" the king shouted.

King Liam inhaled a deep breath, regaining his composure almost instantly.

"Balian," he began, "I know there has been much discord between us in the past . . . a great variance of opinion. But I did not ask you to return to your home and kingdom in order that you would challenge my intelligence . . . or my authority. The day will come when you will indeed be king, at which time you may conjure any manner of delusion you wish with which to entertain your mind and body."

"Father, I have no wish—" Balian began.

"Do not interrupt your king!" his father growled, however.

Balian inhaled a calming breath of his own, resolving that he would not be the reason for his mother's continued weeping.

"Forgive me, my king," he said—though his teeth were yet gritted tight, his jaw clenched firm.

"As I said, one day the throne will come to you, Balian," King Liam continued. "Nevertheless, until I lay dead in my crypt as fodder for beetles and maggots, you will not in the least imply that I would not see—that I *could* not see—a threat and darkness moving toward Vavassour. One dead wolf—which is, in truth, meant to intimidate *you,* not your king—is no evidence that a brother kingdom owns malice toward us. One dead wolf is nothing. And whether or not the kingdom of Mirermith loathes you for your alliance with these animals—though I have no understanding myself why both you and Phillip so concern yourselves over mindless beasts as if they were your own offspring—Mirermith and its king do *not* loathe me. Vavassour has been at peace with Mirermith and King Bramwell since my father died and I rose to the throne."

The king paused a moment and then commanded, "We will have no more of your tenuous speculations of our impending doom, Balian."

The king glared at his son. Balian knew it was expected that he agree to his demands—or, in the very least, to apologize for having disturbed his respite with such conjectures.

But Balian did neither. Rather he looked to his mother, saying, "I am sorry to have distressed you, Mother. Do please forgive me."

Dabbing at the tears on her cheeks with the handkerchief she clutched in her trembling hand, the queen's voice broke with emotion as she said, "Of course, my dear."

Perturbed by what he perceived was Balian's lack of humility, King Liam growled, "Your wolf's carcass is bleeding out on my silk carpet, boy."

Balian looked down at the dead wolf that must still have had a measure of blood in it yet—for indeed the dark crimson of death spread out upon the silk with a gruesome crimson vibrancy.

"You are correct, Father," Balian said. Yet he did not pick up the wolf at once but rather wrapped the soft, silk carpet about its body. Hefting the veiled corpse onto his shoulder once again, Balian turned to leave.

Pausing, he looked back to his father, saying, "You *are* king, Father. Let us all pray the fact remains so."

He did not look back again—not even when his father, the king, demanded that he return to stand before him. No. Balian would not be able to hold his tongue if he lingered even one moment more in his presence. Thus, he strode from the solar, slamming the door behind him.

Making his way to the menagerie, Balian was relieved when he found Phillip already there attending to the animals. He had not wished to go skulking about the castle passageways and hidden doors in search of his brother whilst carrying the heavy wolf over his shoulder.

He knew, at once, however, that the animals in the menagerie sensed the death he carried with him.

Thus, as he approached his brother, he said, "Let us make haste, Phil . . . sir . . . and see this soldier buried properly."

The Monk of the Menagerie nodded. Balian watched as his dark hood glanced about them. Having ensured their privacy, Phillip whispered, "I will see to her, Balian. She shall have a proper burial . . . one befitting a knight of the realm."

"But I would see us both put her to rest," Balian whispered. "She was my wolf . . . my responsibility. I will carve a stone for her resting place and—"

"You carve the stone, brother," Phillip mumbled. "I will see to her eternal comfort. Please allow me to do this thing, Balian. It is important to me."

Balian, still frowning as he had been from the moment he left his father's presence, exhaled a heavy sigh. He knew not why Phillip wished to see the wolf put carefully into the earth, but he would not deny him the opportunity, for it was palpable that the prospect of the act was of utmost significance to him.

"Very well," Balian agreed. "As for my part, I will carve her stone. Yet this evening when I have returned from . . . from . . ."

"From . . ." Phillip urged.

"From a ride out of and away from the suffocating sensation I am experiencing now at being in the castle," Balian finished.

"I take it our father did not hear reason," Phillip growled.

Balian shook his head as his anger flared once again. "No," he said through clenched teeth. "He sees himself too perfect a king for anyone to find flaw in him or his rule. Thus, we can do nothing more than wait."

"Wait? Wait for what?" Phillip inquired.

It was in that moment that Balian owned full remembrance of the truth of his brother's condition. Yes, Phillip was well enough in body—strong and able. He could think as rationally as most men. Even he could conceive such as the improvements he had implemented in the menagerie. But it was fact—one that Balian had attempted to deny to himself since his return—that at times, Phillip's memory, especially of things of recent occurrence, would stammer in like similarity to his speech. Or in the least it would fail to serve him instantly as it had before he had been injured. Phillip physically reacted with swiftness and with power, for the part of his mind that ordered his muscular reflex had not been damaged in the least of it. But Balian silently admitted to himself that his brother—though capable and strong bodily—had not the sharp, rapid reasoning of a strategist, nor the foresight of prediction of outcome that he once owned.

In facing the truth that his brother was yet as permanent in his impairment as he had been from the beginning—though nothing justified the king's hiding his eldest son away or claiming Phillip had died—Balian began to liken Phillip's occasional lapse in quick memory to the condition of a man he had once observed. Balian had witnessed the man be overcome by what appeared to be a curious numbness of speech, movement, and thought, simply by smoking seeds that had been cored from the pods of poppies and crushed. Moreover, Phillip's intermittent numbness of mind, which could in no way be predicted, seemed as inconsistent as the love of a fickle woman. One day he would appear nearly as able-minded as he had been before—his slowed, slurred, and stammering speech the only observable symptom he had been injured with permanence. Yet another day he would stare at whomever was addressing him, an expression of confusion and apprehension lingering on his face as he struggled for recognition—recognition that did always come but oft very gradually.

Thus, in owning great frustration with his father and not wanting to risk becoming discouraged by Phillip's unexpected stammer of thought, Balian answered, "We will discuss it at length another time, brother. For I must take Ewan out riding. We both need a stretch of our legs."

Phillip nodded, though Balian knew by the puckering of his brow that he was somewhat confused yet still focused on the wolf draped over Balian's shoulder.

"Here then," Balian said, transferring the wolf's corpse into the strong cradle of his brother's arms. "You will see to her burial then? With respect and care?"

"Of course," Phillip mumbled. "Enjoy your ride, brother." Looking from the dead wolf in his arms and back to Balian, Phillip's voice seemed to echo from within his cowl as he added, "But be wary. There are those who still believe *you* are wolf on occasion. And if a huntsman is about killing wolves . . ."

Balian smiled, warmed by his brother's concern. "I will be wary, brother. Thank you."

After having changed his bloodstained clothes for fresh ones, Balian had bid Thor and his brood of four to accompany him as he rode. He held no doubt that Thor, Ullr, Freyja, Delling, and Nótt felt as constricted as he spending so much time in the castle—especially following five years of travel and a near nomadic existence.

Therefore, it was, "Som du vil! As you will, my friends!" he called to them as they bounded into the meadow with him astride Ewan. He chuckled as he watched Thor and the others romp and play in the meadow grass as if they were mere pups. He thought of the other wolves—a hundred wolves, less one comrade who had so recently been lost that very morning. He thought of their desire to be free, for he knew they must own such desire, just as any living thing did. For a moment, he considered setting them loose—telling them, each one, to travel to whichever corner of the earth beckoned them. Yet he did not do so—he could not—not as yet. In his soul Balian knew Vavassour was entering a dark mist of threat. And though he could not name it as Mirermith for certain—at least he could not prove it to his father or anyone else in that instant—he knew the threat was there, growing thicker and more malicious with each passing day. And because his mind, as well as his heart, knew that the people of Vavassour—even the soldiers of Vavassour—were not yet prepared to defend their sovereignty, nor their sovereign, Balian could not free his wolf friends yet. He knew they would yet be needed.

Still, the discovery of the dead wolf that morning—his father's insistence the incident was a triviality—still angered and frustrated Balian near to fury, and he knew he must find solace to divert his anger from his father. Hence, he was not astonished in the least to find that he urged Ewan toward the village, toward the cottage once occupied by the apothecary Stuart D'Angelville, in hopes that his wife and daughter still occupied the same cottage. It was only he was experiencing complexity in fathoming an excuse to offer Morgianna D'Angelville once he had arrived there.

And yet he rode toward the village still, determined in knowing that one glimpse of the fair Minnette would calm him. He thought then that perhaps it was the true reason butterflies were drawn to her: the serenity of her being. Oh, certainly she owned the flavor of nectar. Balian owned that knowledge for himself. Nevertheless, as he rode—as he urged Ewan onward at a much quicker pace—Balian realized that even the very thought of Minnette soothed his tired mind and did a bit of mending to his tattered heart and soul. It had been factual since their first meeting—the feeling of tranquility that spread through Balian even at the thought of her.

Therefore, when at last he reached the village, Balian did not linger in attempting to find reason to present for his visit. He simply dismounted

Ewan and, even as several villagers gasped and began to whisper amongst themselves, strode to the cottage door.

"Perhaps it is best if you remain outside with Ewan, my friends," Balian said quietly to the five wolves that had accompanied him. "Best not overwhelm the ladies too entirely, hmm?" Patting each white wolf on the head in turn, Balian gently commanded, "Hvile. Rest. But be ever watchful. Men være nogensinde vågent."

"Balian?" Morgianna exclaimed as she opened the door to see who had knocked upon it. "I . . . I mean, your highness. Whatever finds you . . ." Morgianna frowned near instantly, lowered her voice, and inquired, "Is he well? Should I attend him at once?"

"No, Madam D'Angelville," the prince said, smiling with reassurance. "He is well. I have come for . . . in hopes that you perhaps have a remedy that might . . . that might serve to settle my mother's nerves somewhat. I am afraid she has had a very trying day."

Morgianna felt herself exhale a relieved sigh—for she had thought sure the Monk of the Menagerie were ailing in some way. "Of course, your highness! Of course! Please," she said, standing aside and gesturing that the prince should enter the cottage. "Please do enter. Welcome to our home. I admit to being quite overwhelmed at opening the door to find your highness standing before me."

As Minnette watched Prince Balian enter the cottage she and her mother occupied and worked in, she felt her eyes widen with disbelief—her mouth fall agape.

"Minnette," her mother addressed her, "the prince has come on an errand for his mother, the queen."

"Oh, I . . . I see," Minnette said, rather awkwardly hopping to her feet and sending the length of lace she had been working tumbling from her lap. "Good day, sire," she managed to greet with a smile.

The prince's handsome smile broadened as he looked at her, nodding and saying, "Good day, my lady."

All at once Minnette felt far too warm! Her innards were trembling, and her mouth began to water.

"Please do sit down here, your highness, at the table, and I will fetch several remedies for you to select from for your mother," Morgianna bid him. "Would . . . would *you* perhaps enjoy a cup of something soothing as well while we discuss what will be best for your mother?"

"Of course, madam," Prince Balian answered—though Minnette's heart beat wildly, for he did not glance away from her but rather stared at her with a narrowed, penetrating gaze. "I would thoroughly enjoy it. Much has happened later today that was not near as pleasant as some occurrences early on were . . . and I am, myself, somewhat restless."

Minnette smiled, blushing to her very core when the prince winked at her. It was such a feeling of elation to have him in her home that she felt as if she might burst, squealing with delight.

"Minnette, my sweet," Morgianna began, "do please keep our prince in good company a moment while I brew him a cup of my Serenity, will you?"

"Of course, Mother," Minnette answered.

Taking a seat at the small table across from the prince, Minnette offered, "I am so sorry your day has not been a pleasant one."

Prince Balian's smile broadened a moment, and he said, "Oh, the mid of it was *most* pleasant."

Again Minnette blushed, knowing full well he was implying he had enjoyed their time together—the kisses they shared in the meadow.

"I am pleased to know that," she managed to say in a near whisper. But then she gazed at him, adding, "But it is apparent that a pleasant midday was not enough to carry you through whatever unpleasantness followed . . . and for that I am very sorry."

"It is no fault of yours, pretty lass," Prince Balian assured her. "It is only the thorns of royal life that intrude upon memories of a meadow and a lovely young woman. And it is unfortunate but true that those cannot be avoided."

Minnette's smile faded—even for the fact that she continued to gaze at and linger in the company of the most handsome man she had ever seen. How broad his shoulders were! How square and firm his jaw. Still, he was not settled—she could fair see it—although he tried to appear otherwise.

"Royal thorns indeed, if they have disturbed the queen to such an extent that you have yourself come to visit the apothecary for a remedy, hmmm?" she inquired.

Prince Balian chuckled—only just a little. "Indeed, you are correct," he admitted. "Yet I am determined to procure something from your mother to ease her fretting."

Minnette nodded. "Then Mother will most certainly send you back to her with Serenity," she said. "It is such a wonderful soothing mixture. Even just simmering it over an open flame nearby calms the heart and mind . . . the soul. I myself partook of it near daily just after my father died. Both Mother and I were near inconsolable at his loss." She offered a reassuring smile to him, adding, "Serenity will restore tranquility to the queen, I am sure of it."

Balian could not keep silent. He could not allow Minnette to continue to think he had come to her mother for his mother's sake. For the moment he had seen her, sitting across the room in a chair, working lace, he had begun to feel his anger and frustration waning. His heart had leapt in his chest at the mere sight of her, and when she had joined him at the table, he thought sure he would abduct her—take her home and hide her away as his own secret enchantment.

"It is true that my mother suffers today with, in the very least, apprehension," he said. "But I do desire to be a truthful, honest sort of man, Minnette . . . and the full exactness of it is this. It is *I* who need soothing . . . and I knew you were *my* only remedy. Thus, I rode here direct from the castle and a bitter argument with my father."

Minnette's beautiful green eyes sparkled with delight, and her smile revealed her pleasure in hearing his confession.

"Truly?" she asked in a whisper.

Balian nodded and in a lowered voice answered, "Very truly."

She blushed, and Balian felt warmth enfold him.

"I will admit to being glad—most very glad—that you would seek *me* out . . . especially when your mind is not at rest," she said, smiling at him. "Yet I am still miserable that you are discontented . . . that your argument with your father affected you so ill. Mother's Serenity potion will indeed calm you, sire. Still, I would beg that you would tell me if there is something that I myself can do to help in alleviating your disappointment."

And then it was exactly as if the beauty—who even in that moment, even inside the cottage, had a small yellow butterfly resting on the top of her head—had uncorked the bottle that restricted all Balian's fermenting frustration. Before he could think to do otherwise, he told her, "I have so much churning within me, Minnette. So many secrets I carry, so much care and concern for our people of Vavassour . . . that I wonder that I cannot bear the weight much longer without—"

"Without transforming into a werewolf and devouring whomever may cross your path?" she finished for him, her eyes wide with expectation.

"I . . . what did you say?" he asked—pure astonished that the beauty who had so enchanted him would still hold any belief in werewolves, let alone entertain a notion that he was one.

But when next she smiled at him, a soft giggle escaping her lips, Balian exhaled a relieved breath, having realized she was, in truth, teasing him.

"You see? Humor offers welcome easement of cares and worries, your highness. By use of distraction," Minnette said, the intonation of her voice calm and melodic as that of an angel. "My mother's soothing drink will indeed settle your body . . . aid your mind in resting your cares. They will not disappear, of course. Yet you will feel a reprieve from your disquiet and distress." Reaching across the small table, she placed one warm, soft hand over his where it lay in front of him. Her touch was as a warm hearth on a cold winter's eve, and Balian was awed at the instantaneous comfort that ran through him.

"Here you are, your highness," Morgianna D'Angelville said as she returned. Placing a steaming bowl of liquid before him, she instructed, "Let it cool. I will not have our prince burning his tongue in my cottage. Yet as it cools, I want you to lean over and inhale the warmth of it, the steam. Inhale slowly, exhaling just as slowly. Very well?"

"Yes, madam," Balian said. He did as instructed, leaning over the bowl and inhaling. At once he was struck by the ambrosial scent of the drink as his senses perceived peppermint, lavender, rose root, and sage. Yet there were other fragrances as well—fragrances he could not name but indeed recognized. In truth, he near instantly felt some reprievement of the body and mind. Thus, he exhaled slowly and inhaled again.

"It is soothing, is it not?" Minnette inquired.

Balian looked up to where the butterfly sprite sat across from him. Her hand still lingered on his. Brazenly he turned his hand beneath hers, causing that their palms should meet and enabling him to clasp her small warm one. She blushed, and he delighted in knowing she was pleased with the gesture.

"When it is cool enough, and only when it is cool enough but not too cool," Morgianna began, "sip it. Do not drink it too swiftly—only sip—and I promise you, sire, it will soothe you."

Balian looked to Morgianna and smiled. "It already has begun to, Madam D'Angelville," he said. "Thank you, my lady. I truly do feel more at ease than I did a moment before."

Morgianna's smile broadened with triumph. "I am glad," she said. "I will prepare the ingredients for you, that you may take them home and brew my Serenity for your mother, the queen. It will settle her and assist in her finding a very peaceful night's sleep."

"Thank you, madam," Balian said. But as Morgianna turned to fetch her wares for his mother's sake, Balian caused her to pause in asking, "Might I beg one more boon from you today, Madam D'Angelville?"

"Why, of course, your highness," the lovely woman assured. "What may I do further to serve you?"

Balian did not pause in straightening his posture and asking, "Would you allow your daughter to tour the menagerie tomorrow? In specific, the butterfly pavilion therein? I have it in my mind to see what the menagerie's butterflies will do when your bewitching daughter appears in their domain."

Minnette found she could not breathe! Yes, in fact she held her breath in awaiting her mother's response. She had had no notion that Prince Balian would bring an invitation to the royal menagerie from his own lips, let alone on the same day he had mentioned the idea previous. Oh, how desperate she was for her mother to give permission to the prince! To spend more time with Prince Balian was all she could ever wish for in that moment, and wish she did—however silently.

She watched a rather uncertain smile spread across her mother's face, and still she could not breathe!

It was not until Minnette heard her mother's voice speak, "If your highness wishes for Minnette to visit the castle, the menagerie, then who am I to deny your highness's request?" that she was able to draw breath once more.

"You are her mother, madam," Prince Balian answered. "And as such, you in absolute may deny your permission." The prince smiled at Morgianna, however, adding, "But I pray you do not."

Minnette watched as concern vanished from her mother's face.

"Yes, your highness," Morgianna said. "Minnette may attend the menagerie on the morrow."

"Thank you, Madam D'Angelville," Prince Balian said. "I am truly humbled that you would entrust me with her care. And care for her I will. You have my word; you have my promise."

"Very well," Morgianna said, smiling with sincerity. "I will prepare my Serenity for the queen. And you may discuss the details of your very generous invitation with Minnette. I will only be a moment, my prince."

Once her mother had left the room once more, Minnette looked to Prince Balian to see him smiling at her. His sapphire eyes flashed with allure, and he raised her hand in his, placing a lingering kiss on the back of it. When next he turned her hand over, pressing his lips to her palm, Minnette thought indeed she would expire just there where she sat.

Yet she did not. And when he looked to her again, it was to say, "I fear that should I ingest your mother's soothing drink, I might fall into some sort of unconscious state, so tranquil will I be. For I am already much soothed . . . and that is for the sake of your touch, pretty Minnette."

"Are all princes such accomplished flatterers, sire?" Minnette asked, thinking butterflies had taken to inhabiting her stomach as well as the air around her. For she was entirely captivated by him—enamored of him.

He smiled, and she thought she would melt of bliss.

"Only those who are, in secret, werewolves, my beauty," he teased.

Secrets of the Menagerie

"What is your judgment, Lanval?" Balian asked the captain of his father's guard. "Are my concerns legitimate? Or unfounded?"

Lanval Mordoc shook his head. "No, sire. I feel as you do. There is a threat taking root." The man frowned, bowing his head for a moment as if unwilling to continue.

"What did you find?" Balian urged, for he could see Lanval had uncovered something more—something in addition to the wolf that had been found slaughtered in the wood the previous day—something other than Balian's instinct.

"My brother, Jerrard . . . do you remember him, sire?" Lanval began.

"I do," Balian answered. "He is a strong soldier."

"He is," Lanval assured with a nod. Looking up to Balian once more, he continued, "Jerrard took a wife some three years past, Ermangard. Ermangard hails from Mirermith, sire, and was there to visit her family only six months past. She confided in Jerrard that while there she had indeed heard many rumors . . . countless whisperings that Mirermith's king, Bramwell, means to grow his kingdom, his lands . . . and in vast preponderance. King Bramwell has been heard to say that he will not stand by while certain other kingdoms fall to ruination under— and I beg your pardon, your highness—under the ostentatious, ignorant rule of one the likes who now sits on the throne of Vavassour. Neither will he allow such idyllic lands to be ruled by a monster . . . one who masquerades in human form by day only to roam the land as a beast each full moon."

Balian nodded, even as his frown furrowed in heightened concern. He turned back to Lanval when he heard the man exhale a heavy sigh of his own.

"It is not I who words it thus, sire," Lanval began.

"I know, Lanval," Balian said, reaching to where Lanval sat astride his mount and placing a strong hand of reassurance on his friend's shoulder. "I have been to Mirermith in recent months, and I can attest that many there yet believe in ridiculous notions such as the existence of werewolves. King Bramwell has led his people into the ignorance of such superstitions, and I suspect he has done so intentionally— ruling by fear and threat. Many kings choose to do so."

"Yes, your highness," Lanval agreed.

Balian's frown deepened. "Did your brother's wife offer any further information of value?"

Lanval inhaled a deep breath of discouragement once more before speaking, "Yes, sire. She says that during her visit, she witnessed Mirermith's soldiers in armor, training as if for battle. The king was often in attendance of his men as they trained."

Balian nodded. "Then Bramwell undeniably prepares for combat," he mumbled. "And not defense . . . but for attack."

Lanval straightened his posture. "I am no traitor to our king, my prince," he said. "But I will be damned, or in the least of it hung, before I see Vavassour ill-prepared for defense of our kingdom . . . our people and our lands."

Striking hands with his friend in a powerful grip, Balian growled. "As will I, Captain. As will I. Therefore, proceed with haste in seeing that your men are primed. There is nothing traitorous in preparation, after all. And I am crown prince of Vavassour, a knight of Vavassour . . . and in that I am charged with her protection. Therefore, organize guard posts with messengers available at every viable entrance to our kingdom. Order them to keep watch day and night and send messengers bearing information of any incident, no matter how unsuspecting it may seem. Then we must prepare. We *will* find ourselves in battle, Lanval. And I sense it will not be long before we do."

"Yes, sire," Lanval said.

"I will continue to plead with our own king as well," Balian added. "And let us pray his ears and mind are opened to what you and I can clearly see that he does not."

"Yes, your highness," Lanval agreed with a nod.

As Lanval turned his mount to leave, Balian stalled him. "Oh, but wait, my friend," he called. As Lanval turned to face him once more, in a lowered voice, Balian said, "Send numerous guards to frequent and linger in our village beyond the meadow, Lanval. They that live there are far more vulnerable than those who reside within the castle walls."

"Of course, my prince," Lanval said. "I will see to it at once."

"Thank you, my friend," Balian offered with gratitude.

"I am only glad that you are returned, Balian," Lanval said, showing true friendship in addressing his prince so familiar. "Vavassour would have no hope of surviving King Bramwell's ambitions had you not come back to her."

"Let us hope you are right, Lanval," Balian said.

Lanval smiled a little. "I am right. And you will prevail, my friend. And your men with you."

Balian nodded, attempting to possess a confidence he did not own in that moment.

"Good day, sire," Lanval called over his shoulder as he nudged his horse's flank with his boot and galloped off.

"Good day, Captain," Balian mumbled as he watched his friend go. His heart was heavy in those moments—heavy with worry for the people of his kingdom, heavy with the sense of liability for the life and livelihood of each and every inhabitant of Vavassour.

As Balian watched Lanval ride out across the meadow toward the castle, he heard Thor yip a bit. Looking down to where Thor and the other wolves sat gazing up at him as if they sensed his trepidation and wished to comfort him somehow, Balian did smile—for the expression on each of the five white faces reminded him of years before, when Thor was only freshly widowed and his pups newborn. In that moment, he could have sworn that he saw concern, sympathy, and adoration in each set of wolf eyes—and indeed he did feel comforted.

"Well then, lads and lassies," Balian said, smiling at his wolf comrades. "Shall we fetch the fair maiden and attempt to woo and win her today, hmm?"

All five wolves simultaneously stood, Ullr and Delling panting with excitement, further resembling wolf pups instead of enormous, powerful adults.

Laughing, Balian gathered the reins to the

second horse he had brought with him for Minnette to ride and urged Ewan onward.

"Let us fetch the butterfly sprite then," he chuckled as he rode across the meadow in the opposite direction of Lanval.

Even for the threat Balian knew lurked somewhere beyond the woods, his heart felt lifted by the mere thought of Minnette D'Angelville. It was true; her mother's potion, Serenity, as she christened it, had indeed proved to settle not only the queen's tattered nerves of the previous day but also Balian's. He had slept quite soundly the night before, his dreams filled with the image of Minnette's smile and the sound of her soft, soothing voice. And now he was on his way to fetch her and bring her to the castle. He wondered what the day would hold for her—for them. Would the butterflies in the menagerie fair lose their senses with delight when their fairy queen stepped foot in their pavilion? Would Minnette be pleased with the beauty of the place? Would she be pleased with Balian's company?

Balian found it quite unfamiliar, the manner in which Minnette caused a measure of self-doubt to well in his chest each time he was in her company. Not that he owned an overabundant confidence in his abilities, his strength, and his mind, but in the presence of the apothecary's daughter he found himself quite unable to think of anything but her—not the threat brewing against Vavassour, nor his father's blind belligerence, nor Phillip's lonely existence. It was he wondered then if Minnette would be a strength to him or his weakness. Would she so entirely enthrall and distract him from serious matters pertaining to the kingdom that he would lose sight of some imperative warning of peril? Or would his growing affections toward her add to his strength—find him even more conscious of all things, including menace?

Balian thought the latter would be true—that more time spent in companionship and conversation with Minnette would strengthen his resolve to be the kingdom's champion and protector. After all, Minnette was part of the kingdom, and Balian would move heaven and earth to protect her. Yes, he determined. He was stronger for the sake of knowing her.

He laughed to himself a moment, thinking what opposition he and she were. He was a man charged with the defense of a realm, a man whose best and favorite companions were wolves, a man prepared for battle, a man of skill of weaponry and fighting. Minnette was everything in converse—beautiful, soft, wise, and ever accompanied by the most fragile of creatures. It was, he thought, that she owned everything he did not—and he loved her for it.

"Yes," he said aloud as he rode. "I do love her for it." He glanced to Thor, striding alongside

Ewan with his posterity. "It is many years I have traveled, have I not, my friend? Many people have I met and mingled with. And yet not one woman in all these five years past lit such a flame in me as does this pretty butterfly maiden. You know I must feel deeply for her. For if I am able to deduce what I suspect of Bramwell's intentions—nay, if I can know what I know of the threat that is growing against us—and yet still find such yearning for her company, her image, her kiss . . . then my heart is a prisoner to her will already! Do you agree, my friend?"

Thor glanced up to Balian, his eyes bright with apparent understanding, and again Balian laughed. "I feel that this girl is my deliverance into contentment and joy," he said. "Thus, make haste, my friends. Time is not an expendable reserve, and I am mad with eagerness to see my lady."

"The waterfall implements are simply beautiful!" Minnette could not keep from exclaiming with exuberance. "The great white bear . . . look at him swim! He is fairly giddy, I could swear it!"

She heard the prince chuckle and looked at him to see he nodded in agreement. "Yes. The menagerie has transformed these past years since my absence," he noted.

"Is it the monk's doing?" Minnette inquired.

"It is," Prince Balian affirmed. "One can see his adoration and concern for the place . . . for the creatures herein."

"It is wonderful!" Minnette breathed in awe.

She heard a lion roar then, and her attention was drawn to the habitation across the path from the great white bear. Minnette smiled as she studied the old lion, Apedemak, sitting atop a large boulder surveying all around him. Two younger male lions roared in response, and the lionesses' tails flicked with mild irritation at their rest having been interrupted.

"Oh, look at him there!" Minnette exclaimed, pointing to Apedemak. "Look how regal he is, lounging about on his rock of a throne. How you must treasure him!"

"Oh, but he is not mine to treasure," Prince Balian said, smiling. "Apedemak's loyalty belongs only to . . ."

When Prince Balian did not finish his remark, Minnette offered, "The king?"

The prince shook his head, however. "No. Apedemak is loyal to the Monk of the Menagerie. It is the monk Apedemak favors."

Minnette's smile faded in slight, and she exhaled a sigh of sudden remembered sadness. "It was Prince Phillip Apedemak loved most though, wasn't it?"

Prince Balian's smile broadened, one handsome brow arching with approval. "Yes. Apedemak and Phillip were near as inseparable as Thor and I are. You remember well."

Minnette shrugged. "One does not forget love so easily, if one is a lover of love themselves."

"A lover of love?" the prince inquired.

Minnette giggled quietly and then explained, "Yes, a lover of love. Meaning, one who adores to witness love, who loves love so very much in every condition that one notes it everywhere . . . and remembers it always."

"And *you* are a lover of love?" Prince Balian baited.

"I am," Minnette answered without hesitation. "I see it wherever it occurs . . . such as with your brother and Apedemak. I remember witnessing Prince Phillip tussling about with the great lion one afternoon when my parents and I were ambling about the outer bailey." She glanced up to Prince Balian, adding, "And you were there, as well—you and Thor and the four young wolves." She laughed aloud a moment then and continued, "You appeared as no more than a large boy romping about with giant puppies that day. It was the first time I knew I . . ."

"The first time you knew you what, Minnette?" Prince Balian asked, a knowing grin spreading across his handsome face.

Minnette blushed but maintained her composure and said, "It was the first time I knew that . . . that you loved your wolves, far more than you did most people in your life, I suppose." It was not at all what she had been thinking—not in the least. Still, she was not about to confess to him that seeing him that day at the menagerie with the white wolves of Castle Vargar was the first time her heart had leapt inside her bosom at the sight of him. Had she confessed to him that at the tender age of nine she had begun to daydream of one day meeting Prince Balian and somehow casting a spell over him to cause that he should fall desperately in love with her, he would surely think her mad beyond recovery.

"Is that so?" he asked.

Minnette could see the skepticism in his expression. Still she nodded, returned her attention to the lions, and answered, "Yes."

"Well, then it appears you have always been somewhat of a discerner of souls, hmmm? Or in the least, of hearts," the prince remarked. "For it is true that I do care for my wolves far above most others . . . save my family, of course. And perhaps a very few others," he said, smiling at Minnette.

Just as it had more than ten years previous, Minnette's heart leapt in her bosom—leapt with delight in knowing that the smile he wore was meant for her—leapt with pleasure in the extraordinary attractiveness that was his.

The prince looked down to where Thor stood at his side opposite the one Minnette stood next to. Scratching the large wolf beneath the chin, he smiled, adding, "But, Thor, he is closest to me. Even the others, Ullr, Freyja, Delling, and Nótt, do not share the bond with me that their father does."

Minnette watched as the prince scratched the chin of each of the other four wolves in turn—all of whom licked his hand with thanks. It was an awe-inspiring thing to witness—a man fearless in the company of five great white wolves. Thor himself was quite enormous, and Minnette marveled that she had the courage to stand so near to him. Yet she did not fear him as she had that first day in the meadow. As she gazed into his amber-colored eyes, she thought she recognized an expression of trust in them—as if Thor were silently communicating to her that he had taken her into his circle of those he counted as friend.

"I beg your pardon, your highness."

Minnette looked up to see a lovely young woman standing nearby. Minnette had not heard the young woman draw near, and it was apparent that Prince Balian had not heard her either, for he said, "Hello, Arianna. How is it that you never seem to make a sound when approaching, hmm?"

"Forgive me, sire," the golden-haired, green-eyed young woman said, blushing. "I shall try to walk with a heavier step from now on."

Prince Balian chuckled, however, saying, "Now we both of us know that your proficiency at covertness is paramount to your position here."

"Indeed, your highness," the pretty woman agreed, smiling and blushing an even brighter hue of scarlet.

"What may I do for you, Arianna?" the prince asked.

Minnette tried not to frown, though she could not keep her teeth from clenching tight with growing jealousy. The young woman was very pretty indeed, and she seemed very familiar with Prince Balian. Oh, certainly Minnette knew all women in the world would blush when blessed with a moment of his attentions. Furthermore, Minnette owned no hold on the prince. Yet still she felt the unpleasantness of jealousy churning within her.

"I . . . I was looking for . . ." Arianna began. She glanced to Minnette with obvious evasiveness, however, before continuing, "I was looking for the monk, sire. He had requested that I inform him when I had finished attending to his chambers."

"Oh, well, we have not seen him as of yet," Prince Balian said. "Yet I am certain he is near, so you should come across him promptly enough, I would think, yes?"

Arianna's smile broadened as her expression grew radiant with delight. "Yes, sire. I am sure of it. Thank you."

Arianna turned to be on her way, yet the prince called, "Arianna."

"Yes, your highness?" she asked, looking back to the prince.

"Would you do something for me?" he asked.

"Of course, sire. Anything," the pretty young woman assured her prince.

Minnette silently scolded herself for her jealousy. Prince Balian had always been known for his kindnesses, his considerations of others. It was only he was being courteous to the young woman. It was not as if he were involved in some clandestine affair with her or something the like, surely.

"When you do unearth our dear monk," Prince Balian began, "and when you have finished with him yourself, will you please ask him to meet Miss D'Angelville and I in the butterfly pavilion?"

"Of course, sire," Arianna assured his highness—although Minnette fancied her smile faded somewhat.

"Oh, and forgive my carelessness, Minnette... but this is our Arianna," Prince Balian said then. "Arianna, this is Minnette D'Angelville."

"My pleasure to meet you, miss," Arianna greeted.

"And mine to meet you, miss," Minnette returned.

She watched then as Arianna tipped her head to

one side, her brows drawing together with sudden curiosity.

"Are you kin to the apothecary, miss?" Arianna inquired unexpectedly.

"Yes," Minnette answered. "She is my mother. In truth, my father was the apothecary, Stuart D'Angelville, and my mother, Morgianna, did indeed step into his role when we lost him one year past."

Minnette's eyes widened with astonishment as, of a sudden, Arianna hurried to her, reaching out and clasping Minnette's hands in her own.

"Oh, I am so happy to meet you, miss!" Arianna fairly gushed. Her stunning green eyes widened with admiration as she continued, "You are truly as beautiful as your parents described you to be, and I am so honored to meet you."

"You . . . you are acquainted with my parents?" Minnette asked, confused.

"Yes, miss," Arianna assured her. "And your mother's remedies for illness are pure as wonderful as ever your father's were! I hold your family as a blessing from God himself to those of us who have known pain or illness."

All at once then, Arianna gasped, looking to Prince Balian and saying, "Oh, but forgive me, sire . . . for I have said too much!"

Yet Minnette looked to Balian to see he smiled as if quite amused.

"Not at all, Arianna," he said. "I expect Miss

D'Angelville will be a bit wiser concerning the goings-on at Castle Vargar before she leaves us today."

"Truly?" Arianna asked, her lovely brows arching as if awestruck.

"Yes," Prince Balian assured her. "Now, be off to find that mystery of a monk, will you? And remember to have him attend us in the pavilion. Yes?"

"Of course, sire. Of course," Arianna agreed, releasing Minnette's hands and hurrying away.

Minnette frowned with curiosity. "That was, well . . . in truth, a bit of a strange first acquaintance of persons."

Prince Balian chuckled. "Yes, I suppose it was," he said. "But Arianna is close to someone your father and mother have tended to for many years. I am most certain that is why she was so overjoyed to meet you."

"Really?" Minnette whispered. "Then again, Mother's proficiency with herbs and potions, and Father's as well—many are they who have found comfort from their wares."

"After having myself partaken of what your mother deems Serenity, I am more assured of it than ever," Prince Balian agreed. Then, inhaling a deep breath, he asked, "Are you ready then?"

"For what, sire?" Minnette asked, still somewhat befuddled by Arianna's response to Minnette's parentage.

"To see what the king's butterflies make of the butterfly fairy I discovered in the meadow," he answered.

"I am most ready, your highness," Minnette said. She was still rather disconcerted by the way Arianna had lit up as a star when Prince Balian had spoken to her, but it was she, Minnette, whom prince Balian had invited to the menagerie that day, and she was determined to enjoy every moment in his company.

"Then come along, my beauty," Prince Balian said, taking her hand and placing it at the crook of his strong arm. "And I promise to protect you from any harm their large population and madness to own you might impose upon your petal-soft skin."

Minnette giggled with delight. "I see the werewolf within is in full flattering formation today, your highness," she teased.

She felt something cold and wet at her elbow and glanced to see Thor standing just behind her, the top of his head near even with her own shoulder. He nudged her arm with his soft nose and then licked her elbow with apparent affection.

"You see?" Balian inquired. "It is not only butterflies that crave the nectar that is you, my lady, but also wolves." He lowered his voice, his eyes narrowing as he added, "And their brother werewolves, of course."

Minnette blushed as the prince winked at her with brazen flirtation.

They did not speak for several moments as they walked. In truth, it was not until they reached the entrance to the grand pavilion that the prince spoke once more.

"This is the entrance, of course," he explained. "We must be quick, lest too many of our colorful captives escape as we enter."

Minnette's mouth fell agape a moment as she studied the edifice before her. The king's butterfly pavilion was crafted from very fine net that stretched over an iron skeleton fashioned to support it. The ironwork was almost imperceptible, so covered in green and flowering vines of every sort. Yet it stood pure as high as the West Tower itself and as broad as half again the entire menagerie.

"My . . . the Monk of the Menagerie has sought the most favorable plant life to attract and maintain butterflies with which to stock the pavilion," the prince explained. "And I understand that in the cold months, he has the greater part of the outer region of it covered in protective cloth, and this helps to keep the warmth and moisture inside the pavilion. There are even small fire pits dispersed throughout, and fires are maintained in them when the cold is heavy upon us. This keeps the worms and cocoons from which sprout new butterflies protected and at a moderate temperature. Or so the monk has explained to me."

Minnette's heart began to beat more quickly with the delightful anticipation of stepping into a place she perceived must seem magical indeed.

Looking to the wolves standing behind them, the prince said, "Vent her. Stay here."

Then, taking hold of a part of the netting that hung loose before them, he drew it aside and nodded to Minnette, indicating she should precede him in entering the pavilion.

"Thank you, your highness," she whispered as she stepped through the small opening and into what immediately struck her as an ethereal haven of color and beauty. As the prince stepped into the pavilion behind her, Minnette stood awestruck by the discernable perfume of flowers, the sweet scent of fruit, and a heavy but marvelous fragrance of moisture and green.

"I have never even imagined it would be so brilliant! So beautiful!" she exclaimed in a whisper.

"It does indeed inspire one to feeling near overwhelmed at attempting to take it in all at once, does it not?" Prince Balian said.

"And . . . and there are so many! Hundreds! Thousands, at least!" Minnette noted with astonishment.

"And listen to the quiet," the prince noted. "I understand that it is often my mother comes here to sit, reflect, and rest her cares awhile."

Before taking another step into the surreal garden of beauty and butterflies, Minnette turned to Prince Balian, smiling up at him and saying, "Oh, thank you, your highness! Thank you for inviting me to come here, for bringing me here! I . . . I am pure overwhelmed with gratitude to you and admiration for this heaven all around us. Thank you, sire!"

Prince Balian smiled then, and Minnette fancied for a moment that she might faint from the glory of his superb and unequaled physical form and comeliness! His allure was near unendurable of a sudden, and she envisaged she could near touch the fabric of his masculine prowess and prevailing virility, so heavy did it seem to veil him in that instant.

His eyes—their cobalt blue—the stare of them fair pierced her flesh to look unashamedly on her soul, she thought. And his dark hair, though tousled, fell about his ears and forehead in such perfect disorder that it indeed appeared a contrived provocativeness. All at once, Minnette was cognizant of the pure mass of him—his great height, the unusual breadth of his shoulders, arms, and legs that, though long, boasted an amplitude of strength and obvious musculature unequaled by any Minnette had ever before seen on man.

All at once, her heart began to beat so violent

within her breast, it caused a great aching. Furthermore, a desire—a thirst for his kiss the like they had shared in the meadow the day before—began to well in her so full she began to tremble from its influence over her.

"You are most welcome, Minnette," Prince Balian said. "Yet you have seen but a glimpse of what the pavilion holds for you. Thus, let us amble our way through it, eh?" He looked above her for a moment, smiled, and laughed. "And look here! Your admirers are gathering at the ready."

Desperate to break the spell the prince had unknowingly woven over her, Minnette forced herself to turn from him—to sacrifice further admiration of his immaculate masculinity and consummate handsomeness—to glance to what he had indicated beyond them.

"Oh my!" she exclaimed as she looked up to see hundreds of butterflies had taken flight and were softly fluttering toward them. "They are so beautiful! I . . . I have never before even imagined such a sight!"

"Nor I," Balian mumbled as he stood staring at Minnette.

Oh, but for all the fragile beauty—for all the glory and color of nature in the pavilion—there was nothing to compare with the girl who had, unknowing, captured Balian's attention—and his heart.

In that instant, he owned a notion that he should keep her—that he should seal the entrance to the pavilion and keep Minnette inside to himself for as long as they both could go without drink and nourishment. Certainly it was not something that he could truly endeavor to do, but he did ponder upon it for fair long moments.

"They are so many!" Minnette giggled as wave after wave of fluttering sets of wings affixed to small bodies and tiny, thread-like legs began to alight upon Minnette's arms, shoulders, and head—upon every inch of her being, save her face.

Balian's eyes widened in wonder as in a mere flicker of time, only Minnette's pretty face was visible. What stood before him now indeed favored the manifestation of some ethereal apparition or mythical creature of fairy lore.

"What will they do?" Balian laughed. "For more are arriving, yet there is not one place upon you that they can touch save your face, and they seem to know to leave the beauty of that free for my viewing. I suppose they shall have to share you in turn, hmm?"

Minnette laughed with delight, and the sound was the sweetest to ever have caressed Balian's ears.

"I have never had so many sitting on my person all at once," Minnette noted. "I can feel their weight, infinitesimal though it may be."

"Does it frighten you in any manner? Is it

afflictive to you?" Balian inquired, of a sudden concerned for her comfort.

"Not at all," she giggled.

Balian exhaled a sigh of triumph in pleasing her. He had hoped she would find the pavilion intriguing in the least it. Still, the joy evidenced in her countenance declared she was far more than merely pleased: she was pure elated.

"Good," he said. "Then let us amble further, shall we? You have only stepped inside this magnificent place. I wish for you to enjoy the whole of it."

As Balian gently brushed away several butterflies at the small of her back, in that he could place his hand there to guide her forward, he heard Minnette gasp as all the butterflies that had lingered on her suddenly fluttered up and away.

"I suppose they do not want to share you with me," he said.

But near it was instantaneous that an entirely new wave of admirers descended over her, even spilling onto his own hand at her back and up his forearm.

"You are a mystic being indeed, Minnette D'Angelville," he said as they slowly made their way deeper into the wondrous surroundings, "though I knew that when first we met."

Minnette turned then to look at the prince, near gasping as she saw the approval in his eyes as he gazed at her. Nay, it was more than approval. There was a smoldering essence to his blue eyes that so worked to mesmerize her—a smoldering of admiration—of desire!

She was rendered breathless as the prince put one strong hand to his chest, saying, "I do not warp words, and I am no libertine or seducer of women. And I need you to understand that when I flatter you, I am only speaking my thoughts of you. I have no agenda other than to convey to you the earnest admiration of you that I own."

Minnette frowned a little, puzzled by his sudden serious sincerity. "What is in your mind, sire? For your countenance has altered with such immediacy. Only moments ago, you appeared . . . well, in truth, lighthearted. Yet now . . ."

But Prince Balian seemed to force a smile, shaking his head. "Oh, it is nothing of importance. Only royal matters intruded upon my thoughts of a sudden and . . ." Again he shook his head as if attempting to dispel unhappy thinking. "And I wish only to be here with you. To observe you as you marvel at this beautiful place my . . . the monk has fashioned."

Minnette was fearful of doing so—but surely, when they had shared a kiss only the day before, touching him with the intent to soothe his mind would not find her hanging from the gallows. Therefore, Minnette did stretch forth her butterfly-garlanded hands and took one of the prince's.

"Something is heavy in you, sire," she spoke softly. "I can see it in your eyes. For only a moment ago, they were brilliant and bright with . . . with . . ."

The prince grinned, saying, "With desire?"

Minnette blushed, glanced away a moment, and then looked back to him. "With something other than concern, to say the least. But now . . ."

Somehow she felt that every muscle in his body tensed, and she worried she had disconcerted him.

"I am sorry, your highness," she said, releasing his hand.

Yet he reached out, gathering her hands in his this time and smiling at her. "I am astounded by your ability to see a soul, to interpret a mind or whatever gift it is you have that enables you to sense when my worries are heavy." The prince's grin slowly grew into a smile, and with it the anger, concern, and worry that Minnette had seen take his countenance retreated, and he was calm once more.

"What do you suppose these . . . these delicate worshippers of yours would do to me if I were to impose upon their adulation of you?" he asked.

Slowly his powerful hands traveled from hers that he had held, up and over her arms, until he gently gripped her upper arms, pulling her closer to his own person.

"Do you suppose they will fight for you?" he

asked, his voice low and provocative. "Or will they allow me my own adulation? Will they attempt to fend me off? To save their queen from the wicked intentions of a man? Hmm? Or will they allow me one brief, tender taste of the nectar that is Minnette? Will they share you with me, do you think, pretty fairy?"

Minnette could not draw breath! She was struck silent with wonderment, disbelief that once again the Wolf Prince of Vavassour—the handsome Prince Balian—was gazing at her with a searing desire evident in his beautiful blue eyes.

Barely able to manage a breath of an answer, Minnette whispered, "We cannot know some things, sire . . . until they are tried."

Prince Balian's eyes narrowed, his smile broadening further as he mumbled, "Then it shall be tried. For methinks they left your mouth accessible that I may exact my affection for you precisely there."

Pulling Minnette into the strength of his arms, the Wolf Prince pressed his mouth to hers—lips parted—the strength of him pure evident in his attentive dominance and obvious restraint. As Minnette's mind and body in silent pleaded with her to meet him, mouth for mouth—to return his embrace—she surrendered to her heart's desires—surrendered to Balian, prince of Vavassour, protector of the kingdom, heir to the throne, and the most desirable, alluring, tantalizing man to walk the earth.

Warmth rained over her, coursed through her! As the Wolf Prince's mouth commanded hers, coaxing—nay, begging—reciprocation, Minnette was lost to any thought, any sensation save him. She did not care for butterflies or meadows. She could not think of any other person alive save him. Moist and hot were their blended exchanges—driven, passionate, and intoxicating.

A sudden fluttering of a thousand wings caused Minnette to sense that she and the prince were no longer solitary in the pavilion.

Gasping, she stepped away from the prince, blushing as he smiled at her with satisfaction.

"I believe the Monk of the Menagerie has found us, Minnette," Prince Balian said.

Swallowing a lump of sudden bashfulness that had leapt to her throat, Minnette turned and looked in the direction in which Prince Balian nodded.

There—only mere steps away from where she and the prince stood, only just having been wrapped in each other's arms and mingling mouths in impassioned kisses—stood a tall figure dressed in the cowl and robe of a monk.

Minnette was near overcome with intimidation, for she had never seen the Monk of the Menagerie for herself—only heard tales others told of having seen him, and then only at a distance. She was awed by the height of him, the broadness of his shoulders. Though he was not as large as the prince, Balian, his dark attire and hidden face somehow caused him to seem near as imposing a figure.

"Hello, sir," she managed to greet the man.

The monk nodded.

Minnette heard Prince Balian inhale a deep breath. Then, as the monk extended his hand in greeting to Minnette, the Wolf Prince said, "Minnette, this is the Monk of the Menagerie. My brother, Phillip."

"What?" Minnette exclaimed in unison with a deep voice emanating from within the monk's cowl.

"The time has come, brother," Prince Balian said. The tone of his voice was strong, sure, and imposing. "I know you are not prepared to reveal yourself to the entire kingdom . . . but I would have you reveal yourself to Minnette. Please. I beg it of you."

The monk stood still—as a statue—for long moments as if contemplating what action to take.

"Minnette," the prince began. "Have you ever had the sense that your parents knew something about Castle Vargar that you did not? That no one else knew?"

"Y-yes, but . . . but . . ."

"Phillip did not die, Minnette," the prince

explained. "He was injured . . . changed, yes. But my father could not bear for the world to know that his eldest son was no longer perfect in the eyes of many . . . in *his* eyes. It is why I abandoned my kingdom five years previous, for I could no longer agree with my father that Phillip should remain hidden from all others in the kingdom save our family, your parents, and sweet Arianna, who has assisted him these past ten years."

Minnette turned to look at the prince. For an instant, she wondered if perhaps he had walked so near to madness with grief in missing his brother that he had denied himself reality and concocted some image in his mind that the Monk of the Menagerie was indeed Phillip. Yet her ludicrous musing vanished, even the same moment her mind offered the thought and she saw in Prince Balian's eyes not only truth but also strength and determination.

"Phillip, please," the prince said.

Minnette looked back to the monk—watched breathless and awestruck as the monk reached up and removed his cowl.

"H . . . h . . . hello, M . . . M . . . Minnette," Prince Phillip of Vavassour greeted in a stammering, near-slurred speech. "I . . . I . . . I am . . . I . . . am Ph . . . Ph . . . Phillip."

Darkness enveloped her then. For a moment she was aware of Prince Balian's arms around her—of being laid gently on the path in the pavilion—of a thousand fluttering wings above her and innumerable tiny legs alighting upon her.

The King's Constraint

"Are you indeed certain that you are well, Minnette?" Prince Balian asked.

Minnette glanced to where he sat astride his charger riding next to her. She was glad the horse she rode was smaller and not quite so intimidating as his highness's mount—for, in truth, she did yet feel a bit dizzy.

Still, not wanting to worry the prince, she answered, "Oh yes, sire. I am quite well." She smiled at him, adding, "It is only I am as yet attempting to take it all in—the glory of the butterfly pavilion, the truth that your brother is truly the Monk of the Menagerie . . . that Prince Phillip is still alive." She shook her head, still struggling to believe it was all true. Yet she knew it was, for she had seen Prince Phillip with her own eyes, a moment before she had fainted—and then again when she had been revived.

"No doubt it is overwhelming," Prince Balian agreed. "But a chord was struck deep within me, and I felt compelled to share the secret of Phillip with you . . . and only you." The prince exhaled a heavy sigh—a sigh that breathed of relief, not regret. "Of course, Arianna has known always, for she has tended to his chambers since the day my father publicly announced that Phillip had died. And of course Mother knows."

"And my father knew, did he not?" Minnette offered. "And my mother. Prince Phillip is the reason they were summoned to the castle close after your brother's death . . . his apparent death. They tended him. Mother still attends him when the need arises, yes?"

Prince Balian smiled, nodding and answering, "Yes. And it is evidence of their honor and goodness—the fact neither of your parents revealed the secret of Phillip to you . . . not in all these years."

"No," Minnette affirmed. "They did not." She smiled at the prince, adding, "Though I did not inquire very often, perhaps four or five times in whole. For I knew if it was a secret that required their silence, it must be of great importance indeed. And I too respected them for their loyalty in caching a secret."

"I am sorry you were so overcome that you . . . that you . . ." the prince began.

"That I fainted like a weak-hearted lamb?" Minnette offered, smiling.

"I would not say you were weak-hearted, pretty girl—only overcome with astonishment," the prince offered.

"Well, you are kind to put it so carefully, sire," Minnette said.

As they then reached the large tree beneath

which they had shared their first kiss only the day before, Minnette reined in her mount. The prince's horse followed suit, and Minnette smiled when Thor and his pack instantly relaxed to sitting on their haunches as if they expected to be resting thus for some time.

"Why did you choose me to share the secret of Phillip with, sire?" she asked the prince. "I mean, I am sure you have many friends in the kingdom. It is said that the captain of the royal guard, Lanval Mordoc himself, is your closest friend and confidant. Therefore, I do not understand why in all the world you chose me to . . . to . . ."

"To help me bear this burden?" the prince finished for her.

But Minnette frowned. "Oh no, sire! It is no burden to know that the beloved Prince Phillip yet lives! Not at all!" she assured him. "I . . . I only wonder why you chose *me* to confide in."

Prince Balian inhaled a deep breath—seemed pensive for a moment.

At last he answered her question. "I can only say that I felt compelled to do so . . . and not simply because the secret has been difficult to bear these past ten years. But because something in me sensed it was important that you— in particular you—should know it." He paused, frowning. "There is more, Minnette," he said, having lowered his voice. "And again, I have no explanation as to why I feel you need to know it.

But I listen to what my soul whispers to me and tell you that I sense a darkness, a danger, and a threat is growing against our kingdom. My father will not hear of it. He believes the only threat from another king is attributed wholly to me—to the rumors that still circulate in Mirermith that I am a man by day and a wolf by the full moon. But I know there is more. King Bramwell is no respecter of men. He cares only for land and power, and he has his eyes fixed on Vavassour. He would see me dead and my father tossed from the throne, enabling him to assume rule. But my father will not heed my instincts, or even any thread of proof I have."

At once Minnette felt a fear growing in her bosom. She knew Prince Balian spoke the truth.

"Why will he not heed your words, sire?" she asked. "What proof does he demand, other than your instinct?"

Prince Balian's eyes narrowed as he glanced away from her and to the forest beyond. "It was many times I tarried in Mirermith during my absence. At times, I would disguise myself so that I would not be recognized, and always I heard the rumors, had gossipmongers share with me tales of how pompous and incompetent the king of Vavassour had become—how their own king, Bramwell, should do as he had often said he would do, rise up against Vavassour and King Liam, and take the throne from the Volk family line. After all, the eldest son, Phillip, was dead, and the youngest, Balian, was neither man nor wolf. Therefore, what was to impede Bramwell's taking Vavassour?"

"Truly?" Minnette exclaimed in angry astonishment. "The people of Mirermith are so pompous and greedy that they would tell these things to a stranger?"

"They are," Prince Balian said, nodding. "Furthermore, when last I was in Mirermith, just some weeks past, I arrived as Balian of Vavassour, prince and heir to King Liam's throne."

He paused, his eyes narrowing with fury. "I was accused of being a werewolf, though several in Mirermith had stood witness the night I slept in a cage during the full moon to prove otherwise."

"Did . . . did they speak in a truly awful and disrespectful manner to you, your highness?" Minnette inquired. She was horrified at what the prince was telling her—frightened by what he was telling her.

"Well, yes," he answered, arching one brow. Then he continued, "And they did attempt to kill me, as well."

"What?" Minnette gasped. "Attempted to kill you? A prince?"

"Yes," Prince Balian affirmed. "And now there has been evidence found of malice toward me . . . malice that I believe is meant to distract my father from the truth that the true danger looming is meant for him. The dead wolf that was found in the forest yesterday, though marked as a threat to me . . ." The prince frowned, and he shook his head. "It is not what it seems to be."

"A dead wolf?" Minnette inquired, lowering her voice to a whisper and glancing to the five white wolves sitting beneath the tree. "Do you mean one of the hidden hundred you have throughout the kingdom?"

"Indeed," Prince Balian verified. "She was found in the woods, shortly after you and I met here under this tree, yesterday late morning."

Again Minnette gasped, tears filling her eyes as she whispered, "I think I may have heard this horror."

"What do you mean?" the prince asked, his frown deepening.

"Yesterday, I . . . I watched you ride away," she confessed. Blushing, she glanced away, adding, "For quite some time, in truth. And as I turned back toward the village, as I stepped from the meadow and onto the path through the woods, I heard something . . . a terrible sound." She looked to him, explaining, "I did not know what it was then—though it resembled a bark or a cry of pain that a dog might utter. Yet now I know that it was a wolf being harmed, perhaps killed, for that is what flittered through my mind a moment. Still, it seemed so very preposterous that it would be what it sounded to be that I simply tried to put it from my mind."

Prince Balian's brow furrowed so deeply with concern and anger that Minnette held her breath in awe of the sudden intimidating nature of his countenance.

"You mean to tell me you were close enough to hear the wolf cry out?" he growled.

"Y-yes, sire," she answered. "I am so sorry! I did not know it was something so . . . so horrid for you . . . so significant."

But the prince shook his head, his expression softening, though she was certain he had forced it to do so.

"It is only I am disturbed—greatly disturbed—that the incident seems to have occurred so close to you . . . so close to the village," Prince Balian explained.

The sound of galloping hooves startled Minnette where she sat in the saddle. She and the prince both looked back toward the castle to see a strong charger and large rider approaching.

"My prince!" the man called as he neared. "The king demands you attend him at once, sire."

"Has something happened, Lanval?" Prince Balian inquired, straightening in his saddle.

"I know not the true reason, sire," the armored man answered. The man glanced quickly to Minnette and then turned his attention full on the prince once more. "I have been informed that an ambassador from Mirermith arrived earlier, requesting an audience with the king."

The small hairs on the back of Minnette's neck and on her arms seemed to stand at attention as a sense of dark foreboding traveled over her.

"Captain, see Miss D'Angelville safely to her home please," the prince ordered.

"Yes, sire," the captain of the king's guard agreed.

Turning to Minnette, the prince said, "I am sincerely sorry, Minnette. This day did not go forth as I had intended. Will you forgive me my ill manners please? For I must attend my father, at once."

"Of course, sire," Minnette said, truly concerned by the angry worry apparent on his handsome face. "Of course."

"Thor!" Prince Balian growled. "Komme paa en gang!"

In a flurry of white, the wolves were off, racing across the meadow after their prince.

Minnette looked to the captain. "I can surely walk from here, sir. I well know the way. You may take the prince's horse, and I—"

"I will see you safely to your destination, miss," the captain said. "It is the prince's command."

"Very well. It is this way, sir," Minnette said.

Yet as she rode through the trees toward the village—and although she felt no threat for the sake that the captain was her escort—there was not one part of Minnette that was at rest or calm in any sense.

Prince Phillip was alive! For ten years he had been alive and secreted in Castle Vargar! Futhermore, it seemed that Vavassour itself, as well as her king, was in danger. Most troubling of all, however, was the notion that someone—perhaps an entire kingdom—wished to see Balian, prince of Vavassour, dead!

As she rode toward her home—impatient to be with her mother, to confide all in her—Minnette attempted to keep her thoughts in lingering on the beauty of the butterfly pavilion, on the wonder of the prince's having kissed her again. Yet each time she could nearly taste Prince Balian's kiss once more, the sound she had heard in the forest—the sound of one of the hundred white wolves of the Wolf Prince's secret army being killed—intruded, and what should have been a blissful reverie was brutally tainted.

"There! You see, Balian!" King Liam boomed. Handing the parchment to Balian, the king continued, "There it is . . . with Bramwell's seal upon it! There is no threat directed to me, Balian. It is only Bramwell owns apprehension regarding you! You and that shameful wolf bite years past." Then gesturing toward Thor, Ullr, Freyja, Delling, and Nótt, the king added, "That and your damnable wolf companions here. That is where

Bramwell's trepidation lies—not with me or my rule of my kingdom."

Balian read the writing on the parchment—the veiled threats toward his father if it were proved his son was a monster.

"It is diversion, Father," Balian mumbled. "I told you that Bramwell would attempt to redirect your attention to me. And I stand firm on—"

"Silence, Balian!" King Liam shouted, however. "It is you Bramwell despises, not I! And I will hear no more of your accusations!" The king inhaled a deep breath, exhaling slowly in an attempt to calm his temper. Shaking his head, he growled, "When it was two sons your mother bore me, I never imagined that my blood could run through the veins of such weak men."

"Liam!" the queen scolded in anger. "None of this is Balian's fault. And certainly none of it is Phillip's! I will not continue to stand by while you blame—"

"You will continue to stand by and hold your tongue, Asta," Liam bellowed, "else you find your two sons and yourself exiled from my kingdom altogether."

Balian was infuriated! He had held his tongue all the while his pompous father had accused and blamed him. But to see his mother being treated so ill, he would not endure it.

"You are a coward, Father!" he snarled. "Your ego has grown so large you cannot see it though it is plain on your face and on every other part of your being! And how dare you threaten Mother with exile!"

As his father aggressed upon him, Balian stood strong and straight.

"You will not speak to me with such disrespect and impertinence, boy!" Liam shouted.

But as he drew back his hand intent upon striking Balian, the king gasped when he felt a powerful hand take hold of his wrist.

"You will not strike my brother!" Phillip said through clenched teeth. "You are out of sorts, Father. Contain your temper."

Balian was, in truth, disappointed at Phillip's having appeared and stepped in to defend him. He was well ready to allow his father to strike him, simply for the fact that he would feel justified in striking back. In threatening the queen—in intending to strike his own son—the king pure proved what Balian already knew. King Liam—once a fair, kind, and powerful ruler—had allowed egotism and self-importance to blind him. The kingdom was in danger not because of rumors surrounding Balian and his wolves but because of her king's vanity.

Fair tearing his arm from Phillip's grasp, King Liam growled to himself, glaring at first Balian, then Phillip, and then their mother.

Then leveling an accusatory index finger at Balian, he snarled, "You *will* prove to Bramwell that you are not a werewolf. I have given him my word that a public exhibition will be held in your honor, Wolf Prince. In less than a fortnight, the moon will be full, and you will be imprisoned in a cage through the entirety of the night—wherein every man, woman, or child who wishes to may bear witness to your being nothing more than an ordinary man."

"And when it is proved, your highness?" Balian asked, his voice marked with fury. "When it is proved that I am but an ordinary man, then has Bramwell assured you that his disquiet will be satisfied?" When his father paused in answering—when he saw the king set his jaw firm and defiant—Balian pressed, "Or is there more that he has asked of you, my king? Suffice it to say that already you have shown weakness in even allowing Bramwell to make demands on you, demands to which you agreed, though you well know that I am but an ordinary man."

Balian watched as his father's face grew crimson with wrath.

Yet he continued. "There is more, is there not? The king of another kingdom has walked into Vavassour, handed you down his own demands, has inasmuch commanded you, King Liam of Vavassour, to prove to him that your only heir—in the least, the only one he or anyone else knows exists—is not a werewolf. He has commanded *you* to prove to him—he who has no authority here. He marches into your castle, demanding that you prove the humanity of your heir, your own son, your blood. And not only do you agree to put your progeny in a cage where he can be viewed as no more than another animal in your menagerie collection; even after it is proven that your heir is no monster—no man who turns to wolf in the full moonlight—he places more demands upon you? And you bend to it? You agree to it? What kind of king allows another to determine whether his heir is worthy? Whether or not *he* is worthy."

Balian paused to attempt to calm himself, for his chest rose and fell with such labored breathing of frustration and anger, he feared he might fly apart somehow. He could see his father was wrathful indeed—but also that he saw reason to what Balian had pronounced.

"You will prove yourself no beast the likes of whom you consort with," King Liam growled. "And then you will marry within the month. No woman would knowingly marry a beast, a monster, a creature that has no earthly purpose save it is to do evil. Thus, once you have proved yourself in front of all witnesses, then you shall wed within a month—nay, a fortnight. I will see your ungrateful self wed, and in that there will be the final proving to Bramwell. There will be the dissolution of his worry in the humanity of my heir."

Balian could not keep himself from bursting into astonished laughter. "Father! Are you in earnest? Do you not see Bramwell's agenda? No doubt he offered one of his own kingdom—even his daughter, perhaps. He would see me married to a woman of his choosing and, in that, assure himself your throne! For there I am, wed to some strange girl from Mirermith—a girl who has been ordered to vanquish the life of the Wolf Prince of Vavassour, the werewolf prince. Thus I will lie dead in my marriage bed, and with your only known heir conquered, there is nothing remaining for Bramwell to do but to conquer you . . . and Vavassour will be his." Balian laughed again—laughed in pure disbelief of how ludicrous the entire situation was—of how utterly gullible and blind for his own self-importance his father was.

"Father," Phillip muttered in astonished disgust. "Certainly you did not agree to wed Balian to Bramwell's choice of bride?"

"I did not," the king grumbled. And although Balian saw the color fairly drain completely from his father's face—noted his shoulders begin to droop with the realization of defeat—King Liam said, "I would not agree to wed one of Bramwell's subjects to Balian. *I* will choose whom you marry, Wolf Prince. And you *will* marry whomever I choose, else—"

"Else I be exiled by my king?" Balian interrupted. "As my brother was exiled a decade past merely for surviving tragedy and imperfection? As you only moments ago threatened to exile my mother—the queen of Vavassour, your wife—and for simply speaking in defense of her sons?" Balian sneered at his father, even spat on the floor at his feet. "No, King Liam. I will exile myself from Vavassour before I will marry whom you choose. I will not help you save your throne, Father."

"Balian," the queen cried with desperation. "Please, do not abandon your brother and me again. I could not endure it. I could not!"

Balian closed his eyes, wincing at the pain his mother's unhappiness and pleading drove into his heart. He could not desert her—leave her with only his selfish father to protect her. He glanced to Phillip, and although his brother nodded in silent agreement that Balian should not allow the king to so manipulate him for his own pompous cause, he knew he could not leave his brother to suffer in loneliness any longer.

"You will take to the cage, boy," his father growled. "And you will marry."

As his mother nodded, silently beseeching him through her tears, Balian gritted his teeth tightly before answering, "I will take to the cage, my king. But I will take to the cage for Mother's sake and Phillip's . . . not for yours. And for the sake of Vavassour and all the good people who live freely and in happiness within her green and benevolent borders, I will marry. But I will marry the woman of *my* choosing and no other. Do you understand, my king?"

Stepping forward until he was nearly nose to nose with his father, Balian growled, "I will marry whom I choose, or your kingdom will be lost to Bramwell. And then, my king, I will endeavor to save the kingdom from your pompous, blind ignorance. I will prove it to you, Father. I will prove that this . . . this spectacle of Bramwell's you have agreed to—I will prove that it is nothing but a farce meant to distract you, me, and everyone with any interest in Vavassour. It is meant to distract from his true intention—which, my dear, loving father, is to unseat you from the throne, exile your name, your blood, and any remainder of your progeny to perdition, and rule Vavassour himself!"

"You arrogant fool," King Liam breathed.

And yet as Balian struggled to control his temperament—as he stood in knowing he knew Bramwell's intentions far better than his father would admit to conceiving—he knew he had won. He had won in that he would remain in Vavassour. He had won in knowing that one day he would be king and could then protect his family and his people as he saw fit to protect them. Perhaps he had agreed to marry far sooner than he had expected to upon his return to the kingdom—yes. But was it so miserable a thing when he had already discovered she whom he wished to marry in the first of it? Indeed no. Therefore, Balian had won. He would continue to see the kingdom safe from his place as heir to the throne. He would watch over and protect his mother and one day see his brother revealed to all and standing at his side as Prince Phillip of Vavassour once more. And further, he would marry the butterfly fairy who had so instantly stolen his heart and know such happiness as he could never before have imagined.

"So be it!" the king growled. "Take whomever you choose to wife. I will send word to Bramwell that it will be so. And he will accept it, for it is not I and my rule that concerns him but you and one day yours, Balian." Again leveling an index finger in Balian's face, the king added, "And you will see, boy! You will see that I am a great king—not because I allow another to put my heir to the test but because I do not race off to battle when there is no threat there in the darkness!"

Then, turning on his heels, King Liam shouted, "Phillip! Take your mother and your haughty little brother away from me! I wish to be alone, for there is much required of a king, and I have no more patience for trivialities this day."

Balian noted the frown that at once puckered Phillip's brow—noted how his chest rose with the inhaling a deep, infuriated breath. Yet the queen moved forward, placing her hands on Phillip's strong arm to calm him.

"Come, my darling," she said in a quiet voice. "Let us all retire to my chambers . . . and . . . and rest."

Balian watched as his mother's eyes darted to her husband and back to Phillip. "We are all of us tired," she said. "Perhaps Arianna could serve us a soothing drink. Perhaps some of the apothecary's Serenity, hmm?"

As his mother nodded to him, seeming to be attempting to communicate some unspoken meaning, Balian nodded in return. "Yes, Mother. We will join you in your chambers, Phillip and I."

The queen forced a smile, patted her thigh, and whispered, "Come along, little wolves . . . come along." Without another word to the king, who stood with his back to them huffing and puffing as a pouting child, they left him to it.

Naturally, for the sake that Phillip was with them, the three royals made their way to the queen's private chambers by way of the secret passage leading from the solar to her own sitting rooms.

Balian was not surprised to find Arianna in wait of them, for she often attended the queen, as well as Phillip.

What did astonish Balian, however, was his mother's question as she rather collapsed onto a chaise.

"Is it the D'Angelville girl you are thinking of marrying, Balian?" the queen asked. "Minnette?"

As Phillip, Arianna, and his mother all stared at him in expecting a response, Balian stammered, "Well, yes . . . if . . . if she will have me, Mother. But how did you come to know of my fondness of her?"

The queen exhaled a long sigh. "Arianna, would you be an angel and brew all of us, including yourself, dear, a mug of Morgianna's Serenity, please?"

"Of course, your majesty," Arianna agreed with a curtsy and a smile.

Balian watched, rather confused at the sudden familiarity he felt between his mother, Arianna, Phillip, and himself—as if their father no longer lingered in the castle and all could own peace of mind and spirit.

"Well, darling," Balian's mother began, "I am your mother, am I not? And as such, I am sensitive to your feelings, your musings, your disappointments and delights."

Balian was awed at the change in his mother's countenance. He thought that he should not be awed, for it was ever and always that his mother was near a different being altogether when she was not in the company of his father. It had ever been so.

"I told her of the events in the pavilion today, Balian," Phillip interjected.

"You did?" Balian inquired of his brother. He did not know whether to be angry with Phillip or relieved that he did not have to give explanation.

"He did, my dear," Queen Asta assured him. "And I will tell you that from what I have heard of Minnette D'Angelville by way of her mother—further, by the high character of her parents—well, my darling boy, I am certain you could find no better match for the Wolf Prince than the butterfly girl of Vavassour."

Balian frowned, swallowing the large lump of trepidation that had leapt into his throat. "She may not accept me, Mother. You know this to be true."

But the queen merely shrugged, and it was Arianna who said, "She will, your highness. I saw you in her eyes today in the pavilion. I daresay Minnette D'Angelville was yours the moment she met you, sire."

Balian collapsed into a nearby chair, however. "This is not what I want for her," he sighed. "I do not want this life of royal propriety for her. I want her to run barefoot in the meadow, sip her mother's Serenity, and be ever worshipped by butterflies. Yet to marry me, it will mean anguish, loneliness . . . unhappiness." He looked up to his brother and then to his mother, adding, "And it will mean battle, Mother. For Bramwell means to—"

"I do not want to hear any more of King

Bramwell and his malicious intentions tonight!" Queen Asta exclaimed. She looked at Balian, stared at him, saying, "I know you are correct, Balian. Your father has become arrogant and blind . . . but I have not. I know a darkness threatens us and our good people. But please, I beg you, tonight let us talk of you and your butterfly princess. Let us talk of the day that will come when Phillip is no more in the shadows but standing beside us on the terraces and balconies." The queen smiled as Arianna placed a mug of Serenity in her hands. "And let us talk of Phillip and Arianna. Will you *ever* find the courage to propose marriage to our dear girl, Phillip?"

Balian's brows arched in wonder at his mother's unanticipated frankness. The queen was indeed a different soul when the king was not present—forthright, happy, unafraid to speak her thoughts. Of a sudden, Balian remembered that she had ever been so and that time spent alone in his mother's and brother's company had endured as his favorite before Phillip's accident.

"Mother!" Phillip exclaimed. "Are you indeed attempting to finally frighten Arianna away with permanence?"

Balian watched as his mother smiled, however, sipping Serenity from her mug a moment as she winked at him.

"Not at all, my dear," the queen answered at last. "I am merely attempting to find Arianna where she belongs—in life as my daughter-in-law and in your bed as your wife."

"Mother!" Phillip scolded as Arianna rather juggled the mug of Serenity she had intended to give to him.

Winking at Balian, Asta offered, "Oh, come now, Phillip. It is not as if you and I have not discussed it—at length—for years now. Balian is wondering when you will find the courage to propose to Arianna as well. Are you not, Balian?"

Balian looked from Phillip's humiliated expression to Arianna's hopeful one. "I am," he said—for he had known since the first moment he had seen them together upon his return that something between his brother and Arianna had blossomed into adoration—love and the anticipation of passion.

"Balian! Brother! Do not tell me you have gone mad in harmony with our mother," Phillip exclaimed. "Why . . . why, Arianna has no more care for me in an amorous regard than she does a stray dog."

"I would ask you, please, Prince Phillip," Arianna began then, "not to make assumptions on behalf of my cares."

Phillip's eyebrows leapt to arches. He stood entirely dumbfounded before the girl.

Breaking the silence, the queen said, "Why not take Arianna for an amble in the butterfly pavilion, Phillip dear?" Winking at Balian once more, she added, "I hear it is quite the perfect venue for a romantic interlude. Hmm?"

"Shall we walk, your highness?" Arianna inquired of Phillip.

Phillip, rather dazed in appearance, nodded, and Arianna took his arm as she led him toward the hidden door in the chamber that led to the secret passageways of the castle.

When Phillip and Arianna had disappeared into the passageway, the queen again patted her thigh, calling to Thor and the others, "Come here, puppies. I have missed you warm, furry darlings so terribly."

Balian watched as first Thor, then Delling, and then the others deposited themselves at the queen's feet where she sat. Placing her mug of Serenity on a small side table, Balian's mother began to pet and rub each wolf in turn—just as she had always done when the opportunity presented itself in the time before Balian had left.

"Now, Balian, my sweet," the queen began, "tell me the tale of how you have only been returned a matter of days and yet have managed to find yourself in love?"

Balian chuckled. What sort of insanity was running rampant throughout the castle that would find him in fiery, verbose battle with his father one moment, Phillip and Arianna bound for a romantic tête-à-tête the next, whilst he lingered in the quiet solitude of his mother's chambers, with her querying him concerning Minnette and treating his ferocious wolves as if they were pups the very next?

The Dog-Intrepid

"In truth, I could see that Mother was so relieved to at last be able to share her secret with me," Minnette explained to Balian as she carefully worked in crafting a small wreath chain of wildflowers. "She told me that it was not a hard thing to do at all, to keep the truth of your brother a secret before my father died—for she and he both cached the knowledge and could speak of it to one another, at least. But when Father passed away, Mother began to feel quite alone in bearing the burden of Phillip's tribulation."

Balian smiled as he watched Minnette connect the final two flowers of the wreath she had been working. Smiling, she reached over and placed the wreath on Freyja's large white head.

"There you are, milady," Minnette said, stroking Freyja's back. "Now you are as festooned as your comrades."

Balian chuckled as he studied his ferocious white wolves. He would have sworn to all the earth that Thor wore an expression of disgusted patience as he sat with the wreath of purple and yellow flowers bedecking his head—disgust at having been festooned with flowers, patience for the love of she who had placed them there.

Continuing to lounge comfortably beneath the great maple on the edge of the meadow, Balian gazed at Minnette as she spoke. It was very glad he had been to find that Minnette's confiding in her mother of having herself become aware of the truth of Phillip of Vavassour had offered her mother an obvious respite of the mind. It was a comfort to Balian, as well—to know that Minnette shared his opinions of his brother's circumstances.

For the hour they had already lingered together beneath the tree in the meadow, Balian had imparted lengthy explanative descriptions of his frustrations with his father concerning Phillip's invisibility to the kingdom. Minnette had listened, truly intent upon his words, sincere in her interest and attentiveness, ever offering assurances and understanding of his grievance, while still able to work delicate wreath chains from flowers with which to ornament the wolves. Balian found that simply the ability to talk freely to someone concerning Phillip—discuss anything and everything to do with him and his circumstances—greatly lessened the resentment, animosity, and anger that often simmered inside him pertaining to the fact.

Furthermore, Balian found true gladness in knowing that Minnette's mother now had a confidant as well. It was no easy burden the king had placed on Stuart D'Angelville and his wife,

Morgianna, ten years previous. It was cruel, in truth—selfish. Yet Balian knew that his father's selfish manner would not change. At least, not easily.

"Thank you for confiding of Phillip with me, sire," Minnette said of a sudden. "It soothes my heart to know he is not dead . . . that you still have him." Her smile broadened as she added, "And I am refreshed in knowing that your mother has had him all this time, as well. I so very often could not bear to think of the poor queen, her anguish at having lost a son. For though I do not have a child, of course, I could always imagine a tiny measure of the hurting she must have endured . . . and it broke my heart to think on it."

Balian grinned at her with admiration. "I too am heartened to know that I, like your mother, now have someone to share my secret with. It near can cause a man to rupture—owning such knowledge of a great and powerful injustice the like that Phillip endures." He paused, frowning as determination rose within him. "I will see Phillip freed, Minnette. I will see him able to walk the bright castle halls instead of the dark and dank hidden passages. I will have him at my side in public view whenever he and I choose it. I will have him live comfortably with the sun on his face, riding out during the day." He smiled and winked at Minnette, adding, "And I will see him happy in marriage to Arianna—with a loving wife and children to bounce upon his knees."

Minnette smiled, giggling, "Oh, I wish I could have seen his face when your mother tattled on Phillip of his affection for Arianna. How mortified he must have been! And the queen! I have only ever seen her stoic and with serious expression or forced smiles. I had no idea she could be so playful and impish." Minnette laughed a moment and then said, "I love her for the cheerful, mischievous soul she keeps so well hidden."

Balian laughed, yet only in brevity, for he was, of a sudden, reminded of his father's bowing to King Bramwell's demands, and it pure irked him.

Minnette noted Balian's laughter died away, his expression hardening, his handsome brows knit together in a manner of discomfited thinking.

"What is it that haunts you today, sire?" she asked. "For I can fair see it in your countenance—that there is more pricking at your mind than the injustices heaped upon your brother. Please, speak in confidence to me, for have I not proven myself a loyal confidant thus far?"

The prince nodded, grinning a little. "Indeed, you have, Minnette." Still he paused, until Minnette reached out, placing one of her hands over his where it lay in the grass next to where she sat.

"Come now, your highness," she playfully coaxed, relishing the feel of his warm, strong hand beneath her own. "No one is about, and your wolves are resting at ease with their newly worked head ornaments. Thus, tell me what wrinkles that stern brow of yours today. Is it yet concern for Phillip? Persistent frustration with your father?"

The prince inhaled a deep breath, exhaling it slowly.

"King Bramwell of Mirermith has laid down demands at my father's feet," he rather growled. "I am to prove myself to our people and any of Mirermith who wish to witness. I am to be caged again at the next full moon eleven days hence."

"What?" Minnette gasped. "That is absurd! Your father knows you are no werewolf! Why ever has he agreed to this preposterousness?"

"Because Bramwell threatened him with battle. At least that is my assumption," the prince answered. "And it is not that I am loath to be caged. I would welcome the opportunity to dispel ignorance among *our* people if any still exists . . . which it does not. The people of Vavassour are faithful followers of Christ, wise folk who know there is no such thing in all the world as a werewolf . . . or in the very least of it know that I am not one. But even if there remain some among our people who yet hold to superstition, I would cage myself as proof to them and gladly. But to be forced to prove it to the conniving, malevolent king of another kingdom . . . to *his* subjects? And simply for the fact that my father is too arrogant and self-important to see that Bramwell only attempts to distract him from his exact intentions?" The prince shook his head with disgust. "*That* is what I find so repugnant, so thoroughgoingly irksome."

Turning his hand so that he now tightly grasped Minnette's, he inquired, "Will you attend me again, Minnette? In my hour of public viewing . . . will you attend as you did before, when you were much younger? It would be far more tolerable a night of incarceration were I able to gaze upon your lovely face amidst the crowd of gawking gatherers."

Prince Balian then smiled such a smile that, had Minnette not already been seated in the cool, fragrant grass, the numbing weakness the sight of his provocative smile infused directly into her knees would have found her collapsed there soon enough.

Gazing at him for long moments, Minnette thought she would grant him *anything* he asked of her! He was so strong, so very handsome and able, so concerned for the people of the kingdom—more concerned for them than even his father was! And although she had never observed him in battle, she could well imagine what a powerful warrior he was. She thought of the day she first met him—thought of him first running through the meadow with only his trousers to clothe him—thought of the intimidating presence he was when garbed in light armor and sitting astride his charger. Oh, it was certain that Prince Balian—for all his gallantry, restraint of cruelty, and gallant escort of her through the butterfly pavilion—was not a man that any other, no matter how strong or how skilled with weaponry, would wish to face in battle.

"Of course I will attend, sire," Minnette answered. "For I would not leave you to endure the dark night alone."

"Thank you, my butterfly sprite," the prince said, smiling at her with marked appreciation.

Of a sudden, an unanticipated notion leapt into Minnette's mind, and she spoke out loud of it without pause.

"Why not invite someone to remain in the cage with you, your highness?" she offered with enthusiasm. "Surely that will even more deeply intrigue all who are witness to your examination, as it were—in particular those who hail from Mirermith to observe, will it not? If they are ignorant and prejudiced enough to believe you are truly a werewolf, then why not really give them what for? Have someone linger in the cage in company with you, all through the long night—someone they might fear you may devour entirely if your werewolf self appears!" Minnette giggled. "And think how disappointed they will be when the sun rises and your companion is left unmarred, hmm? Oh, that would be delicious! Would it not?"

So delighted was Minnette with imagining the expressions manifest on the faces of those of another kingdom who traveled to Vavassour with expectation in seeing a man transform into a wolf and also observe what the outcome would be for an innocent caged with him, she did not pause for the prince to comment on her suggestion, only continued, "Oh, how foolish their king would seem to them then. How weak King Bramwell would appear to his subjects at having accused our king of harboring a monster! How imprudent the world in its entirety would think King Bramwell! What say you, my prince? Will you keep a captive with you in your cage? Just to prove King Bramwell an incompetent for all who attend the preposterous viewing?" Clapping her hands together with pleased anticipation, Minnette laughed as she thought of the pompous King Bramwell proved to be a fool to his own people.

Balian smiled, chuckling with amusement and pleasure. How vivaciously Minnette was speaking; her entire countenance was radiant with delight in thinking of King Bramwell being bested, humiliated before his people. It seemed there was a bit more of the imp in her than Balian had suspected—and he adored her all the more for it.

"What think you, sire, of my mad proposal?" Minnette asked him, her eyes fair glistening with anticipation of his response.

"I think it a brilliant strategy," he answered full truthful. "Yet to beg some other poor soul to linger in a cage the full of the night—would it be cruel, do you think? For I am loath to be pent up for even a moment; nay, it is I am fearful of it."

"You, your highness?" Minnette exclaimed, however. "You? Fearful? Never! I do not believe you are ever fearful. And how could being kept in a cage for just one night find you afraid?"

Balian shrugged where he lay stretched out in the cool meadow grass. "Oh, it is not for myself that I fear but for others—for my family, the people of the kingdom."

"But why ever would you worry for others when *you* will be he who is captive, sire?" the beauty sitting next to him inquired.

"For the duration of the long night that I am caged, then who will watch over the people and the kingdom?" he explained.

"I do not understand, your highness," Minnette said. "Or is it that you see yourself as our guardian . . . you alone?"

"I know what is in your mind, Minnette," Balian began. "You are thinking, *Why would he worry about our welfare now? For he abandoned us to whatever harm could take us for near five years. Yet now he returns and decides we are not safe without him?* And you are correct in thinking me weak and low—a coward for having left the kingdom to any and every threat these past five years. Still, I will say that I did not know my father's arrogance had so magnified during my absence. I assumed, though I see now that one must never assume where anything at all is concerned, that he was yet as cautious and wise a king as he had been before Phillip's accident. For even after Phillip was injured—even after I began to understand that my father's pride was why he had exiled my brother to a life of invisibility—I yet thought he cared more for the people of Vavassour than he did himself. Yet it was not so, and I abandoned our people for these five years past." He paused, his eyes narrowing as he stared at Minnette, covenanting, "And to be caged, even for one night—to be unable to take up arms if someone is threatened—that is what causes fear to rise in me, Minnette. Only that."

Minnette was not smiling, yet Balian noted the manner in which her eyes lingered on him—traveled the length of him with admiration and esteem.

He was astonished—nay, awed—to even greater esteem toward her when she next spoke to him, saying, "*Territi sunt oves, et proximus sunt lupi rapaces. Ego sum canis-intrepidus maneo.* The Volk family motto—the sheep are frightened, and the wolves are close. I am the dog-intrepid."

"I am moved that you would recite our creed with such reverence, angel that you are," Balian told her—for it was true. Never had he heard any voice, outside that of his own family, speak the Volk motto with such emotion—emotion that revealed thoroughgoing understanding.

Minnette smiled. "I am happy to have pleased you," she said, blushing. "Further, I understand that only you—you more than anyone else in your family since your great-grandfather, King Roldan, proclaimed the motto—understand it, live to consummate it in its literal meaning. I admit that having looked into your brother's eyes yesterday, I am confident in suggesting that he too holds to the heart of your motto . . . that if life had not dealt to him such tribulation, he too would uphold the motto to his dying breath."

Balian was, in truth, mesmerized! How could the beautiful young woman so intensively know the thoughts and desires of his heart? Of his very soul? And after mere days of acquaintance? It was a wonderment to Balian—nay, even a miracle!

"Who is the flatterer now, my fairy?" the prince asked, smiling at Minnette with narrowed, alluring eyes. "And how do you know so much about the motto of my family? I daresay, most that reside in Vavassour are not even certain what the translation is from Latin, let alone the deep meaning it holds."

Minnette smiled, blushed, and felt the presence of not only the butterflies that lingered on her shoulders and in her hair but also those that were fluttering about in the pit of her stomach. Prince Balian, still clasping her hand, raised it to his lips, pressing a firm, lingering kiss to the back of it.

"How do you know so much about it?" he asked. "And how do you know that I hold it as my life's motto—my creed, my province, and my calling—when others in my family have or do not?"

He kissed her hand once more, and Minnette thrilled at the bliss palpitating through her limbs because of it.

Yet she did manage to answer his inquiries. "My father was a wise man, sire. He was a student of King Roldan's writings, opinions, and history. It was my father who told me, years ago, on the very night you first were caged under suspicion of being a monster. It was then that my father said, 'Prince Balian is no werewolf! Indeed not! Balian is the truest dog in the Volk royal family!'" Employing her best imitation of her father's deep, commanding voice, she continued, "'It is Balian who bears the creed true, Balian who runs to face danger and threat . . . runs toward it, instead of away from it. As the dog that the shepherd keeps.'"

"I am truly fascinated, pretty fairy," Prince Balian said, still smiling at her. His blue eyes were warm, inviting, filled with approval. Yet he teased, "Pray, go on. Tell me why your father measures me to be a dog."

Minnette giggled. "Oh, do not attempt to jest with me . . . to infer that my father's naming you the dog is in any way offensive to you. You recognize it to be the greatest compliment, sire . . . and you know why! You of all people know you are irrefutably the dog—not the sheep, nor the wolf." She paused, laughing again before adding, "Though not so many dogs keep company with wolves the way you do, sire. Still, you are the dog, not the sheep, and though it might appear otherwise to those who do not know you in the flesh, you are unquestionably not the wolf."

Prince Balian nodded with concurrence. "No, I am not the sheep, nor the wolf. But did your wise father—and if he were here I would grasp his hand in thanks for complimenting me so—did he further elucidate concerning the sheep, the wolf, and the dog when he so named me?"

Minnette smiled as the prince raised himself to sitting next to her. Her skin tingled with gooseflesh at being so near him—at the provocative nature of his gaze at her.

"Of course, sire," she assured him.

"Why not enlighten me then, Miss Fairy?" the prince prodded. "For it may be that I am having a stupor of memory in regard to the profound and true meaning of my family's creed. Hmmm? Why did your father name me the equivalence of the dog?"

Minnette's heart was pounding with such rapid fury, she wondered for a moment if she would be able to continue to speak! He was so very near to her—so very enticing by his very nature.

Still, at last she managed, "My father named you the dog because he knew that is what you are."

"More please," the prince said, leaning closer to her—staring at her mouth.

"Sheep . . . they do not want to know there is danger in the world, nor malicious intent. They do not want to recognize their own vulnerability—the truth that they can be killed, their lives taken. The sheep wish to live in peace and ignorance. It is they only desire to graze and chaw on the lush grasses the shepherd leads them to. They wish only to grow their wool and eat, to live safe and unaware of impending danger. Further, the sheep know of the wolf, but in their desire to live in blissful ignorance, the sheep believe the wolf will never come. The sheep say, 'Oh, that wolf! If he exists, he will never intrude upon us, for we have lush green grasses upon which to graze. What more is there in life if not our perpetual pleasantries?' Yet the sheep do see the dog, and they oft do not like him."

"Why do the sheep not like the dog?" the prince baited, grinning at Minnette.

"The sheep do not like the dog for many reasons," Minnette explained, however needless explanation was to the prince. "In the first of it, the sheep do not like to be herded by the dog, and they oft resent him for it. Moreover, the dog rather resembles the wolf. In truth, the dog, like the wolf, owns sharp fangs . . . and a tendency toward hostility, bloodshed, and the aptitude for violent behavior. Thus, the dog is an ever-present admonition to the sheep that the wolf truly does exist. Yet there is vast opposition between the wolf and the dog—opposition that the sheep oft choose to ignore. For as the wolf will enter the flock, murder sheep, and devour their flesh, the dog lives only to protect the sheep . . . to keep the wolf at bay. The dog would not harm the newest lamb; in any regard, he would not harm a sheep. Nay, in fact, the dog would give his life for any sheep in the flock . . . even for the fact they do not like him. And still the sheep are not easy with the dog in their midst. The dog is ever circling the border of the flock. He barks at things the sheep cannot see. And he is ever prepared for and expectant of battle. And in truth, battle is what the dog lives for. Honorable battle only, of course . . . righteous battle to what end? The safety and preservation of the flock. The dog is the warrior, and the dog was born a warrior—

chose to remain a warrior—one who loves his people, loves his flock so earnestly that he will engage his propensity for battle and bloodshed and, willing, confront cardinal evil, even battle and defeat it, and return to his flock intact . . . and oft unappreciated as the sheep return to their preferred ignorance, believing that no wolf will ever intrude upon them. The dog cannot change his nature, and he would not if he could. For he is driven to watchfulness, awareness, and vigilance. He is driven to battle when the wolf comes, and he knows the wolf will come. Hence, the dog endures the sneers, the jeers, and the condemnation of the sheep. He endures their chosen ignorance and lack of preparation for the wolf's arrival—for the wolf will come."

Minnette sighed, gazing deep into Prince Balian's bewitching blue eyes. *"Territi sunt oves, et proximus sunt lupi rapaces. Ego sum canis-intrepidus maneo,"* she said. "The sheep are frightened, and the wolves are close. I am the dog-intrepid," she spoke. Then in a whisper, "*You* are the dog-intrepid, your highness. I have known it since the night my father spoke of you as the dog . . . since the night I stood witness to your caging years ago."

Balian's heart swelled so intensively within his chest, he fair thought it would burst from his body completely. She knew him! Minnette

D'Angelville knew him as no other on earth had ever known him.

It was true that her father had recognized the dog in him, and he owned further respect for Stuart D'Angelville even than he had before. Yet it was he could see himself—his own reflection in the ethereal green of Minnette's eyes—and she *knew* him. She perceived his very soul.

In that instant, Balian owned divine confirmation that the girl before him—the beautiful young woman who, even now, was worshipped by in the least twenty butterflies—was the woman who was meant to be his wife.

Unquestionably he was reluctant to take her from her quiet, lovely little cottage home—from her mother and their tranquil life of working lace and preparing herbs. Nevertheless, his heart, mind, and spirit knew it was what was meant for him—what was meant for her—what was meant for them both.

The culminating affirmation welling within Balian of a sudden melded with his fierce, all-consuming desire for Minnette, and he could keep himself from her no longer! Thus, driven by passion, admiration, comprehension, and love to a depth he had never before conceived, the Wolf Prince of Vavassour reached out, vigorously gathering the butterfly sprite into his arms and against his body as he claimed her nectar-laced mouth with his own thirsting one.

• • •

The prince had no need of forcing his kiss upon Minnette—even if he had intended it. For she had seen desire in his eyes as he gazed at her, his attention oft lingering on her lips as she spoke. Hence when he reached for her, she freely, readily, blissfully surrendered into the strength of his arms.

"Minnette," he mumbled against her mouth.

"My prince?" she asked, breathless.

She knew he smiled, for she could feel the curve of his lips against hers.

"Oh, I think we are far beyond such formalities, my sprite," he breathed. "I am Balian to you, your own dog to make the flock discomfited. Surely you will call me Balian, my precious lamb . . . for I do so wish to hear my name from your sweet lips."

Minnette's heart ached inside her bosom—ached with rapture in knowing the Wolf Prince owned affection for her.

Gazing for a moment into the depth of the blue that was his eyes, Minnette whispered, "Very well . . . Balian."

Her whisper seemed to be his undoing, for with a groan of savage emotion and desire, Balian presented a reclamation of her mouth—of her kiss—of her body held tight against his.

Oh! Such blissfulness! Such rapture and euphoric sensations washed over her as Minnette had never known—even on the previous occasions of being blessed by Balian's magnificent and far more than merely proficient kiss! Warm—nay, hot—and moist was his mouth as their lips blended in shared impassioned commutation.

Their somewhat maladroit position of sitting was swiftly resolved when Balian laid Minnette down in the grass, all the while continuing to slather her with adoration in impassioned kissing. Oh, but his proficiency in enchanting seduction caused that Minnette began to feel moderately dizzy! Yet she cared not, for where was she to fall if her mind whirled out of control? Being that she was already founded on a bed of grass—the fervor of romance and affectionate reciprocity between her and Balian fanning to steadily mounting flames of emotional and physical intensity—Minnette knew she could not tumble from the edge of the earth there in the meadow. So she ignored the dizziness of ecstasy swirling her mind in vibrant colors of every hue. To Minnette, there was only Balian—his arms about her—his mouth hot and demanding against hers.

It was not until she felt something cold upon her forehead that slowly she became aware that one of the wolves was sniffling in her ear.

Balian broke the seal of their lips, gazing down at her with an expression of pure marveling in his countenance.

Something soft fell onto Minnette's face then, and she giggled when she realized it was the flower wreath she had bestowed upon the head of Thor.

Balian chuckled as well, saying, "Methinks my friend Thor has had his fill of flowers adorning his head for now."

Rising to his feet and taking Minnette's hand as he helped her to her own, Balian spoke, "A true epiphany has been gifted me this day, my pretty fairy. And I thank you for it."

"Then you will have someone attend you when you are caged before King Bramwell?" Minnette asked, happy that he thought her proposal clever enough to implement.

"We will see," Balian responded, bending to place a firm kiss on her forehead.

For all the rest of her charms and virtues, his fairy was a witty lass as well. Yet he would not disappoint her in that moment by confessing that he could never allow someone to linger in the cage with him on the night of the full moon. For although his father believed Bramwell only demanded supplementary proof of Balian's full and incontestable humanity, Balian suspected otherwise. For what more uncomplicated manner could there conceivably be in which to assassinate the Wolf Prince of Vavassour than to find him caged for a full night long?

No. For as clever as Minnette's notion of a companion to attend him in the cage, Balian would never place anyone between him and those who meant to kill him. For the dog would never hazard the life of even one lamb to stay the wolf from slaying him.

Brushing a strand of hair from Minnette's soft cheek, Balian said, "But for now, know this. The sheep are frightened, and the wolves are close, my pretty lamb. Yet I will weather the caged night well, for I am ever your dog . . . intrepid."

As Minnette threw herself against him, her arms tight around his waist as she clung to him, Balian knew she was yet anxious for his well-being. Still, as he brushed a blue butterfly from the top of her head, kissing her there, and then resting his chin upon her, he feared nothing—neither his father's ignorance nor King Bramwell's malicious strategies. He was the dog, and the people of Vavassour were the sheep he loved. He would protect them—all of them—even his self-important father. But it was his lamb he would battle impervious to protect.

"Baa baa," Minnette giggled.

And even for all that was burdensome in his mind, Balian laughed. For as King Bramwell was the envoy of malevolent hell, so Minnette was the plenipotentiary of pure paradise.

Arianna's Overture

Morgianna lifted the candelabra from the table at which she and Minnette had been crushing and mixing herbs. The sun had set near an hour previous; thus both Morgianna and her daughter were curious as who was knocking quietly on the cottage door.

"Perhaps it is Balian," Minnette whispered as she followed her mother across the room.

"I would not think it could be," Morgianna quiet said. "For the two of you have already shared company near the whole sum of the afternoon. And I would hope the prince was abed by now. He will need his rest if he is to keep awake the entirety of tomorrow night."

It was true. Minnette had spent hours lingering with Balian in the meadow that midday and afterward. Over the past ten days—since King Liam had commanded that Balian would be caged through the first night of the full moon—Balian had come to the meadow to rendezvous with her each midday. It was hours and hours they would sit in discussing any and seemingly every topic two people could possibly conceive to converse. And, of course, there were the physical affections they shared—kisses so marvelous they warmed the very air of the meadow around them.

Still, though her mother was obvious in her assumption that Minnette had remained in Balian's company for pure sufficient—nay, pure bountiful—time that afternoon, Minnette knew that, would she be blessed with spending every moment forever with him, it would not satisfy her.

Hence, she hoped it was Balian come to call—thought that it well could be he. For she knew he felt as she did—their time together was far too brief, no matter the length and measure of it.

Peering through the darkness to where the candlelight flickered as her mother called, "Yes? Who is there?" Minnette held her breath in curious anticipation at what voice would respond.

"It is I, Madam D'Angelville. Arianna of Castle Vargar," Arianna's voice answered.

Instantly, Morgianna swung the cottage door open. Indeed, it was Arianna standing just beyond the threshold.

"Arianna!" Morgianna exclaimed in a whisper. "Is all well? Am I needed at the castle?"

"No, madam," Arianna assured her. "But may we enter and speak to you in privacy?"

Minnette frowned in like manner as her mother, curious.

"Of course, my dear," her mother answered. "Yet who accompanies you? I see only—"

Minnette gasped, astonished when the Monk

of the Menagerie—even Prince Phillip himself—stepped from the blackness of the night to stand behind Arianna.

"Your highness," Morgianna breathed. "Whatever are you doing here at my doorstep?"

"M-m-may w-w-w-we en-enter?" Prince Phillip stammered.

He was, as ever, clothed in his black robe and hood. Yet Minnette thought it quite extraordinary—the manner in which the prince's deep, resonate voice commanded attention, even for his slurred stammering.

"Oh yes! Of course, of course," Morgianna said. Stepping aside, she bid them both, "Please enter. And forgive me. I am simply so thoroughly astonished at finding you here, sire."

"And we are apologetic for disturbing you, Madam D'Angelville," Arianna began. "It is only that . . . well, his highness was compelled to speak with Miss Minnette this evening. He has much he wished to convey to you both, if . . . if you will allow it of him . . . and if you feel that you may spare the time and patience required to listen."

"Oh, I am always delighted to linger in your company, sire. As well as yours, Arianna," Morgianna said, smiling. "It has been quite some time past since you and I have shared conversation."

"Yes, Madam D'Angelville," Arianna confirmed.

"Please. Please do join us for some refreshment. And we are eager to hear what your highness has to say to us, are we not, Minnette?"

Minnette nodded with earnest assurance, saying, "Oh yes! In particular I . . . for I have only met your highness once before." Looking to Arianna, she added, "And that did not bode well for a first impression of my person, I am quite certain."

She blushed, remembering when first Balian had introduced her to the Monk of the Menagerie—for she had fainted near dead away.

"M-m-my im-immm . . . impression of y-y-you w-w-was t-to b-b-be pl-pleased for m-m-my br-brother's sssake, M-M-Minnette," Prince Phillip assured her as he entered the cottage behind Arianna.

Again Minnette blushed—yet also sighed with reprieve in knowing she had not disappointed Balian's brother too terribly upon their first meeting.

"Do please join us at the table, your highness . . . Arianna," Morgianna said, leading them further into the small cottage.

Quickly, Minnette cleaned the table of the herbs and utensils she and her mother had been working. "Do sit wherever you would feel most comfortable," she said.

She smiled and looked to her mother, who also smiled, as Phillip held Arianna's chair for her as she sat, pushing it in at the table afterward.

"Thank you, Phillip," Arianna said, smiling at the prince.

Prince Phillip then repeated the gesture to Morgianna in turn and finally Minnette.

Morgianna giggled a little, took one of Arianna's hands in her own, and began. "*Phillip* is it now, hmmm?" She looked to Prince Phillip, her smile broadening as she said to him then, "I see you have, at last, found your courage where your beautiful Arianna is concerned, eh, your highness?"

Phillip nodded—pushed back his monk's hood to reveal a smile donning his handsome face. "M-m-my m-m-mother fffound th-the c-c-courage fffor m-me, I am a-a-afraid."

"Bravo for the queen, say I!" Minnette exclaimed. "And bravo for you, your highness, for soldiering forward with it."

She was delighted when a warm glow rose to Prince Phillip's cheeks as Arianna gazed up into his handsome face and smiled, oh, so very lovingly.

Prince Phillip looked to Minnette, and even before he spoke, she remembered that Balian had told her that if she listened with her heart instead of just her ears, she would learn to hear him as if he did not struggle to speak clearly at all. And so, as he did begin to speak, Minnette focused her attention not on his mouth, nor even the words he would speak, but on his eyes. She would hear his heart and soul as he spoke; she was determined.

"M-m-my br-brother," Prince Phillip began, his blue eyes sparking with emotion. "H-he t-told me of your suggestion . . . that he have someone stay the night with him in the cage Father is forcing him to be imprisoned in tomorrow night."

Minnette smiled, happy that Balian had been correct in his promising her she could hear beyond Phillip's slurred stammer—hear only his words and his intention if she tried.

"Yes?" Minnette prodded.

"When he told me of this strategy, I was immediate to agree with you, Miss D'Angelville," Prince Phillip explained. "In truth, I planned to be the one to remain in the cage with my brother tomorrow night. For would not the presence of the Monk of the Menagerie lend intrigue? Further intimidate King Bramwell—if the oaf can be intimidated at all?"

"What a brilliant notion!" Minnette exclaimed. "Yet why do you say you planned to remain with him? Have you since chosen not to?"

Prince Phillip shook his head, saying, "No. Balian tells me he will not allow it . . . for he fears the entire affair is simply a thing Bramwell contrived to ensure that Balian would be vulnerable to attack . . . to assassination."

Minnette and her mother gasped in unison, "What?"

"It is what Balian fears," Phillip continued. "And once he had presented the prospect to me, I too am able to see the danger."

"Then he must not stay in the cage tomorrow night!" Minnette exclaimed. "I cannot believe I did not fathom his being vulnerable before." Then, as fear washed over her entire being, she asked, "Pray . . . did he agree to forgo the caging? It is a preposterous notion in the first of it!"

Prince Phillip inhaled a deep breath, and Minnette realized that, in truth, it was wearing for him to speak for long periods—for it was difficult for him.

"No," he said. "Balian will be caged . . . even for the peril . . . for he knows . . ."

When Phillip did not continue, Minnette responded, "That it is Bramwell's hope to dethrone your father and deprive him hope of your family's ever reckoning . . . by killing his only known heir."

Minnette's blood seemed to run cold as Phillip answered, "Yes."

Desperation gripped her then—as surely as she reached out, gripping Prince Phillip's strong arm. "We cannot allow him to be caged, sire! We cannot! It is true. I too see it clearly now. King Bramwell will, no doubt, employ an archer, a knight, even a peasant—he will see that someone kills Balian tomorrow when he is caged! I know it! Please, sire, how do we act? What do we do to stop Balian from entering that cage?"

"We do not stop him," Prince Phillip stated.

"But your highness! He will surely be killed!" Minnette cried as tears escaped her eyes, streaming over her cheeks.

"No," Prince Phillip rather growled, however. "He will not be killed. For he will have guards at the ready . . . dressed in the manner of villagers so as not to be noticed by Bramwell and his men. Lanval Mordoc for one. He is captain of the royal guard, Balian's friend, and a far superior soldier than any in Bramwell's command. And I will be there, as well. It is I have an aptitude for remaining unnoticed, passing as a shadow and without detection. I will keep Balian safe for you, Minnette. It is why I wanted to speak with you this evening . . . to assure you that I will not allow anyone to harm him."

Yet Minnette was little soothed in truth. How could Prince Phillip and Captain Mordoc protect Balian when he would be caged, like an animal that had been hunted and caught? She thought then that even the animals in the king's menagerie were not so vulnerable as her Balian would be.

"You will not be able to stop it, if Bramwell arrives well prepared," Minnette offered. "It is impossible to protect him when there will be so many gathering to gawk at him."

It was Arianna who reached out, taking one of

Minnette's hands in her own then. "My prince will protect yours, Minnette," Arianna said, "even as yours has always protected mine. All will be well. And when it is done—when the sun rises once more, again proving that Balian the Wolf Prince is naught but a man—then King Bramwell will have failed. The known heir to the Vavassourian throne may, at last, persuade his father that there is malice in the heart of the king of Mirermith."

But Minnette shook her head, even as she clutched Arianna's hand in gratitude. "You mean to say, if Balian's heart still beats when the sun rises."

There was nothing but fear, dread, and despair in Minnette's mind and heart at that moment. She could not imagine a greater peril awaiting Balian anywhere than to be caged—to be made a manageable target for arrow, sword, or dagger. In the cage King Bramwell had manipulated King Liam into placing Balian in, he would have no means of defense whatsoever. His life would be for the taking at the whim of King Bramwell's servant.

"I have a notion of something that may help Balian," Arianna offered, lowering her gaze. "It will not please you, Phillip, and Balian cannot know of it, but it may serve as distraction while your brother is caged . . . perhaps enough that any assassin would be far less willing to be captured while making an attempt on Balian's life."

"What is it, Arianna?" Prince Phillip urged.

Still, Arianna paused, and Minnette could see she was apprehensive.

"I do not want anyone in this room to believe me insipid, heartless, or simply lacking my wits," Arianna ventured.

"None of us here could ever think that of you, Arianna," Prince Phillip said. Minnette's heart warmed at the sound of love in his voice as he spoke to his lady. His eyes glistened as he looked at her, as well—just as Arianna's did when she gazed up into his handsome face.

Minnette perceived that this was a love built over many years—forged by triumph over adversity, shaped by mutual respect, admiration, and attraction. The love that was evident between Prince Phillip and Arianna was a most beauteous love—one to be envied by most all who walked the earth.

"Please, Arianna," Morgianna encouraged. "Please speak. Do not worry that any of us will think ill of you . . . ever . . . no matter the circumstance."

Prince Phillip smiled at his love, nodding to her to indicate she should continue. Therefore, after inhaling a deep breath, Arianna bravely spoke. "It is that I think Minnette should indeed linger in the cage with Prince Balian tomorrow night."

"What?" both Morgianna and Prince Phillip exclaimed.

For her part, Minnette smiled—for she surely agreed with Arianna.

"Why ever would you suggest this, Arianna?" Prince Phillip kindly inquired. "After all, we have only just discussed the danger to Balian—his unwillingness to allow even me to remain with him in the cage. Yet you would propose that he allow Minnette to?"

"Oh, he would never, not in all his long life, allow Minnette to remain with him in the cage," Arianna elucidated. "I do not recommend that we ask his permission for her to do so . . . only that she does so."

"But, Arianna—" Morgianna began, painful worry evident in her countenance.

"Madam D'Angelville, Phillip, please understand me," Arianna began once more. "I propose that Phillip not tell Balian that Minnette will be with him. I propose that Phillip tell the king, his father, who will, no doubt, be delighted to present a greater spectacle than was even anticipated by King Bramwell. I propose that when Phillip begins to fasten the bolt of the cage—for if the Monk of the Menagerie should do so, it will be wildly intriguing to the public, which King Liam will embrace eagerly—then I propose that Minnette quickly slip into the cage with Balian, just before Phillip locks it. I know the king will agree—nay, will welcome the scene—women of Mirermith gasping in horror, thinking they will witness a prince transformed to a werewolf only to devour a pretty maiden."

"Go on," Phillip urged, though Minnette could see the tears welling in her mother's eyes.

Arianna cleared her throat, brushed a strand of loose flaxen hair from her cheek, and proceeded. "Phillip will stand guard—obvious guard—menacing, intimidating as he ever is, so tall and broad-shouldered and bedecked in his black robe and hood." Looking to Phillip, she added, "You will have no need to lurk in the shadows then, my love. This way, you may be ready at hand and with your hawk's eyes see any threat before you . . . and before it has an opportunity to reach Minnette or your brother."

"It is set then!" Minnette exclaimed. "I will endure the werewolf's cage with Balian. And when King Bramwell's assassins—if there are assassins about—fail and Balian does not turn to a werewolf in the light of the full moon, King Bramwell will surely know he cannot slither into Vavassour under pretense of claims the Wolf Prince is no proper heir to King Liam's throne. Bramwell will know he cannot rain malicious destruction upon us!"

"Minnette, my love," Morgianna began, however, "you cannot possibly attend Prince Balian in the cage. It would mean that any assassin might strike you down in pursuit of him."

"No," Prince Phillip interjected in a deep, commanding voice. "I swear to you, Madam D'Angelville, as you have so many times come to my aid—nursed me, even preserved my life—so will I protect your daughter's life with my own." He leaned toward Minnette's mother, continuing, "Arianna possesses a sharp wit, a keen mind that I very much admire. And though my own ability for strategy is not a breath of what Balian's is—nor Arianna's, for that matter—her plan would enable me to stay close to Balian, to watch the gatherers for threat, to defend him . . . even to free him from the cage if danger draws too near. I cannot perform any of those services if I must lurk in the shadows outside of the crowd."

Tears were streaming over Morgianna's beautiful cheeks. "Minnette, it is too perilous. I cannot . . . I cannot allow you to—"

"Would you have done any less for Father, Mother?" Minnette asked, yet with empathetic understanding. "Would you do any less for me?"

Morgianna brushed the tears from her cheeks, even as she shook her head. "No, I would not pause to do the same, and more, for you . . . as I would have done anything to protect your father."

Prince Phillip rose from his chair then and made two small strides to where Morgianna sat, trembling with trepidation. Kneeling on one knee at her side, Prince Phillip took her hands in his.

"I will protect Minnette with my own life, Madam D'Angelville," he said. "We are, all of us, of Vavassour. We are all in profound peril at the hand of King Bramwell's malice and my father's refusal to see reason. As it is my duty, and joy, to protect my brother and your daughter, so is it the duty of every soul residing in our peaceful kingdom to do whatever they must to preserve that peace . . . that freedom. My brother, Balian . . . he will triumph where I fear my father now fails. Thus, Balian's life must be preserved at all cost . . . even at the cost of my life. And that same life I will give in protecting Minnette. This I swear to you, Madam D'Angelville."

Minnette watched as Prince Phillip kissed the back of her mother's hand and then stood straight once more.

Her mother then clutched Minnette's hands so tightly, her fingers were turning blue. Yet with tear-stained cheeks, she managed to choke, "Very well, Minnette. Very well. Were your father here . . . I know he would agree with Arianna's plan. I know he would trust in Phillip to protect you, to see you returned to me, safe, when the sun rises."

"And you need not fear for my Phillip's life either, madam," Arianna said, rising from her own chair, gazing up into Phillip's face with all the admiration of a woman who had given her whole heart to her lover. "For Phillip ever triumphs. No one will be harmed while Prince Phillip of Vavassour stands guard." Arianna giggled, adding, "No harm will befall one soul when the Monk of the Menagerie stands guard either."

As she pondered Arianna's plan, Minnette found not one shred of fear in her. Not one. Rather, she felt hope and excitement begin to grow in her bosom. With an innocent in the cage with Balian, not only would the prince be a more difficult target to strike, but it would allow Prince Phillip—donning his disguise as the Monk of the Menagerie—to linger close at hand. Balian would safe endure his night of captivity. And afterward, if King Bramwell continued to press King Liam about the worthiness of his heir, perhaps King Liam would at last see the threat as clearly as did Balian.

"Are you certain she will be safe, Prince Phillip?" Morgianna asked.

Minnette could see by the lack of color in her mother's face that fear for her daughter's safety still gripped her.

"Madam, I am certain," Prince Phillip answered.

Morgianna inhaled a deep breath, nodding as she assured herself more than the others. "I will put my faith in you, my prince. For I do know what a great man you are, how powerful and true, in every regard." Forcing a smile, Morgianna looked to Arianna a moment before rising from her chair, moving to Phillip's love, and embracing her.

"And do not wait to wed, my dears," Morgianna said. Releasing Arianna and embracing Phillip, she continued, "Wed as soon as you are able, in secret if you must. For though I know Prince Balian has vowed you will be known to your people again, my prince, do not waste a moment alone . . . not one more moment alone when you could have your love at your side in every moment to come, forever. Very well?"

Prince Phillip smiled, and Minnette felt her heart swell with emotion, for his eyes were filled with gratitude and happiness—a happiness Minnette well knew the secret prince had not known for a very, very long time.

She could see—visibly see—that Prince Phillip felt just as she, Minnette, did—alive, hopeful, happy for being in love. For a moment, cruel thoughts—the fact that Balian was indeed heir to the Vavassour throne—intruded upon her joy and the pleasure she owned in loving him. Yet though she knew it was inconceivable that both princes of the kingdom would choose to marry common women, she prayed that God would intervene on her behalf—grant her the miracle of one day being Balian's bride. Oh, Minnette knew it was at best a far-fetched notion. Yet she wondered why she had ever been put in Balian's path if not for a reason. And oh, how she prayed both day and night that the reason was for the sake that she and the Wolf Prince were meant to be husband and wife—lovers—eternally.

Thus, after Prince Phillip and Arianna had left the cottage to make their way back to Castle Vargar—after she'd said good night to her mother—Minnette lay in her bed, gazing out the cottage window to the clear but black night sky, watching the stars wink their silver glints at her and wishing upon every lovely twinkle that, somehow, Balian, Wolf Prince of Vavassour, could be hers—that she could belong to him.

Minnette D'Angelville had no design or desire to live in a castle. She had not one whit of a wish to live the life of royalty. Indeed, she much preferred to daydream of being married to Balian and living quietly in a small, isolated cottage on the far side of the forest. Still, if a castle was his home and monarchy his trade—whether by birth or the necessity of Vavassour's one day needing a wise and able king—she would endure. She would live in a castle of stone instead of a cottage of thatch. And she would share the man she loved with the people of the kingdom—for better to have Balian as her own and live anywhere in all the world and under whatever circumstances living life brought to her than to weather one hour of life without him.

Minnette sighed, smiling as she studied the kaleidoscope of slumbering butterflies perched amid the slats of her window shutters. More butterflies rested on the bed at her feet. She would miss her pretty friends when the cold months descended upon Vavassour. Yet even as she closed her eyes, a vision of the menagerie's beautiful butterfly pavilion hovered in her mind. Winter was the time of cocoons in the meadow, and she wondered how many cocoons the pavilion protected from the cold. And as she too drifted off to sleep—as one large blue butterfly fluttered in through her open window to alight on her shoulder to nap through the long night with her—Minnette continued to think of the butterfly pavilion—and of Balian kissing her there—of Balian kissing her and kissing her . . . and kissing her . . .

Passion and Connivance

"And it is not enduring the night in a cage, in itself, that so irks me," Balian growled, ranting his frustration to Minnette there in the meadow. "It is my father's bowing to Bramwell's demands that full infuriates me!"

Minnette watched as Balian paced back and forth through the grass before her. She almost smiled as she glanced to Thor and the other wolves, sitting in repose near her beneath the grand maple—their heads moving from one side to the other and then back as they watched their master march to and fro with frustration.

It was that Minnette felt happy in knowing Balian chose her to be his confidant. Naturally, she was not happy with the situation before him; she was terrified for his safety, in truth. And as the sun sat lower and lower in the westmost sky, Minnette's apprehension grew, as well. Yet she would not speak of it—not in that time—not when Balian was so fair wound tighter than a toddler's top and needed to give vent to his aggravation.

Of a sudden, Balian dropped to his knees before the place where Minnette sat. Taking her hands in his, a stark and intimidating frown upon his brow, he asked, "How can I make him see what is there before him, Minnette?" Shaking his head, he continued, "He will lose the throne if he does not see into Bramwell's malicious heart! Worse, he will lose our people—plain hand them over to a foul and cruel dictator who cares only for wealth and nobility. Bramwell has no great love, in the least, for the common people. He sees them only as a means to grow his own riches and power. And my father refused to see it."

Balian exhaled a heavy sigh of discouragement, released Minnette's hands, and sat back on his heels, defeated in countenance.

"I know," Minnette said softly, reaching out to place a calming hand to his cheek. "But by the sun's rise in the morning, King Bramwell will be thwarted, and perhaps your father will see reason." She knew, as well as Balian did, that King Liam was blind to reason—in particular where his own pride was concerned.

Still Balian smiled a little, his sapphire-blue eyes regaining a bit of their sparkle.

"You are either much more hopeful in my father's character than I," he said, "or perhaps it is that you simply were born to be a court jester. For you and I both know that my father will simply feel he has proved what Bramwell set him forth to prove and dismiss the entire affair as inconsequential. Meanwhile, Bramwell will have readied his men, and though he may not strike at once, he will most certainly attack Vavassour. And my father will gasp in disbelief that such a thing could have transpired under his rule."

"Well, at least you will have your brother near to you," Minnette offered in attempting to encourage her love. "And that is something you have not known in a very, very long time. Perhaps you can find a bit of comfort or . . . or . . . an additional perseverance of some sort in knowing Phillip will be so close at hand."

Minnette's heart leapt in her bosom as she thought of the prospect of lingering in the cage with Balian through the night. She did not care what speculation her doing so would cause—what the old hags and gossips would whisper in her wake once the event was done. She knew only that she wanted to be with Balian—to simply sit in his presence, every moment that she was able. And though she had said nothing to Phillip, Arianna, and certainly not her mother, Minnette fully intended to guard Balian's life with her own. She would step in front of him and take the assassin's arrow or blade—and without pause. For Minnette understood, just as Balian did—and possibly even more—what would become of Vavassour and its people if their heroic Wolf Prince, Balian, was murdered by Bramwell. Hope would indeed be lost. Further, Minnette valued Balian's life more than anything—more even than her own—and she would move what earth and heaven she could to protect him.

Therefore, she too was far more anxious within herself than she appeared to be without.

Still, she smiled, taking Balian's hand as he spoke, "Yes. It is good to know Phillip will be close at hand. Yet in the same breath, I worry for his safety far more than for my own."

Minnette watched as Balian's handsome brow again furrowed with an angry frown. "I own a mind to simply reveal Phillip to all myself!" he exclaimed in anger. "Father has treated Phillip miserably—fair taken the fullness of life from him. And now that he has Arianna—now that the two of them are intending to wed—I truly think to reveal him to Bramwell and all who attend this insipid display tonight! When the sun rises, it is in my mind to pull that mask of a hood from his head and announce, 'Here is my brother, the first prince of Vavassour!' After all, what will my father do if I reveal Phillip? Kill me? There in front of Bramwell and all the people of our kingdom? Nay, he will not! For he should as easy hand the kingdom over to Bramwell in that moment . . . for Phillip would never agree to rule." Balian shook his head. "Phillip has no desire to rule. He never has. I have no desire to rule for my part of it either. But I will not leave our people to the wolves, so to speak."

Minnette smiled, her love for Balian expanding

in her heart so fully she feared the organ might burst with loving him so complete!

"You will not leave your sheep to the wolf," Minnette gently said. "You will not leave them without their dog. And Phillip knows you are the dog they need, Balian. Phillip, great and capable as he is . . . he comprehends what his injuries took from him. It is one reason he loves Arianna so, I believe. She compensates for what he lost, with patience and love . . . for she would not love him if he were perfect, if he were the heir to the throne of Vavassour and not you. She would not be happy as queen, and he would not be happy as king, for he would feel clumsy and awkward because of his speaking impediment and loss of . . . of . . ."

"Loss of memory and strategic wit," Balian said, his shoulders sagging.

Minnette felt tears well in her eyes, her heart aching with compassion. Balian did not desire to be king either. Yet he would never allow his sheep to be devoured by the hungry wolf Bramwell, nor any other evil, conniving wolf.

"It does fall to me then, does is not, my fairy?" Balian asked.

Minnette brushed a tear from her cheek as she nodded. "Yes. It does."

Balian inhaled a deep breath of renewed resolve and fairly leapt to his feet.

"Then I have played the sulking shirker enough

today," he said. He offered a hand to Minnette, assisting her to feet. And the moment she stood once more, he gathered her into his arms.

Smiling as he gazed down at her, he said, "At least I shall have my butterfly sprite there to watch over me tonight, hmm?"

"I would watch over you *every* night if I could," Minnette said. At once she was regretful at having spoken aloud her thoughts. Balian was prince of Vavassour! And though she knew he cared for her—even she knew he cared deeply for her—it did not give her sway to speak so intimately. In truth, she feared that he might end their embrace, having been made to feel as if she owned too much hope in what he could offer her—in how long he could offer it.

Balian did not release her, however. Instead, his smile broadened and his powerful arms banded all the more tightly around her small frame.

"Is that so?" he asked, his eyes narrowing in the provocative manner she so adored.

"I . . . I . . . forgive me," Minnette stammered, blushing to her toes with discomfiture at having spoken so plainly to him.

"Oh, please do not ask me to forgive you the most tempting thing I have ever heard pass from those beautiful, soft lips of yours, dove," he chuckled. "For I would watch over you every night as well . . . if I could."

Still, Minnette was ill at ease. "But I had no

right . . . no, I should not have said such a thing to you."

"Of course you should have, Minnette," Balian assured her in a lowered, alluring voice. "You should say whatever you desire to say to me, my pretty butterfly maiden."

He was sincere. Minnette could see sincerity in his whole countenance—sincerity and desire!

"Of a sudden, I am not so overly concerned with what lies before me this night," Balian said. He bent, pressing a warm and lingering kiss to her throat. "In truth, I am, in this moment, numb to the ravages of anger and frustration . . . careless of my father's idiocy."

Balian placed a firm yet tender kiss to her lips, stripping Minnette's breath from her in an instant!

"Here," he breathed, "in this instant, standing beneath this tree, the meadow grasses soft and fragrant beneath our feet . . . there is only *you* to me, Minnette."

Balian kissed her lips once more, mumbling, "Oh, that it could ever be thus—you in my arms . . . the taste of your mouth mingled with mine."

Minnette, for her part, was wholly undone then! As Balian's mouth captured hers in a ravenous, intimate kiss heated with the fiery passion of yearning desire, she melted against him. Oh, how marvelous was his mouth—warm, moist, and flavored with all essences possessed of the Wolf

Prince: attractiveness, allure, power, virility, foresight, and intelligence!

As Minnette bathed in the bliss that was Balian's kiss—in the felicity of being in his arms—she dared to dream that he was hers and she his, that they would live out their lives together in genuine, lasting happiness. Oh, what paradise it would be to wake to Balian's handsome countenance every morning, to hear his laughter and see his smile, to feel his mouth pressed to the soft hollow of her throat in a hot, impassioned kiss as it was in that moment—to know that same thrill every sunset forevermore!

Balian's mouth returned to hers, driving such a potent and powerful kiss upon her that it robbed her of her breath!

"Did you mean what you said, Minnette?" Balian's lips mumbled against hers.

"What?" Minnette gasped in a whisper, overwhelmed with emotion and a palpable craving to remain in his arms.

"When you said you would watch over me every night if you could . . . did you mean it?" he asked, his voice low and filled with desire.

"I . . . I did," Minnette breathed. "Though I know I should not have said it . . . I did mean it, with all my heart."

Balian pressed a long, firm kiss to her neck, just below her left ear.

"Then I must away," he said, releasing her,

"for I'm meant to prove myself a man and not a monster tonight. And you, my butterfly fairy, have given me influence and inspiration, and I now most assuredly know what I must do to save Vavassour from my father's ineptitude as king."

"And what do you mean to do?" Minnette asked, still breathless from Balian's affections—yet at once remembering that he would be made vulnerable once caged before sunset.

Yet Balian only chuckled, calling, "Come, Thor! Ullr, Freyja, Delling, Nótt! We make for Castle Vargar and all that will unfold there at the rise of the full moon!"

Mounting Ewan with skillful ease, Balian smiled, seeming of a sudden rejuvenated and near inspired toward adventure.

"Oh, pretty butterfly queen," he laughed, "you cannot know what passion and actuation you evoke in me." Laughing again, he called, "At the next sun's rise, Bramwell will not be so bold as to attempt to manipulate my father further . . . and all because of you, my pretty fairy! I will wait to see you amidst the gatherers before I have my brother cage me. Thus, I hope you are as prompt as ever I have known you to be!"

Minnette smiled as Balian called, "Wolves! Come at once! Komme paa en gang!" urging Ewan into a gallop across the meadow with five wolves close at his heels.

"And you cannot know what passion and connivance you have evoked in me, my love," Minnette whispered to herself. And of a sudden, any lingering trepidation she owned about putting her life at risk for the sake of Balian's flittered from her mind and heart, as quickly as the soft flittering of butterfly wings.

The Proving Plot

"There are men here I do not recognize," Morgianna whispered to Minnette.

"Yes," Minnette agreed. "It is as Balian feared. Many from Mirermith have come in the hopes of seeing a man turn to a beast."

"Or to assassinate either," Morgianna added.

"And yet the king sits upon his chair confident that caging the Wolf Prince for one night will find Bramwell satisfied," Minnette grumbled.

Everyone who had gathered in Castle Vargar's main bailey wore expressions of excited anticipation. It was pure obvious which persons were of Vavassour and which had traveled from Mirermith—at least to Minnette it was. For all who were of Vavassour frowned with distaste at King Bramwell and his company, casting glances of disapproval at their own King Liam. All in Vavassour knew that the Wolf Prince, Balian, was no werewolf. For one, few in Vavassour believed in such superstitions. For another, it had been proved before—years before—when first Prince Balian had been caged during a full moon.

"I pity him in a manner," Minnette said to her mother.

"Whom do you pity?" Morgianna asked. Yet as

her own gaze followed her daughter's to arrive on King Liam's person, Morgianna exhaled a heavy sigh. "You pity the king . . . for being made to look the fool by King Bramwell."

"Yes," Minnette admitted, "for he believes it will be King Bramwell who will look foolish when Balian does not transform into a werewolf. Yet our people know, even as Balian knew before us, that King Bramwell is only in manipulation of King Liam's pride."

"Indeed," Morgianna agreed.

"Phillip is coming," Arianna said quietly as she strode to greet Minnette and Morgianna. "He has instructed me to tell you to place yourself in front of the gatherers, Minnette. Once he opens the door and Balian steps in, he asks that you make haste to enter after him . . . preferably before Balian has turned to face the crowd."

"Yes, yes . . . of course," Minnette said, nodding. Inhaling a deep breath of anticipation of Balian's being angry with her, she said, "He will be livid . . . enraged with me."

Of course, Minnette had ever known Balian would be angry with her for allowing Phillip to imprison her in the cage with him. Yet she could not stand by and watch him endure such vulnerability. Therefore, she had reconciled herself in knowing that she risked losing Balian's affections—his trust and care—in endeavoring to protect him. Yet the thought of losing him, even for the fact she did not truly own him, began to terrify her in that moment.

"He will be furious. This Phillip knows, Minnette," Arianna said, placing a hand on Minnette's shoulder in comfort. "But his rage will be bent upon Phillip, not you."

Minnette frowned, near bursting into tears. "But I do not wish him to be angry with his brother. Only today he said he might . . ."

Minnette was glad she was able to hold her tongue—that she did not speak of Balian's jesting over revealing his brother's existence once he was freed from the insipid cage. For in truth, as her mind had lingered on the notion Balian had presented, whether in jest or not, when she thought of the exuberance that had overcome him just before he had left her in the meadow, she surmised that perhaps the Wolf Prince truly did mean to make known his brother yet lived to all in attendance. And she wanted nothing to taint the profound revelation. Minnette did not wish for Balian to be angry with Phillip, not ever, and certainly not on this night—not when Phillip was willing to die in defense of Balian.

Closing her eyes a moment, however, Minnette inhaled a deep, calming breath. It was all as it must be; she knew it was. Phillip must risk not only Balian's anger but even his own life if the Wolf Prince were to be kept safe. In like manner, she must also risk her love's anger and her own life as well—and she was ready to do so.

"Are you quite prepared, Minnette?" Arianna asked.

Minnette opened her eyes, offering a nod of confirmation to Arianna and a loving smile to her mother.

"Oh, my sweet girl," Morgianna began, her eyes filling with tears.

"You must stand dispassionate, Mother," Minnette whispered, "for my sake as well as the prince's. All will be well, for Phillip is before us. Yes?"

Morgianna swallowed hard and nodded. "Of course," she muttered. "All will be well. I know it will."

"Good people of Vavassour," King Liam's voice boomed.

Minnette looked to see he had risen from his chair. Dressed in all manner of elegance—his fingers stacked with golden rings, his breast ablaze with the glint of the setting sun on the jewels round his neck—the king smiled.

"As you know, our friend King Bramwell of Mirermith has requested of me that my heir, even Prince Balian Volk of Vavassour, be shown worthy to inherit the throne of our great kingdom," King Liam fair bellowed.

Minnette's eyes fell to Queen Asta standing at his side. There was no smile on the queen's face. In truth, Minnette saw only angst and contempt simmering in her lovely eyes. Queen Asta glanced to her husband the king only once, and that glance was filled with such revulsion that Minnette wondered if all in attendance had taken notice of it.

Yet when the queen looked to Phillip, the Monk of the Menagerie, standing barely discernable in the heavy shadows to one side of the cage that was to imprison the werewolf prince for the length of the full moon night, she nodded, and a slight curve adorned her pretty mouth. Minnette was somewhat soothed in recognizing that the queen—Balian and Phillip's mother—was also soothed. For she knew that Phillip would watch over and protect Balian, just as Minnette would.

Then, of a sudden, Queen Asta looked unswervingly at Minnette, offering a slight smile and nod—as if the queen herself owned an awareness of the design Prince Phillip, Arianna, and Minnette were planning to exact. Uncertain as to whether the queen's gaze was resting on her incidentally or with certain knowledge, Minnette smiled, dropping a slight curtsy as the queen continued to gaze at her. As Queen Asta's smile broadened—as she offered a second, graceful nod to Minnette—Minnette knew with confidence that the queen herself was well aware of the plot to ensure Balian was as protected as he could be during such a state of vulnerability.

"Thus, though all of us of Vavassour have seen it proved before, our Prince Balian has insisted that he be allowed to prove, once again, this time to King Bramwell and the people of Mirermith that he is no such thing as a werewolf," King Liam announced.

It was rare that Minnette's temper flared too quickly or too blistering, but the king's words pure exasperated her and incensed her to near mad anger!

"Coward!" she growled quietly. "He will not admit to his own pride and action even to himself, I am convinced."

"Hush, my precious, lest you be heard and hanged for treason for speaking against the king," Morgianna softly warned.

It was with great difficulty that Minnette calmed her temper. She wished that the sun were not setting so quickly, for in that very instant, she realized how great a comfort her delicate, colorful flutter-by companions ever were to her. She wished that some were near—that even one would alight upon her shoulder to soothe her. But dusk was turning to night, and the flames of the fire pits and torches had frightened them away. And Minnette longed for their calming company.

The gatherers of Vavassour applauded in support of their heroic Wolf Prince. And as their cheering began as well, Prince Balian strode into their midst, his five white wolves encircling the large cage and adding a thoroughly threatening presence to any would-be assassin.

As Balian strode to stand before the crowd of gatherers, his attention rested on Minnette a moment, and he smiled, offering a nod of reassurance to her. The simple gesture served to significantly buoy Minnette's courage, and she smiled at him, dropping a mild curtsy and a nod in return.

Raising one hand in a gesture to the people that they should quiet themselves, Balian's deep voice resonated, "My good people of Vavassour." At once the crowd dropped silent, and Balian continued, "As you have by now come to understand, King Bramwell of Mirermith does not think me of sound mind and body."

A low rumble of aggravation and resentment toward Bramwell rippled through the Vavassourians gathered in the night. Yet Balian again raised one powerful arm in bidding all to be silent and listen.

"He believes, as many in Mirermith do, that by the light of the full moon, I transform into a monster—a werewolf—and in that form I roam the countryside murdering and devouring human flesh. All of my fellow Vavassourians know this to be pure rubbish, malicious gossip spread by ignorance and envy."

King Bramwell fair leapt from his chair to his feet, his face crimson with anger and indignation.

Yet Balian continued still. "However, for the sake of maintaining alliances with King Bramwell and the people of Mirermith, I have committed myself to another exhibition of my humanity here, this night, in this cage . . . with as many looking on through the rising of the full moon as would wish to attend."

Minnette's brows arched in awe as Balian then began to strip himself of his belts, baldric, tunic, and shirt, tossing them to the ground before King Bramwell.

"I go now into the cage," he said, glaring at Bramwell. "Yet do not worry over me, my people, for if there are those in attendance here this night who mean me harm—who will see me caged and captured to vulnerability—I will be well. For I have not only the wolves of Vargar Castle to defend me but also he who will see no man or woman approach the cage. My people, I give you the Monk of the Menagerie, and he will serve as not only my turnkey but also my guardian through the entirety of the night."

Minnette smiled as Prince Phillip, shrouded entirely in black, strode to stand next to Balian. The gatherers were awed to silence, for few had ever glimpsed the monk at such proximity, and the monk was a most intimidating presence.

"It is as you put forth, my king and father," Balian said. "When first it was determined I should be caged, my father insisted that I have an able warden at hand."

"I did indeed insist upon it," King Liam claimed.

"Oh, this was brilliant!" Morgianna whispered to Minnette. "To have involved the king's ego? Balian and Phillip are no fools."

"No, they are not," Minnette quietly agreed. "And even for Prince Phillip's injuries of the mind, they are both most certainly superior in intellect to their father. Balian himself is superior in every regard to any man."

She watched as Balian strode forward to stand directly before King Bramwell. "Therefore," he began, towering over the villain, glaring at him with an expression of mocking determination, "it is for your benefit, my people—as well as for King Bramwell's fulfillment in knowing Vavassour's heir is not only human but also powerful, resilient, wise, and ever the protector of Vavassour and her kingdom—that I now invite you to spend a most tiresome and monotonous night in staring into a cage wherein your prince will sit in boredom for the length of it. Thank you, my good and loyal people. And I bid you good night."

Balian turned, pacing back toward the cage, the ominous Monk of the Menagerie in his wake.

The moment was upon her, and as Phillip opened the door of the large iron cage, Minnette quickly scuttled up behind him.

As Phillip moved aside for only an instant, Minnette stepped into the cage just at Balian's heels.

Phillip then slammed the cage door closed, drawing down the large iron bolt, sending the echo of impenetrability rumbling through the night.

"Pray do not be angry with us, sire," Minnette begged in a whisper, tears of trepidation filling her eyes. She did not want Balian to be disappointed or angry with her—not in the least.

Yet when Balian turned to face her—as a grin of mischief and perception spread across his handsome face—he asked, "Do you think I cannot see what is in your mind? Yours and my brother's, my fairy?"

Minnette frowned with discombobulation. "How could you possibly . . . ?" Minnette breathed with bewilderment.

And even for the fair amount of commotion and raised voices from the crowd outside the cage, Minnette could hear King Liam explaining that he owned such confidence in his heir to the throne that he had granted him a companion during his confinement.

Minnette could also hear Balian explain, "Oh, I was, shall we say, filled with worry when Mother revealed that Phillip and Arianna had convinced you to set your own proposal to rolling forth, placing *you* in this damnable cage with me to discourage would-be assassins. Yet my mother owns a wisdom my father does not, and in the end, she convinced me to comply . . . for she and I crafted a strategy of our own, my sweet."

"And what strategy would that be, sire?" Minnette ventured.

"That strategy, Minnette, will be implemented in due course," Balian assured her. "And I am no sire or your highness to you, remember?"

Exhaling a breath of relief that Balian was not angry with her, Minnette whispered, "Yes, Balian."

Minnette and Balian each turned to face the gatherers then, however, when of a sudden Thor and the other wolves stood growling in defensive postures.

"You would put a maiden in a cage with a monster?" King Bramwell bellowed. "You would sacrifice one of your own subjects to being devoured before a crowd of witnesses?"

Yet King Liam puffed out his chest, near shouting, "My son is no monster, Bramwell! And this night he shall prove that which needs not proving, yet again! And why not suffer the boy to have companionship and conversation with a pretty young woman during his confinement? She is in no danger from my son . . . for he is no werewolf! At sunrise that fact will be proven for good, and you will have no cause to doubt my bloodline!"

"Look there," Balian whispered to Minnette, nodding toward one edge of the crowd. "You see. Lanval has already found a lurker, armed and ready to attack."

Minnette watched as Lanval Mordoc, captain of the king's guard, dressed as a simple villager, indeed placed one strong arm around the neck of a man Minnette did not recognize. In sheer moments, the body of the man in Mordoc's hold grew limp and sagging—unconscious. Two other men dressed as villagers appeared as if from the very air, assisting Mordoc to hold the man upright.

"Too much ale for this one," one of the disguised men said when those in the crowd began to turn and look on with curiosity. "Best get him home and put to bed."

The gatherers were convinced that all was well and returned their attention to the two kings standing breast to breast, looking akin to two proud peacocks at odds.

"Good, Thor. Good. Good wolves," Balian said, reaching out of the cage to pat the top of Thor's head. "The wolves will alert Lanval and his men—Phillip as well—to any that would even think to harm you," Balian explained.

"Harm me?" Minnette asked in a whisper. "Do you never think of yourself, Balian? You are the one in danger here! Not I."

Balian smiled, however, and brushed a strand

of hair from her cheek, saying, "Oh, I am quite selfish, pretty fairy. For if I were not—if I did not want to spend every moment in your nectar-laced company—Mother would never have been able to convince me to allow you in this cage with me."

"Chestnuts? Roasted and delicious chestnuts? There is not price for my chestnuts tonight! As my hail to our Wolf Prince, you may indulge without compensation to me. Chestnuts?"

Minnette looked to see the chestnut peddler pushing a small cart filled with his wares toward the crowd. He was set upon at once.

"Why, that is Jon, the chestnut peddler," she spoke. "Yet why would he offer his wares for no compensation? He will be left destitute!"

Balian smiled with admiration for the remarkable young woman sharing the cage with him. There she stood, imprisoned with a would-be werewolf, and yet her concern for the struggle of the chestnut peddler was foremost in her mind.

"It is I have asked him to bring his wares here this night, for should not the people who attend me be entertained in some regard?" Balian whispered in Minnette's ear. "And do not worry, sweet girl, for earlier in the day, I more than compensated him with gold and silver coin for so generously distributing his goods."

The smile on Minnette's face—the expression

of approval and admiration for him—was worth far, far more than all the wealth in the world to Balian, let alone the small satchel of coins gifted to a deserving chestnut peddler.

"Furthermore," Balian added, "note how distracted the gatherers are. The peddler causes that Lanval and his men might more easily detect those who are in King Bramwell's service."

He watched Minnette return her attention to the crowd just as several men who were not tempted by the lure of complementary foodstuffs moved closer to the cage. At once, Thor growled, setting his stance strong and defensive. Yet Lanval and his men were upon the miscreants at once, besting them with ease and dragging them off into the shadows before any other person noticed.

Minnette smiled at Balian. "My! You are a sly trickster, are you not?"

"Not at all, my fairy," he assured her, however. "Only wary of danger . . . ever wary of it."

Balian winked at her then, and Minnette's heart leapt with the thrill his small gesture sent rippling through her limbs. She realized that she, Phillip, and Arianna had been simpleminded indeed to presume the Wolf Prince would not find his way to knowing of their plan. And it caused her pride in Balian's wit and foresight to swell in her.

And as the sun sent its very last rays of light cascading over the landscape, Balian's wisdom and skill in strategy was further proved. Ever there was something about to entertain and distract the people there. The court jester arrived, performing feats of physical oddities as well as daring. A traveling minstrel was in attendance, singing ballads of King Liam's accomplishments and accompanying himself on his lute. Other peddlers were there, offering their wares with no compensation. And all of it was of Balian's coordination—to both entertain the gatherers and distract King Bramwell and his compatriots, thereby revealing any and all who intended on carrying out Bramwell's malicious stratagems.

In all, Captain Mordoc and his men waylaid twelve of Bramwell's lurking henchmen before the full moon rose to its height directly over the cage wherein Balian and Minnette lingered in conversation. Yet once the moon was full and fully risen, the gatherers began to return their attentions to the cage and its captives.

Minnette looked to see her mother was well, seated with the queen and Arianna near to where King Liam and King Bramwell sat drinking ale and devouring turkey parts as if they were but two ill-mannered fools rather than monarchs of great kingdoms. Morgianna looked to her daughter, and Minnette offered a reassuring smile to her mother. Her mother nodded, and Minnette knew she was somewhat soothed.

Of a sudden, however, someone in the crowd

shouted, "Lo! The full moon is at its peak! Will the Wolf Prince transform?"

Of a sudden, all attention—every set of eyes looking out through the darkness of night and torches—was fixed upon the cage.

"Be wary, Phillip," Balian quietly said to his brother. "Pure a dozen have failed, and time is waning. No doubt a blatant attack is forthcoming."

In the very next moment, as if Balian possessed some manner of divination, two men wielding broadswords burst from the crowd of gatherers and toward the cage.

Minnette gasped and the women of the gathering screamed and shrieked as the two iniquitous miscreants charged Prince Phillip. Yet no one, not even Minnette, expected with what speed, skill, and accuracy the Monk of the Menagerie pulled from his robes two daggers, wielding one in each hand. Before mere moments had passed, it seemed, the monk had not only evaded the assassins' sword strikes but also managed to slit each man's throat ear to ear simultaneously with his daggers.

As both nefarious villains crumpled to the ground in quick-pooling blood at the monk's feet, the Monk of the Menagerie simply slid his still-bloody daggers into sheaths beneath his robe. Folding his arms across his chest, the monk straightened his posture to an intimidating pose.

Every mouth in observance of the attack and its abrupt conclusion stood agape and staring, stupefied, at the Monk of the Menagerie.

"Who are these men who dare to attack my . . . the monk?" King Liam roared. Turning to King Bramwell, he demanded, "Explain yourself, man, before I run you through with my own sword."

But King Bramwell, posed as astonished as every other onlooker present, merely shook his head, feigning confusion and horror. "I have nothing to explain, Liam! I have no knowledge of these men, nor their intent."

"Then who are these men that charge the cage wherein my son is captive?" King Liam shouted.

"I believe another distraction is in order. Do you agree, my fairy?" Balian asked, his blue eyes glinting with the exhilaration that so brightened them when he was about his mischief. "Feign fear, my sweet," he chuckled.

Uncertain as to what Balian's thoughts were, Minnette merely nodded her agreement—though she knew not what she was agreeing to.

She startled then, nearly leapt from her skin, when Balian bent over, shouting—nay, howling—as if he were in great agony.

At once, all attention turned from King Liam and his accusations of Bramwell to the cage.

"The pain! I cannot bear the pain any longer!" Balian shouted. "I must turn! I must! I cannot fight it when the moon is thus full and risen!"

"He is turning!" a man's voice shouted from among the throng of witnesses. "He is beginning to transform to the werewolf!"

Phillip spun on his heels, took hold of two of the cage's iron bars, and growled, "Wh-what are y-y-y-ou about, br-brother? Are y-y-you mad? Bramwell will think he is ppr-proven!"

Balian looked up to Phillip only for a moment, saying, "Prepare yourself, my brother . . . for all we know is about to clatter into chaos." Balian then howled, causing that Thor, Ullr, and the others took to howling with him.

"The werewolf comes!" the anonymous man from the crowd shouted. "Look! Watch! He will turn! And then he will devour the girl! King Liam has sacrificed one of his people to a monster!"

Minnette caught sight of Captain Modoc then. He was midst the throng and pummeling a man with his fists. Instinct whispered to her that the man being bested and silenced by the king's guards owned the malevolent mouth voicing accusations of Balian.

"They are vanquished, sire!" Captain Mordoc called from his place in the crowd.

Instantly, Balian stood erect once more, and the five white wolves of Castle Vargar ceased in howling.

"Take them all and drop them at the feet of their master!" Balian shouted with a voice that no man would ignore.

As Captain Mordoc pushed his way through the crowd, incendiary in hand, the other guards in disguise as simple subjects of Vavassour made their way toward King Liam and King Bramwell's position, as well.

"Phillip . . . raise the bolt," Balian said to his brother.

He turned to face Minnette then and, dropping to one knee before her, said, "Will you be queen of Vavassour one day, my love? Will you accompany me all the days of my life here, and forever, as my bride? I know that there is no desire in you—not one thread of it—to live the life put upon a monarch. Yet I pray that there is enough desire in you toward me to endure such a life . . . if it is to be endured with me. Will you marry me, beautiful butterfly princess? I want you for my wife, Minnette. Please say you will make it so."

Minnette could not breathe! She could not move! For an instant, she thought she might have fallen asleep while keeping Balian company in the cage and was only dreaming he was kneeling before her proposing marriage. Yet as he took her hands in his, placing a firm kiss to the back of each, the warmth—nay, the fire—his touch sent racing through her body assured her she was full wide awake.

When at last she found her breath again, she whispered, "Are you in earnest, Balian?"

"Always with you, my love. Always with you," he said, his voice low and alluring as ever it was when his emotion was deep.

As tears spilled from Minnette's eyes, she nodded, sobbing, "Yes! Yes, of course! You know I want nothing more than that . . . than you for my husband!"

Balian rose, gathering Minnette into his arms and driving such a wanton, sweltering kiss to her mouth that she was again rendered blissfully breathless!

It was the silence that she noted then. As Balian broke the seal of their lips, it was Minnette noted the silence all around them.

Taking her face in his powerful hands, Balian spoke to her, "There is much that must be attended at the moment, my love. But fear not. After this miserable night is finished, I am hopeful that Bramwell will taste his defeat miserably and ride back to Mirermith at sunrise, with his tail between his legs as a beaten dog." He kissed her again and then turned, pushing the door of the cage open.

Through her tears of joy, Minnette could see the gatherers. All were stunned into silence. Not only had they borne witness to the Wolf Prince of Vavassour offering a proposal of marriage to a common village girl, but they likewise watched as Captain Mordoc and his men deposited the twelve bound bodies of King Bramwell's yet-living henchmen, the two dead bodies of the assassins who attacked the monk, and the boisterous incendiary in a pile before King Bramwell and King Liam.

"Good people! Are you astonished?" Balian shouted, stepping out of the cage. "Do you stand in awe that, instead of a werewolf, you now view wicked intent toward our kingdom and our king? Are you inspired that you will soon have a new princess, chosen from among the common people of Vavassour?"

Still the people stood too astonished, too confounded to speak or react.

"Well, this night is one that will be remembered for generations to come!" Balian shouted. "For you have not one prince and his princess that will be wed posthaste but two!"

Minnette smiled, for she knew Balian's intention. And when he reached out, pulling the cowl from his brother's head and revealing to all that Prince Phillip of Vavassour yet lived, her heart swelled with such joy, it forced all the more tears from her eyes.

An audible gasp rose up from the crowd, and Minnette heard the whispers. "It is he! It is truly Phillip!"

"Balian!" King Liam roared.

"Yes, Father?" Balian asked, an air of defiance about him. "Would you tell the people why Phillip has been masquerading as the Monk of the Menagerie for a decade? Or shall I?"

It was pure obvious King Liam was unsettled—nay, appeared near mad with agitation.

"No," King Liam growled. "I will tell the tale at midday on the morrow . . . when both of my sons are wed to the women they have chosen for themselves."

"Your heir means to wed a commoner?" King Bramwell pompously asked.

But it appeared King Liam was not the fool he had been even an hour before. For turning to Bramwell and inhaling a deep breath to ease his temper, King Liam said, "Gather your miscreants and dead assassins, Bramwell. The captain of my guard will see you escorted to our borders."

"You would dare to—" King Bramwell began.

Minnette watched as Balian advanced on Bramwell then.

"You would be wise to leave now, Bramwell," Balian growled, "else the Wolf Prince sees you turned to fodder to feed the beasts in my father's menagerie."

"Liam! Are you going to allow your son to so threaten a king?" Bramwell raged.

"You mean a king who endeavored to have my son and heir murdered in my own kingdom?" King Liam growled.

When King Bramwell did not respond—only stood huffing and puffing with furious indignity—King Liam ordered, "Balian . . . Phillip!

My sons, see to it that King Bramwell and all who have accompanied him here are expelled from our borders."

"At once," Balian said. "Captain Mordoc, gather your men! We have intruders to rid the kingdom of!"

Minnette looked then to her mother—her mother, who stood next to the queen, who stood next to Arianna—all three with countenances of mingled awe and joy.

"My good people," King Liam bellowed then, "I invite you to the north bailey at midday on the morrow to witness the marriages of Prince Balian to his betrothed and Prince Phillip to his betrothed. Then and there will I reveal to you the purpose of Prince Phillip's clandestine existence these ten years past. Now off with you! To bed! For tomorrow we celebrate the marriages of my sons!"

Minnette was awed to silence. In a miniscule measure of time, Balian had revealed the truth of King Bramwell's malicious intent, unmasked his secreted brother, and proposed marriage to her! And she was to wed Balian on the morrow? It was pure inconceivable.

Yet as Balian returned to her—as he took her shoulders between his powerful hands, kissing her full on the mouth before all that stood witness to the spectacle—her heart soared with rapture!

"Please, my love, accompany your mother back

to the cottage and wait for me there," Balian said. "I will see Bramwell delivered to Lanval's men, and then I will come to you." He kissed her again, mumbling, "And soon we will be wed, and I shall carry you to our marriage bed. And oh, you have no notion of how I will love you, my butterfly queen."

The Battle of the Meadow

The people of Vavassour did indeed erupt into cheers and applause. Merriment of every sort surrounded the newly wed Prince Balian and now Princess Minnette, as well as Prince Phillip and now Princess Arianna. A veritable raining of colorful flowers and fern fronds descended over the two regal couples as all those in attendance of the royal wedding tossed offerings of goodwill and best wishes over them.

For Minnette's part, she was so overwhelmed with how swiftly the entire event had evolved and concluded, she felt near dizzy the majority of the measure of time that elapsed between Balian's proposal in the werewolf cage and the friar pronouncing "man and wife" over her and her beloved Wolf Prince. She was married to Balian—truly married to him! Minnette was awed to near stunning with lingering disbelief as Balian and Phillip stood waving to the people of their kingdom and the cheering continued. Still, as she ventured a glance to Arianna, she noted that her newly acquired sister-in-law appeared quite as astounded as Minnette herself felt.

Yet as Arianna looked to Minnette then, it was she smiled, Minnette returning her smile, for each knew she had somehow managed to achieve her greatest dream come true. They had each, only moments before, been given in holy matrimony to the man each loved. And it was a blissful knowledge to own.

Minnette felt tears brimming in her eyes—tears of inexpressible joy. And as Balian again bent, kissing her firm on the mouth there before the king and queen and all of Vavassour, she sighed with resplendent contentment.

"My people!" King Liam called. "Good people of Vavassour!"

Slowly the crowd quieted, anxious to hear King Liam, who, as far as the people of Vavassour knew, had thwarted King Bramwell's attempt to murder the heir to the Vavassourian throne and exiled him from the kingdom's borders in shame.

"This is indeed perhaps the greatest day of my life since I met and married your beautiful Queen Asta—since my sons, Phillip and Balian, were birthed! And as I promised at the full moon's rise last evening, I will explain to you now why it is that your Prince Phillip was hidden these ten years past."

The crowd applauded, and King Liam raised his arms in a gesture they should grow silent once more.

When the crowd had quieted again, King Liam announced, "Pray, gather with us beneath the North Tower balcony so that all may hear my voice as I tell you the tale, so that all may well see our beautiful new princesses and their princes, for I know not all have clear viewing of them now. There is no need for haste. I will wait until all of you have assembled before I begin. And thank you, good people of our great kingdom of Vavassour!"

As the crowd began to thin—as those who had attended the royal wedding of Prince Phillip and Prince Balian began to wander toward the north bailey in order to gather beneath the North Tower, Balian took Minnette's hands in his own, gazing down at her with such passion simmering in his deep blue eyes, it sent gooseflesh rippling over Minnette's limbs.

"You are mine, at last, pretty fairy," Balian said, his voice low and provocative. "I shall never have to leave you in the meadow again." He chuckled, grinning and saying, "I shall never have to sleep in my bed without you again."

"Is this truly happening, my love?" Minnette asked. "I . . . I feel as if I will wake of a sudden, only to find I dreamt it all . . . that I am only dreaming that you . . . that you . . ."

"That I love you beyond anyone or anything in all of earth and heaven?" Balian interrupted. Smiling, he said, "No, my pretty fairy, you are not dreaming. For I do love you . . . love you infinitely more than mere words can express."

"As I wholly as I love you?" Minnette ventured.

"More so," Balian affirmed.

But Minnette shook her head, smiling and saying, "That is not possible, my love. For in measures of time past or forthcoming, no woman has loved a man as full desperately as I love you."

Balian bent, capturing her mouth in a moist, ravenous kiss that weakened Minnette's knees and fair stripped her from any ability to draw breath.

"Then let us away to the North Tower with expedience," he said. "For until my father has told his account of Phillip's need to remain hidden—whether he tells the truth or weaves some sort of fib that will, no doubt, become legend—it is I know I cannot have you for myself until it is done. Thus, make haste, my love . . . to the North Tower with me."

"Yes, let us hasten what must be done, for I am aching to be in your arms, Wolf Prince of Vavassour . . . my lover," Minnette whispered.

Balian smiled, brushing a strand of hair from her face as he gazed at her. "Your mother has accompanied mine, and Phillip is in escort of Arianna. Thus, let us walk together, you and I—our first amble as husband and wife, hmm?"

Minnette nodded, and Balian took her hand. And as they started for the North Tower, Balian called over his shoulder, "Come, my friends. Kommer, mine venner." The five white wolves—

companions to the Wolf Prince and his Butterfly Princess—fell into step behind their masters.

It was not long before the Volk royal family stood on the balcony of the North Tower solar, watching as the people of Vavassour gathered in the bailey below.

Minnette reached out, taking her mother's hand and squeezing it with affectionate reassurance. Morgianna brushed fresh tears of mingled joy in her daughter's happiness and heartache at her own loss.

She would live alone in the cottage without Minnette now. Oh, it was true Balian, as well as King Liam and Queen Asta, begged Morgianna that she should dwell in chambers in Castle Vargar henceforth. After all, she was the mother of the Princess Minnette and as such was welcome, and even in a small measure expected, to reside with the monarchy. Yet Morgianna was determined she would be much happier continuing in the cottage in the village—the home built by her late husband—the home in which she and Stuart D'Angelville had conceived, birthed, and nurtured their beloved daughter. It was her home. It was where her heart and soul desired to reside. Therefore, graciously thanking the king and queen for their kindnesses, Morgianna would not dwell at Castle Vargar—and Minnette was happy for it. For she knew the wonder and comfort of the cottage and would not wish her mother to reside anywhere else.

Thus, there they stood—King Liam with Queen Asta at his right, Phillip and Arianna at his left. Balian and Minnette had chosen to stand near the queen, at her right hand, Morgianna to the right of them. And so, with the royal family gathered on the solar balcony of the North Tower, King Liam raised his arms to collect the attention of all who had gathered below them in the bailey.

"My good and worthy people," the king loudly began. "It is true that your first prince, Phillip, has been alive these past ten years. It is true that he is strong and able. Yet it is also true that your king has been a proud and selfish man. And though that is behind me now"—the king glanced to Balian, nodded, and continued—"I see the sinful error of my ways, ways that near saw our kingdom in ruin, had it not been for the foresight, courage, and action of my son Balian . . . your Wolf Prince of Vavassour."

A sudden commotion at the far end of the bailey distracted the king's attention for a moment.

"It is Lanval," Balian noted as he saw his friend, armor and horse bloodied from battle, ride into the bailey.

"Captain Mordoc!" King Liam shouted. "What has happened?"

The moments following the king's calling to the captain of the guard flew by so quickly, Minnette had not one instant to react on her own.

"Archer!" she heard Balian shout.

She then felt her husband push her and her mother back with such brutal force it sent them both tumbling to the floor of the solar behind them. It was then that the king fell—King Liam fell—an arrow having plunged deep into his broad chest near his right shoulder.

Minnette stared at the king a moment, horrified at the sight of the arrow's shaft protruding from his body.

Arianna lay on the floor on the other side of the king, having no doubt been pushed by Phillip as Minnette and her mother had been pushed by Balian.

The queen was on her knees beside the king near instantaneously. "Liam!" the queen cried.

"Bind him! Bind him at once!" Minnette heard Balian shout to the people below on the bailey. "Lanval! What has happened?"

"We were attacked, your highness!" she heard Captain Mordoc's voice call to Balian. "As we were escorting Bramwell from the kingdom, his soldiers lay in wait, and we were attacked! They will be upon us at any moment, sire—Bramwell and his men! And I have lost twenty of my men at least in the battle to stay them. They are just beyond the meadow forest now."

Minnette, tears streaming over her cheeks, fear gripping her heart, watched in terror as Balian called, "Thor! Come at once! Komme paa en gang! Komme paa en gang!"

Ever near his master, Thor hurried from his place near the hearth with the other wolves to Balian. "Thor, indkalde dem alle! Summon them all! Inkalde dem alle! To battle! Til camp, Thor! Til camp!"

Instantly, Thor raised his head and howled a great, long, and powerful howl. Over and over he howled, and soon the other four wolves joined him.

Balian looked over the edge of the balcony once more. Then turning to Phillip, he said, "They have the archer bound, Phillip! Loose your lions, brother, and ride with me and all the wolves loyal to me into battle. Ride with me in defense of our kingdom and those we cherish with all our hearts . . . and those we cannot live without!"

"I will ride with you, brother!" Phillip said, placing a strong hand on Balian's shoulder. "I will ride, and I will battle!"

"Phillip!" Arianna cried. "You have not been to battle in a decade!"

Phillip dropped to one knee before his bride. "I am strong, Arianna. And I am a prince of Vavassour. The kingdom and all who dwell here are in danger, and when I shed that black robe and hood of shame last night near the werewolf cage, I swore I would never hide again—not from any man and certainly not from evil. I will triumph,

Arianna, my love. Know that I will return to you as soon as our people are safe."

Minnette wept for Arianna. Yes, she wept for all that was transpiring—for the king, the soldiers that had been killed, and most of all knowing Balian would soon be in battle. Yet Minnette's heart wept sore for Arianna, for she understood that Arianna had spent ten years in serving Phillip—in assuring he was never found out and never in danger. And now she must send him to battle on the very day they were wed. Thus, Minnette's heart was so crushed with pain, she thought she might not draw a full breath again.

"Liam?" the queen cried. "Liam?"

"I am here, Asta," King Liam moaned.

"Oh, Liam!" Queen Asta wept as she dabbed at the moisture on her husband's forehead with her kerchief.

"Balian . . . Phillip," the king groaned. "Bramwell means to—"

"We will fight him, Father," Balian growled. "He will not reach the walls of the castle! He will be vanquished, Father, for we have good men prepared for battle . . . and an hundred wolves to fight with them."

"I will attend you, sire," Morgianna said, making her way to the king.

Balian turned to Minnette then, took her chin in one powerful hand, and said, "I will return,

Minnette. I will! And when I do, nothing will part us again! You know this, do you not?"

"I-I do," Minnette stammered, tears of fearful trepidation rolling over her cheeks.

"I love you, my fairy," Balian said. He kissed her then—long, deep, and driven.

And once he had released her, he shouted, "Thor! You, wolves! Til camp! Til camp!"

Balian whistled, and Thor, Ullr, Delling, Freyja, and Nótt turned, racing from the solar and down the tower stairs.

Balian for his part, however, returned to the balcony. "Lanval! You are wounded! Pray stay and guard my bride and family."

"But, sire, I can yet battle!" Lanval shouted.

"Yes, but I need *you* here to protect the king and queen, the royal family of our kingdom," Balian shouted.

"Yes, sire. I will protect them," Lanval called at last.

"Then pray come at once!" Balian ordered.

Balian turned, gazing longingly at Minnette for a moment. His beautiful blue eyes were bright with determination and power.

Minnette gasped when, instead of following his wolves down the tower stairs, Balian reached out and with both strong hands took hold of the thick cording of one of the great royal banners that had been unfurled from the balcony in honor of the wedding. Without pause, the

Wolf Prince leapt over the side of the balcony.

"Balian!" Minnette shrieked, leaping to her feet, as did Arianna when Phillip followed suit of his brother. Both princesses of Vavassour dashed to the balcony in fear for the well-being of their lovers.

Minnette exhaled a sigh of respite when she saw Balian was there, safe on the ground, racing toward the stable where Minnette knew Ewan awaited. Phillip found his feet with ease a mere moment later and was also running across the bailey toward the West Tower. And in the next instant, Thor and his offspring were at the heels of their master and his brother.

Of a sudden, a great howling began, and Minnette looked to the meadow. Pure an army of white wolves was pouring into the meadow from all sides of the forest. Once gathered in the center of the meadow, the wolves stood howling—calling for their master.

"Minnette," Morgianna said, drawing Minnette's attention to the circumstance in the solar.

Turning, Minnette's thoughts turned to the task at hand, tending to the wounded King Liam—though every part of her being feared for her husband's safety.

"Yes, Mother," Minnette said, brushing the tears from her cheeks.

"We must remove the arrow, stop the blood

from escaping further, and tend to the wound," Morgianna's calm voice instructed.

"Of course," Minnette agreed, nodding.

It was Captain Mordoc had made his way to the solar. Standing in the threshold, he spoke, "No enemy shall pass, my queen."

"Thank you, Lanval," Queen Asta said—ever polished, even for her tears.

"Pray, keep him safe, God in heaven," Minnette whispered as she knelt beside the king. Several large butterflies of brilliant and varying colors flittered in through the balcony breach then, alighting soft upon Minnette's shoulder and arm—and she smiled. For therein was her assurance, therein were her comforters sent from heaven, and she knew her lover Balian would be safe and preserved—that Balian would return to her from battle well and whole.

Balian turned, a triumphant smile curving his mouth as he saw Phillip approach. His brother was garbed in his own battle armor, mounted upon his charger, twelve great lions subsequent in his way.

"Let us beat this Bramwell to a bloodied bone, brother," Balian said as Phillip reined in before him.

Thor, Delling, Ullr, Nótt, and Freyja sniffed the air, at once recognizing their old friend, Apedemak. Though the wolves stood off from the lions, Balian was pleased to see neither species in fear of or agitated by one another. There seemed an understanding between them—an understanding that their friends and masters, the two great princes of Vavassour, were in need of their assistance. Thus, wolves and lions stood allies.

"Indeed, brother Balian, we will!" Phillip growled.

As Balian placed his own helmet on his head, Phillip asked, "Are you pleased, brother?"

Humbled at Phillip's thoughtful insight, effort, and skill, Balian nodded with affirmation of his gratitude and admiration in his brother's gift to him. The wolf pelt Phillip had tanned, cared for, and affixed to Balian's helmet armor would indeed appear fierce, wild, and intimidating to any foe.

"I am, my brother," Balian said, thick emotion rising in his throat. "The first casualty of this battle brought to our threshold by Bramwell and his malice . . . it is appropriate that she accompany us . . . that she join her brother and sister wolves in fighting in defense of our beloved kingdom."

The wolf who had been found murdered in the forest by the Vavassourian huntsman mere weeks before now crowned Balian's helmet—its head, ears, eyes, snout, and fanged upper jaw affixed to the top of the helmet to face forward as did Balian. The fur front legs and paws lay across Balian's broad shoulders, bound together at his chest with a leather strap. The back of the wolf's pelt, hind legs, and tail swathed Balian's armor at his back, spreading out over much of Ewan's hindquarters. Though some may think it a gruesome tribute, a tribute it was, and Balian was pleased to have the lost sister wolf ride into battle with him.

"The men are assembled just beyond the moat, your highness," a guardsman said as he rode to meet the princes.

"Good. I will address them briefly, and then . . . then we ride to the meadow to meet Bramwell—nay, to obliterate Bramwell and his malice toward my father and greed for Vavassour's throne in finality."

"Yes, sire," the guard said, turning his mount and riding toward the meadow.

"Well, my brother," Balian began, striking hands with Phillip, "it is not only your freedom we fight for today but for the preserved freedom of all who dwell in Vavassour!"

"Let us ride, then, brother . . . Wolf Prince of Vavassour!" Phillip hailed.

Turning their mounts toward the main bridge of Castle Vargar, Balian shouted, "Wolves! Komme paa en gang!"

Then urging Ewan into an immediate gallop, he heard Phillip shout, "Lions attend me!"

Balian heard Apedemak's powerful roar—heard

the shouts and calls of his men as he and Phillip crossed the drawbridge to enter the meadow.

Indeed, Vavassour's soldiers were an intimidating sight! Balian felt pride swell in his bosom as he saw the glint on their polished armor—watched their mounts tramp at the meadow grass, rearing and stomping with impatience.

Raising his hand to indicate the men should settle themselves and prepare for instruction, Balian determined to ensure King Bramwell never again dared to threaten the king of Vavassour, nor any other king. Balian gritted his teeth, dauntless.

The men quieted, and Balian began, "Men of Vavassour, warriors, keepers of the kingdom! Our sheep are threatened by the wolves of Mirermith and their monster steward, King Bramwell!"

The Vavassourian soldiers shouted with anger! And when they had quieted once more, Balian continued, "Yet we are the dogs of Vavassour . . . the protectors! We are they who run toward malice, menace, and mortal danger! We are the dogs of Vavassour—the paramount, the impenetrable, the conquerors of evil—and we will triumph over the evil that is Bramwell! We fight as men, as wolves, as lions, and we will see Bramwell run, else reduce him to naught but a hoard of bloody bone!"

The men roared with affirmation they would

battle to the death to see Bramwell bested and gone.

Urging Ewan to rearing, Balian drew his sword, wielding it high above his head and shouting, "Territi sunt oves, et proximus sunt lupi rapaces. Ego sum canis-intrepidus maneo!"

Then every man gathered to battle wielded his own weapon, shouting, "The sheep are frightened, and the wolves are close. I am the dog-intrepid!"

"Ride, men of Vavassour!" Balian shouted. "Ride to battle! Ride for Vavassour!"

"Hail the Wolf Prince! Hail Balian of Vavassour!" the men shouted unison.

Then, with the thunder of a thousand charging hooves, with the howl of a hundred great white wolves, and with the roar of the great lions of Prince Phillip, the army of Vavassour rode into battle.

As Queen Asta and her mother tended to the king—the arrow having been broken and then hammered through his chest, Lanval Mordoc having pulled the shaft through his body from his back—Minnette stood on the North Tower balcony, clutching Arianna's hand.

"Bramwell's men have made the forest!" Arianna cried.

Minnette watched as King Bramwell, leading the Mirermithian army, indeed breached the trees of the forest on the far side of the meadow.

And though her heart was hammering with terror—fear for the safety of every man of Vavassour riding toward battle, her soul begging God to protect her love, Balian—Minnette spoke. "But look, Arianna. It is the white wolves of the Wolf Prince and our soldiers advance as a wave of havoc and destruction. I know naught of battle, but even my eyes can discern Bramwell is already defeated."

The great clash of sword and shield echoed over the meadow to the North Tower. Men plighted in combat, wolves snarling, lions roaring—all of these sounds mingled into one great and abhorrent noise! The cries of men in pain, bloodied, maimed—men howling with lament as if the Reaper himself were upon them—sent Minnette's blood running cold with grief.

"Look! It is King Bramwell! See his charger?" Arianna exclaimed. "Just there, in the midst of the fighting! It is Balian battles with him!"

"Then Bramwell is dead already," Minnette whispered. She held her breath—strained her vision—watched as the Wolf Prince skillfully wielded his sword, striking King Bramwell's throat, near severing his head.

Exhaling as the dying king plunged from his horse to lie in the once fresh and fragrant meadow grasses—meadow grass now stained with mud and blood of brutality—Minnette whispered, "It is ended. King Bramwell is vanquished—and his vile, malicious intent toward my love exists no more."

Burying her face in her hands, Arianna began to sob. Looking up then, she smiled through her tears, "And Phillip is unharmed! See him? There, with his lions now surrounding him!"

Minnette looked from Balian only long enough to see Phillip astride his charger, Apedemak and the other lions of the Castle Vargar menagerie encircling him—roaring with triumph.

"Prince Balian will claim Mirermith for his father," Captain Mordoc said, stepping up to stand behind Minnette and Arianna. "In his lust and greed for power and land, King Bramwell sacrificed his own people in the end."

"But the conquering of King Bramwell by the princes of Vavassour will prove a blessing to his people, there is no doubt," Minnette noted.

"No doubt whatsoever, your highness," Mordoc agreed.

It was then that Minnette and the others heard the voice of the Wolf Prince rise over the meadow. Though she could not discern his words, she understood their meaning. For as the remaining soldiers of Mirermith surrendered to those of Vavassour, the hundred white wolves of Prince Balian perked their ears to his voice. And once he had spoken, the hundred white wolves began to disperse into every venue of departure through the forest that there was. In mere moments, only five wolves remained, larger than the rest and standing in watch of their master, the Wolf Prince.

"He has freed them," Minnette said, speaking her thoughts aloud. "He has freed the hundred for serving to save Vavassour." Then as she continued to watch Balian shout out orders to his men, Minnette of Vavassour smiled when the Wolf Prince paused and turned his mount toward the north, wielding his sword high with one hand, placing his other hand over his heart, and bowing his head.

Tears spilled from Minnette's eyes as she stretched her arm high, waving to her love in return. And as butterflies began to alight not just on Minnette of Vavassour's person but upon Arianna's as well, the small crowd that had lingered in the bailey during the battle began to cheer as Queen Asta appeared on the balcony.

"King Liam lives! And our kingdom is preserved!" the queen called to her people.

Such an uproar of joy and relief, of pride, wafted into the air that Minnette was certain heaven itself had heard it, and she thanked God for his divine intervention—for the life of her love, the Wolf Prince, Balian of Vavassour.

Would he come to her that night? Minnette wondered as she lingered on the balcony of Balian's bedchamber.

It had been hours and hours since the battle with King Bramwell had ended with Bramwell's beheading at the hand of the Wolf Prince. Hours during which the physician had attended to the wounded king, Queen Asta ever at her husband's side. Hours since Captain Lanval Mordoc's injuries had been full ascertained and dressed, even hours since Prince Phillip had returned and narrated details of the battle won to his father the king. Even hours since Phillip had retired to his chambers with his new bride, the Princess Arianna.

Yet Minnette was still in wait of her husband's return. Of certain there were particulars to be addressed, messengers to be sent to Mirermith, all manner of grandeurs and minutiae to be recorded. Still, Minnette thought positive Balian would have come to her by now.

Morgianna D'Angelville had been safe escorted to her beloved cottage in the village by none other than Captain Mordoc and the great white wolf Thor himself. Thus, all was as it should be in Minnette's mind; all was ripe for Balian's return from the duties and obligations of a prince who had just bested an enemy. Thus, she again wondered what kept her lover from her.

A warm fire burned in the hearth of the Wolf Prince's bedchamber, and Minnette had bathed in lavender-fragranced waters, combed her hair, and dressed in a beautiful nightgown of pink silk—a gift from her mother-in-law, the queen. More and more butterflies flittered in through the open balcony, and Minnette wondered if they had been bewildered at arriving at the cottage bedroom in the village to find her missing. Yet as she watched several of them alight upon the bed canopy, felt two or three alight on her shoulder, Minnette smiled, silently prayerful that beautiful flutter-bys would always seek her out—find her worthy of their company.

Minnette gasped then—startled when the enormous oak door of the bedchamber swung open of a sudden.

"Balian!" she cried, tears filling her eyes as her lover closed the door behind him, drawing the bolt. "I was growing anxious for your return. I feared—"

The Butterfly Princess was struck silent, however, when her husband began to stride toward her. It was plain he had recently bathed, for the fact that his hair was yet wet and tousled—for the fact he wore naught but a pair of trousers.

"Battle is a brutal, taxing thing, my pretty fairy," he said.

Minnette bit her lip, pure delighted by the low, alluring intonation of his voice.

"Bramwell did not know what he had done whence he interrupted my wedding day, now did he, my lovely?" Balian said, gathering Minnette into his arms immediate and crushing his mouth to hers in a fiery, wanton kiss!

Instantly Minnette was swept up into the powerful cradle of Balian's arms. Continuing to rain impassioned, consuming kisses over her mouth, her cheeks, her throat, her shoulders—revealed when the silk dress slipped from them upon his advance—the Wolf Prince laid his bride upon their bed.

"Forgive me in being so belated in coming to you, pretty fairy," Balian mumbled against her mouth.

Caressing the breadth of his shoulders—reveling in the smooth warmth of his skin—Minnette smiled beneath his kiss, beneath his body as he stretched out the length of her, placing lingering kisses to her shoulders once more.

"I knew you would come to me when you could, my love," Minnette breathed, conquered by love and desire.

"With all that has transpired these past hours since the moon rose previous, I have thought of nothing save having you, Minnette. Even in battle, my ambition was to vanquish Bramwell and his threat with the utmost precipitance so that I could be here, where I am at this moment—consuming you with the love and passion that is in me for only you, Minnette . . . the Butterfly Princess of Vavassour."

Minnette smiled, sighed with elation as she

buried her hands in her husband's hair at the back of his head. "The Wolf Prince and the Butterfly Princess, is it?" she softly laughed. "It is sure the birth of legend, is it not?"

Balian paused, gazing down at her with naught but fathomless love mirrored in his deep blue eyes.

"Their love will be the birth of legend, yes," he said, his manner exuding powerful passion. "And our loving the inspiration of it."

And then, there in the North Tower of Castle Vargar—in a warm, fire-lit room of comfort and tranquility, as abundances of butterflies found their rest upon the canopy of the marriage bed of the Wolf Prince and the Butterfly Princess—a legend was indeed stirred, inspired, consummated into eternal everlastingness.

Epilogue

"Your grandfather King Liam passed into the next world only ten days after the Battle of the Meadow," the dowager queen, Asta, said. Tears filled her eyes as she gazed upon the enormous painting of her love, Liam. "See how handsome and strong he is there, Freyja, my sweet? It is ever how I remember him—this way, the way he was when your father and King Phillip were only boys and we, all of us, were happy and free of care and worry."

"Grandfather was handsome indeed, Grandmother," the young princess, Freyja of Vavassour, noted. "And I know how you miss him."

Freyja took several steps to the right of her grandfather's painting. Standing before the next painting in the hall of kings, she smiled.

"Yet this one . . . it is one that I favor near most above all others," Freyja sighed.

"Ahh yes!" Queen Asta agreed, gazing at the painting. "It was commissioned just after Thor was found, having died in his sleep and at a grand old age indeed."

"That is Thor, there," Freyja said, indicating the image of her father—the head of a large white wolf crowning the helmet of the Wolf

King, Balian of Vavassour. The massive pelt of the great white wolf, forelegs drawn together at the king's breastplate, hung far down the king's back—testament to the magnificent size of Thor, the white wolf of Castle Vargar.

"Yes," Queen Asta affirmed as emotion rose to her throat. "And that is Apedemak," she added, motioning toward great lion head and pelt that adorned Phillip's helmet and armor. "Apedemak was wounded in the Battle of the Meadow. He died the very hour that the king did."

"The Wolf Prince and his brother, the Lion Prince," Frejya breathed. "How handsome my father is, Grandmother. And King Phillip." Turning to face her grandmother, Freyja inquired, "Is it true that the people of Mirermith cheered when my uncle took Bramwell's throne?"

"Yes, it is, my love," Asta answered. "The people of Mirermith had been ill-treated to a great degree by the covetous Bramwell. So it was when your father was crowned king after your grandfather's death that he named Phillip to be king of Mirermith . . . for he knew that Phillip would rule kindly and well. And he has." Asta's smile broadened as she next spoke. "His people have loved him with all their hearts, hailed and esteemed him always . . . no matter his benign imperfections."

Freyja smiled, slowly moving to stand before the next painting in the hall.

"And this painting . . . I love it most of all," she said.

"I would think you should, love," the queen said, smiling and stroking her granddaughter's long dark hair.

"The Wolf King and his Butterfly Queen," Freyja sighed. "Oh, how I love the story of Father and Mother's first meeting . . . the courtship. It fair causes gooseflesh to prickle my arms at times."

Asta laughed softly. "Yes, it is quite a story, is it not?" She looked to her beautiful granddaughter Freyja a moment—studied her kind and loving countenance. Her smile broadened at the three butterflies lingering upon her arm.

"Even now they are in the meadow," Freyja said, "beneath the large maple near the path to Grandmother Morgianna's cottage."

"What?" the queen asked. "And how can you be so certain that is where they are, love?"

Freyja smiled, reached up, and patted young Forseti on his white furry head. Forseti at once dropped to the floor, rolling onto his back and panting in wait of a scratching of his belly.

As Freyja giggled and knelt to comply with Forseti's demands, she said, "It is where they ever are when they are not to be found, Grandmother."

"Ahh yes," Asta said. Then singing as the traveling minstrels did, she began, "Beneath the maple in the meadow . . . round aboutet by gossamer wings . . ."

Smiling up at her then, Freyja joined, "Lingers she, the butterflies' mistress . . . in the arms of the brave wolfen king."

The laughter of the dowager queen, Asta, and her granddaughter, the princess Frejya, echoed throughout the hall of the kings, wafting through windows and out into the air of the bailey.

After long moments their merriment subsided, in sound, at least, and Queen Asta said, "Let us away now and find your brothers. For I have no doubt they are knee-deep in mischief, my love!"

Freyja nodded, stood, and took her grandmother's hand. And together they walked along the remaining portraits hung on the west wall of the hall of kings.

Whilst over in the meadow, beneath an ancient maple, the Wolf King, Balian, and his love, the Butterfly Queen, Minnette, lay together on a bed of fragrant green grass, lost in the sharing of affection—as four white wolf pups romped and wrestled beside them.

Author's Note

I wrote *The Wolf King* while under, as the saying goes, extreme duress. And although I hoped said duress wouldn't come through in the book, I realize now that it did—most likely through Balian. Balian's anger and frustration is a reflection, I believe, of my own.

Now, were I to list the reasons for the pressure, stress, and, again, extreme duress I was under while writing this book—well, that would be a book in itself. However, there are a couple of contributing factors that I think were perhaps the heaviest—the most distracting.

The first of those is the situation with my mother. As you most likely already know, my mom began showing signs of dementia and Alzheimer's as long as thirteen years ago. However, the past two years have marked her far more rapid descent into the cruel abyss of those diseases. For those of you who have lost a loved one (especially a parent or spouse) to these horrid conditions, I know you already understand the agony, the frustration, the constant mourning, and the anticipation of further loss as well as final loss that accompany it.

For those of you who have not personally

endured it, I won't dwell on negative or sad things too long, but I will tell you that it is like unto losing one of the people you love most in the world daily. To me, it's as if my mom has died somehow, yet the mourning never ends. There's no peace in me because I know there's no peace in her. I see the fear in her eyes when—and this is a visible thing—everything is suddenly gone. Her brown eyes suddenly look black and empty, and I know she's frightened, scared to death.

It's not the fact that she doesn't know me that upsets me most; I understand that. What upsets me is when she realizes she should know me—that I'm her daughter—and she has forgotten. It literally wounds me to see her slip further and further away, become more and more frightened, not recognize my dad. (Though it was sort of funny when she told my dad one night as he joined her in their bed that she couldn't sleep with him because she was a married woman and shouldn't be sleeping with strange men. Funny and then so sad I cried . . . then funny and my sister and I laughed . . . then cried . . . then laughed . . . then sobbed.)

I'm not going to dwell on my mom too long. I don't want to ruin your "happily every after mood" completely. What a meanie I would be for that, right? But I did want to reveal to you that I think Balian's frustration and anger—his protective nature where his brother is concerned and his fury at what he sees as injustice to Phillip—all stems from my constant mourning, anger, and sadness over my mom. Most every night I weep for her as I try to get to sleep. If someone asks me about her, it takes every ounce of strength I can muster not to burst into tears, if I manage to avoid it at all. That kind of duress, my dear, is the definition of extreme, right?

Now, moving on, because I'm sobbing and need to regain some sort of composure. (Hold on, I'm changing my playlist. *A Charlie Brown Christmas* oughta do it! It's one of my soothers, you know.) Another additive to my extreme duress status during this book is the fact that *both* of my sons are now law enforcement officers—not just the oldest but the youngest, as well.

I am so proud of my boys—so proud I'm near to bursting! I've heard it said that being a cop is one of the very hardest jobs to obtain and yet one of the easiest to lose, and those of you who have law enforcement ties know how exact that statement is. And as proud as I am of my boys—as much as I brag on what exceptional officers they are—it's *terrifying,* especially in the day and age we live now! When my oldest son is arresting people with $250,000 worth of weed on them, arresting drug cartel guys and people with meth shards the size of bananas—let's just say I pray a lot! When my youngest son is dragging (as kindly as possible) naked crazy guys out of the shower and trying to calm them down, driving out to the middle of nowhere with no backup to check on a car someone had thrown Molotov cocktails into, responding to "shots fired" and driving out onto the mesa at one a.m. to find grown men playing Pokémon Go, or transporting eleven prisoners by himself—well, let's just say, I really do pray a lot!

However, this particular "mother of two cops" piece of my duress is a lot more obvious in *The Wolf King*. In fact, it was intentional and a *huge* part of my inspiration for the story in the first place. Some of you may already recognize why.

I'll start by quoting the Volk family motto: *Territi sunt oves, et proximus sunt lupi rapaces. Ego sum canis-intrepidus maneo.* "The sheep are frightened, and the wolves are close. I am the dog-intrepid." You may find the motto sounds a bit familiar, at least to some degree. If you do, then I'm about ninety-nine percent sure you have a family member who serves or has served in law enforcement or the military.

For my part of it, though I do have many family members and friends who have served in our military, it's obviously my two heroic sons who directly inspired me to build a heavy thread of the analogy of the sheep, the wolves, and the sheepdog (i.e., the dog) in *The Wolf King*.

On Combat: The Psychology and Physiology of Deadly Conflict in War and in Peace by

Lt. Col. Dave Grossman, U.S. Army, was released in 2008. Since its release, this book has proven an invaluable tool to those men and women who are "the sheepdogs" in our society. Easily the most quoted portion of this book is Grossman's passage on the analogy of the sheep, the wolves, and the sheepdog. Grossman explains that a retired Vietnam veteran shared with him the analogy, and therefore, I don't know who the actual original author of the idea was. But I can tell you that it is spot on! You've read my own simple version of the analogy here in *The Wolf King*. Still, I would ask you to read the passage in its entirety, for it is extremely insightful, is fully true, and explains a lot of what is wrong with society today. Here is one web address where you can find the Grossman passage: https://www.policeone.com/police-heroes/articles/1709289-Book-Excerpt-On-Sheep-Wolves-and-Sheepdogs/

Now, with everything that is going on right now—with so much anti-cop stuff out there, so much violence and hatred directed toward the men and women that serve and protect us—being a cop mom is probably more stressful than it ever has been before! My two sons put their lives on the line for people every day, and as I said, there's a lot of prayer for their sake in my life, as there is for any of those who are protectors of the law, our lives, and truth and justice—prayers for the sheepdogs.

One thing that helps me cope a bit is that I've known in my heart and soul for nearly their entire lives that each of them was a sheepdog of some sort. Ever the protector of the picked-on and bullied, the unnoticed, the unaccepted, the handicapped, both of my boys began as sheepdog puppies. You have never met more patient, truly caring boys—even if they did struggle with frustration, anger, and intolerance toward those that caused others to be unhappy. There were so many incidents throughout their lives that were clues to me—hints, revelations, epiphanies, or whatever you choose to call them—that forewarned me they would both be sheepdogs as adult men.

Such as, you may ask? Well, both of my sons instinctively run toward danger in defense of others and always have. I'll share one example that was an affirmation to me of what I'd always sort of felt and, as a mom, dreaded.

One lovely autumnal November afternoon in 2011, I had managed to corral my family into taking a family photo. Our oldest son had been married six months before, and we had a little grandson who was heading toward two. So we all gathered down on the banks of the Rio Grande River, under the ancient cottonwood trees gloriously bedecked in their autumn-gold leaves, and managed to get a fun family photograph together. (It was quite a feat, considering we had to wrangle a two-year-old boy who was enjoying his first time down on the banks of the river!) We all drove back to the apartment complex where my oldest son and his wife, as well as my daughter, her husband, and their little cutie, were living at the time. (Not all in the same apartment, of course.) We had all parked our various cars at the complex and then carpooled to the river, so we carpooled back to the apartment complex. My son-in-law was driving and pulled over to one side of the parking lot to allow the rest of us to get out and go to our various cars. He looked in his rearview mirror and saw a Jeep pull up behind him. But it stopped and seemed to be waiting for everyone to exit the vehicle. However, when I opened the backseat door behind the driver to get out, the Jeep pulled around us, flooring his gas pedal and nearly ripping the car door, not to mention my left arm, clean off. Did the guy in the Jeep stop to make sure we were okay? No!

But as my son-in-law was helping me out of the car and checking to make sure we were all okay, I looked up to see my own two sons running "hell-bent for the horizon" after the fleeing Jeep. Both my sons were wearing jeans, Converse high-top tennis shoes, and red T-shirts that day, looking like six-foot burley buff twins. As I watched them "hauling it" around the corner in pursuit of the Jeep and its driver, I was overwhelmed with a sensation and a profound voice in my mind telling me, *They didn't pause. They're running toward danger in protection of us all and justice. And this is what they will always do.*

I know that that moment was one of many little hints I had been given along the way to help prepare me for the careers my boys chose to pursue. There's more, of course—the fact that they both act and react with remarkable physical reflex, quick thinking, and incredible skill with firearms (they're both "top shots"); the fact that both of them seem to be the person all others are drawn to, confide in, calm down for, respect, adore, and trust.

These things and many more speak to me of there being more to my boys' choosing to be sheepdogs. They were born with a desire to protect, no matter what. Now, that is not to say that they will always remain in law enforcement. The sickening ingratitude, disrespect, and unwarranted violence toward law enforcement these days may indeed find them too discouraged in people to be able to continue doing what they love. But even then, they will be sheepdogs—and I'm proud of that! Scared to death for their safety, yes—but very, very proud!

Balian is a sheepdog. I worried at first that readers might not think him tough enough in the beginning of the story. I mean, the Crimson Knight comes out of the chute knocking people's teeth out of their heads, you know? Yet as you read further, were privy to Balian's thoughts, saw the things that were plain to him, that his father (a big old idiot of a sheep) couldn't see at all, I'm sure you began to see how strong he really is—that he is indeed the sheepdog. Bramwell is a wolf and King Liam a sheep, who only in the end, when it's far too late, recognizes that wolves do exist—learns that Prince Balian, the Wolf Prince, the Wolf King of Vavassour, is truly a sheepdog in royal clothing.

I hope you enjoyed *The Wolf King*, more than I enjoyed the things life was pitching at me while I was writing it! I hope that if you reread it, you'll envision little girls delighted and mesmerized by the enchantment of a frozen meadow—that whenever you see a police officer, you'll think of my two handsome boys, knowing that they (and others like them) are often the only ones who will run toward danger, risk their own lives, to protect you and yours.

I hope you don't mind that I revealed so much personal stuff in this Author's Note. But I do believe it's important that we ever and always consider that most people are dealing with very heavy emotional and physical burdens that we have no idea even exist for them. I hope it gives you some insight into my writing process, my characters, and my life.

One of my friends wrote to me after reading over an editor's copy of *The Wolf King* saying that she felt the reader really had a lot of insight into the hero in this book. And it was then that I realized that *The Wolf King* is perhaps the first book I've ever written where I identified most with the hero instead of the heroine. What do you think?

Well, I'm off to finish up *Romance with a Side of Green Chile* now. It's a lighthearted contemporary book with a lot of humor, and I think I'll enjoy writing that right now for a while. And wait until you find out from whence my inspiration for *that* one hailed! (Winky face!)

Yours,
Marcia Lynn McClure

Snippet #1—The meadow in *The Wolf King* holds a special significance to me beyond simply being the sunny, colorful, warm, and wonderful meeting place where Balian and Minnette often rendezvous. One of the most vivid memories in my mind of my mom is how nostalgic and excited she would get whenever she'd tell me the story of "the frozen meadow"—an experience she always held tucked in her heart as one of her most treasured memories of childhood. Although I was nearly certain I had a written account of the frozen meadow via a letter from my mom, I can't seem to find one anywhere, and so I'll just have to tell it to you from memory. But first let me share a bit of my mother's beautiful heart and angelic spirit. This is an excerpt from something she jotted down in 1991—long before dementia and Alzheimer's ravaged her mind, cruelly stripping her of these memories she so deeply cherished. I may have shared the following first paragraph with you before, in one of the Ipswich Trilogy books dedicated to my mom. Still, I hope you'll read it again, for it will give you a sense of my mom's heart.

Thus, at a very impressionable age, I was transported to the vicinity of my beloved Westcliffe and Sangre de Cristo Mountains—land of spacious prairies, towering mountains, green verdant meadows, pure white diamond-studded snows; crystal clear streams and lakes; crisp, clean, fresh air; lingering twilights; beautiful wildflowers (especially the blue columbine, my favorite, which is also Colorado's state flower); and the ever quivering tall, slender, white-trunked quakies (Aspen) . . .

I could go on and on with this part of my life. It was a wonderful time; I still long for those mountains. Whenever I have an occasion to get even close, something pulls me, and it is difficult to keep from veering off the road and heading for Westcliffe. I believe the last time I was there was in 1976 when my parents, siblings and their families, and my daughters and I went camping at DeWeese Dam and the next day went up into the Sangre de Cristo Mountains and eventually on up to Hermit Lake, which is yet another story. On the drive up there from Colorado Springs, as soon as we came within fifty miles of Westcliffe, I recognized the feel of the evening air, the shadows, the twilight—which my dad always said lingered longer than in any place he had ever been. It was coming home to me, and for the short time we were there, something inside was content.

As for my mom's beloved frozen meadow, it began with a heavy rain, followed by a very late spring freeze. During the previous winter months, my grandpa and grandma would bundle my mom up and haul a little sled to the meadow. The meadow was frozen for most of the cold months, and my grandpa would take hold of the rope tied to the front of the sled and run around on the icy meadow, pulling my little mom around on her little sled as my grandma looked on, cheering and calling out excited encouragements. One day, my grandpa decided to really give my mom a thrill. As he pulled the sleigh as fast as he could, he stopped in his tracks, using his strength to send the little sleigh sailing past and ahead of him as he held the rope. But the rope slipped through his hand and my little mom went sailing right toward a barbed-wire fence. My grandpa scrambled, throwing himself on the ice, sailing after my mom on his stomach, and catching hold of the sled's rope an instant before it would've sent my mom hurtling into the barbed-wire fence.

That was a scary story of the meadow. But it's the story of the year the meadow flooded and then froze that always captured and held my imagination. As in *The Wolf King*, there was a heavy spring rain at the foot of the Sangre de Cristo Mountains that year (approximately 1941). The heavy rain flooded the meadow, and as the temperatures dropped drastically and way below freezing that evening and through the night, it froze the meadow—and it froze everything in the meadow with it. Mom always talked about how her dad and mom took her out there the next morning, and they spent hours tiptoeing carefully across the fragile ice and looking down to see little frogs, snakes, crickets, and mice encased in the ice. Mom's face would light up with remembered intrigue and happiness anytime she told me about the frozen meadow the year she was so small and innocent, living blissful in the company of her parents, the farm animals, and the beauty of the Sangre de Cristo Mountains she loved so much.

So you see, this is why the meadow in *The Wolf King*, as well as Minnette's memory of the beauty of the frozen meadow, is so close to my heart. My mom had such a marvelous gift of description!

I think it's why description is so important to me—whether in writing my books or simply in my thoughts or speaking. It's a gift I was given from my mom, and I cherish it so much. In my innermost and very private thoughts, I think it's my way of hanging onto my mom as her mind continues to slip away from her—from me—from any and all whose lives she blessed with her beauty of spirit and gift of description.

Snippet #2—I first heard the name Balian in the movie *Kingdom of Heaven*, a story rather loosely based on a real-life crusader noble of the Kingdom of Jerusalem, Balian of Ibelin (1143–1193). The movie had many historical inaccuracies, but in real life Balian d'Ibelin was quite the badass. After reading up on the real Balian of Ibelin, I loved the name all the more and decided I definitely wanted use it for a hero in a book. So I jotted the name down and waited for inspiration. Then, early in 2016, wham! *The Wolf King* began to simmer in my mind, and I knew Balian would be named Balian!

Snippet #3—As for King Liam's name—well, Liam Neeson was also in the movie *Kingdom of Heaven*, so his name just popped into my mind when I first introduced his character. Not very exciting, but maybe fun to know. Right?

Snippet #4—While serving a full-time church mission in Las Vegas, Nevada, my youngest son, Trent, and the guy working with him at the time were out one day to keep an appointment with someone who had asked to meet with them. The neighborhood wherein the appointment was scheduled to take place was very run down, crime-ridden, and, as Trent would say, "sketchy."

As Trent and his companion approached the apartment complex where they were supposed to meet with someone, they saw a middle-aged woman hanging clothes on a clothesline outside one of the bottom-floor apartments. She was very familiar with missionaries and with what their purpose was and struck up a friendly conversation with them.

Trent, as always, was kind and friendly and willing to speak with anyone. Thus, the three began a nice conversation.

After they had been talking a while, the woman asked, "Hey! Do you guys want to see my wolves?" She explained that she had rescued two baby wolves (though Trent doesn't remember exactly how or from where she rescued them).

Trent responded, "Yeah, sure, we'd like to see them."

Of course Trent suspected that the lady had a couple of Huskies or some other kind of wolfish-looking dogs and that the lady was just a sweet, lonely little thing that loved her dogs. And so, excitedly, the kind lady led Trent and his friend to her apartment to show them her "wolves."

However, neither of the young men was prepared for what met them at the threshold when she opened the door. There before them stood an enormous white wolf! Truly! Trent (about six foot two with his shoes on) said the wolf's head hit him square at about the lower part of his chest.

As Trent and the guy with him stood staring at the wolf, the little lady said, "You can pet him if you want."

Not wanting to appear too freaked out, and also not wanting to offend the lady, Trent said, "Okay." He reached out and began petting the top of the wolf's head. As he did so, another wolf appeared from inside—a smaller female, yet still large enough to, you know, tear a man's throat out. Furthermore, as Trent continued to pet the large male wolf, he began to sort of growl, the sound emanating from deep in its throat.

"He won't bite you," the lady said as Trent casually drew his hand away from the big old wolf's head. "But did you know that a wolf can bite right through small bones? He could tear your hand right off, but he won't."

Needless to say, Trent and his companion very politely bid the kind lady and her giant wolves goodbye and went on their merry, if not a bit rattled, way.

It was the day that Trent was telling this story to Kevin and I that the white wolf thread for *The Wolf King* began to simmer in my mind.

Snippet #5—You might already know this, but Balian's wolves are all named after gods in Norse mythology. Thor is the one I'm sure you recognize, being the Norse god of thunder and battle. Ullr is the Norse god of winter and hunt, Freyja is the goddess of love, fertility, and battle, Delling is the god of dawn, and Nótt is the goddess of night. I chose to name the five main wolves after Norse gods because of the fact that King Liam received Thor and his mate from some great king of the north country. Also because the wolves hailed from the north and were named after Norse gods, Balian speaks to them in Danish, being that the language of the Vikings was Old Norse—the parent of the modern Scandinavian languages of which Danish is one. And just in case you might have missed one or two of the translations when Balian is speaking to Thor and the other wolves (or in case I forgot to translate them in the text of the story):

> Gå skjule. (Go hide.)
> Tilflugt. (Take refuge.)
> Komme paa en gang. (Come at once.)
> Husker henne. (Remember her.)
> Træde tilbage. (Stand down.)

Vent her. (Stay here.)
Hvile. Men være nogensinde vågent. (Rest. But be ever watchful.)
Kommer, mine venner. (Come, my friends.)
Indkalde dem alle. (Summon them all.)
Til camp. (To battle.)

Snippet #6—You might have guessed the reason for Phillip's name—you know, Prince Phillip. If it doesn't hop right out at you or if you didn't already know this, I just always feel like Prince Phillip in Disney's animated *Sleeping Beauty* got a bum rap, you know? I mean, he's one of my favorite Disney princes, if not my very favorite! Why? Because he's awesome, *and* he's not perfect. I think it's great that the fairies help him out when he's chained up by Maleficent. He still has the courage and loves Aurora so much that he goes up against a dragon, right? Plus, I love the way he surprises Aurora in the forest. Great singing voice too! (He was voiced by a guy named Bill Shirley. Surely you can't help but adore Bill Shirley's singing voice, right? I mean, surely you love it! And don't call me Shirley.) And so cute!

Snippet #7—Something about my creative process is what I like to call "the simmering phase." This is the time following the moment the initial inspiration for a story hits me (i.e., my son tells me a story about big white wolves, and I think, *Hmmm, a prince who has wolves for friends*) but before I start jotting down ideas for scenes and character on old store receipts, torn envelopes, or whatever is close at hand when a thought hits me. During the simmering phase for *The Wolf King*, I was enjoying a rare moment in my life—that being time by myself and being a couch potato in front of the TV and watching a documentary and enjoying a little PBS thingy on the Tower of London. Now although I learned a ton about the history of the Tower of London, the one vein of the documentary that really caught my interest was the part about the Royal Menagerie. I had never heard of it, but the moment I did hear of it via the documentary, I knew exactly how Balian was going to come by owning five large white wolves. The Tower of London menagerie first recorded lions residing at the Tower of London in 1210. From there the menagerie grew and grew until it was quite the zoological spectacle in 1816, with guidebooks, tours, and so on. By 1932, there had been multiple incidents wherein animals escaped and attacked people, and so the animals were taken to the London Zoo. Naturally, King Liam's menagerie—so well and wonderfully kept by the Monk of the Menagerie—boasted much more humane, if you will, habitats for the animals and was much better kept.

Snippet #8—This is the "too much information" snippet! My body was hitting pre-menopause or something the entire time I was writing *The Wolf King*. I felt overheated for months and months—the entire time I was writing this book! Therefore, know this (and you can ask Kevin if you need further proof of the truth of what I'm about to reveal): I wrote ninety-eight percent of *The Wolf King* dressed only in my underwear! True story.

About the Author

Marcia Lynn McClure's intoxicating succession of novels, novellas, and e-books—including *Shackles of Honor*, *The Windswept Flame*, *A Crimson Frost*, and *The Bewitching of Amoretta Ipswich*—has established her as one of the most favored and engaging authors of true romance. Her unprecedented forte in weaving captivating stories of western, medieval, regency, and contemporary amour void of brusque intimacy has earned her the title "The Queen of Kissing."

Marcia, who was born in Albuquerque, New Mexico, has spent her life intrigued with people, history, love, and romance. A wife, mother, grandmother, family historian, poet, and author, Marcia Lynn McClure spins her tales of splendor for the sake of offering respite through the beauty, mirth, and delight of a worthwhile and wonderful story.

Center Point Large Print
600 Brooks Road / PO Box 1
Thorndike, ME 04986-0001 USA

(207) 568-3717

**US & Canada:
1 800 929-9108**
www.centerpointlargeprint.com